"IRRESISTIBLE."
The Kirkus Reviews

"Brisk, delirious dialogue; meticulously placed wit; and a lively spin on the by now jaded academic mystery angle. Thomas is just the kind of professor you wish you'd had."
Booklist

"Just when readers think they know the score and interest begins to peak, a plot twist changes the whole picture and lifts this detective thriller into the realm of biting political-social satire. . . . Features snappy send-ups of academia and the porn industry, as well as some deep meditations on eros and on pornography's dehumanizing effects."
Publishers Weekly

PEEPING THOMAS

Robert Reeves

IVY BOOKS • NEW YORK

Ivy Books
Published by Ballantine Books
Copyright © 1990 by Robert Reeves

Library of Congress Catalog Card Number: 90-32478

ISBN 0-8041-0779-3

This edition published by arrangement with Crown Publishers, Inc.

Manufactured in the United States of America

First Ballantine Books Edition: October 1991

For Mother, Linda, and Christine

Part I

Hard-Core Classics

1

Early one Saturday morning in late summer, Emma Pierce, a feminist historian, political activist, and new head of the women's studies department at Wesley College, surprised me with a telephone call. She asked me an odd question.

"Professor Theron, have you ever heard of the First Amendment?"

At least that's what I *thought* she said. Her call had roused me from the oblivion of a bourbon-induced slumber, not to mention the more general oblivion of my first academic sabbatical. My brain slowly surfaced from the depths. What came from my lips wasn't speech, but an unintelligible croak.

"I apologize if I woke you," Emma Pierce said, once again identifying herself. "Please understand, I wouldn't call if this wasn't important."

"Excuse me," I finally wheezed, "Professor Pierce? I . . . uh, could you just give me a minute?"

I staggered into the bathroom, cupped my hand under the faucet, and drank until I was breathless. Through gummed eyelids, I squinted in the mirror and groaned. Sallow, bleary-eyed, two days' growth of beard. Brain parched, eyeballs scorched, as if some macabre spirit of the night had marinated my entire head in alcohol, then served it flambé. I tapped four aspirin into my palm and stared at them with-

3

out much hope; the cure for a headache of this magnitude wasn't aspirin but general anesthetic.

In a moment I stumbled back to the phone, searching my memory, wondering who in the hell's free speech I'd suppressed. The First Amendment? Emma Pierce? Easy, Thomas, I told myself, easy. Don't be so defensive. She's probably making a courtesy call. Wants to say hello to a junior colleague. Ask a few questions about the Bill of Rights.

"Professor Pierce, hello, good morning. Just what can I do for you?"

"The First Amendment," she repeated. "You know where it is, correct?"

"Where?"

Had I finally lost one brain cell too many? I said, "The free exchange of ideas, the ACLU, Nazis in Skokie, *that* First Amendment?"

"We don't seem to be on the same wavelength this morning, Professor," she replied. "The First Amendment is the name of a bookstore. Alleged bookstore. They sell pornography."

"I see," I said slowly, not seeing at all.

"I was under the impression that you'd be familiar with it."

"You have the impression I frequent porn shops?"

"Nothing personal, Professor Theron, but your reputation precedes you. There's a consensus among your colleagues that, however fine a teacher you may be, your true calling is . . . slumming?"

I gently massaged my eyelids. So that was it. It wasn't much of a reputation, I supposed, and it was a little out of date, but it was all mine. Not so long ago, whenever the narrow walls of academia threatened to imprison me, I'd escaped into the seamy underworld of Boston life, feeling very much like an explorer of old, priding myself on an unhealthy curiosity about anything unspeakable, unthinkable, or unprintable. There were consequences, of course, not the least of which were a lingering reputation for marginal behavior and a résumé unlikely to appear in *Who's Who at American Universities:* Thomas Carlyle Theron, professor of American civilization, habitué of seedy bars, chronic horseplayer and railbird, furtive patron of strip clubs, devotee of professional wrestling, perpetual enthusiast of the spiritually exotic. For better or worse, I possessed the heart and soul of a Peeping Thomas.

"It's not slumming," I corrected her affably. "Think of me as a Diane Arbus who doesn't take photographs."

"I assure you, Professor, this is a friendly call. I'm trying to ask a favor. I know I'm popping this on you out of the blue," she continued, "but would it be convenient for you to meet me here, say, within the hour?"

"Meet you where?"

"In the Combat Zone. I'm calling from a phone booth just across the street from the First Amendment."

I sat on the edge of the bed, trying to concentrate despite the rhythmic throbbing in my head. Professor Emma Pierce, author of half a dozen works of significant historical scholarship, not to mention the virtual best-seller *Phallacies,* a celebrity academic who'd been lured to Wesley by the prospect of heading the first women's studies department in the Ivy League, a woman with whom I'd exchanged no more than two dozen words of formal introduction at the faculty club, wanted me to meet her at a porn shop in the Combat Zone?

I said, "Professor Pierce, is everything okay? You're not in some kind of trouble, are you?"

"No, no, nothing like that. I suppose I'm in trouble, yes, but only in the sense that we're all in trouble. What I have to ask you may sound a little odd."

"It already sounds odd."

"I imagine that it does. But I'd be grateful if you'd just drop by and hear me out. I can't fully explain over the phone. There's something I want to show you."

"Yes?"

She said, "A pornographic movie. More than one, as a matter of fact."

With that, I decided not to ask any more questions. I poked around in the ashtray on the floor next to the bed. I found a fair-size butt, lit it, inhaled. When I stopped coughing, Emma Pierce said, "The First Amendment, Twenty-three LaGrange Street, between Tremont and—"

"It's been a while," I said, "but I'll find it."

"Splendid. You can't miss us. We'll be on the sidewalk right in front."

"Us?" I said. "We?"

But she'd already hung up. So I heaved myself out of bed again, pulled on a pair of jeans and a white shirt, gulped two more glasses of water, and headed for the door. It wasn't until I stood on the T platform in Wesley Square that I began to have second thoughts. Had I dreamed the entire conversation? Hallucinations had never been a side effect of my drinking before, but there was always a first time.

A minute later the train eased into the station, and I boarded it, deciding, no, the telephone call couldn't have been a dream. Not even my subconscious could conjure a renowned feminist inviting me to the sleazy part of town to watch dirty movies.

2

The Incredible Shrinking Combat Zone.

In its heyday, the Zone was a thriving adult-entertainment district, a small area of downtown Boston set aside in the sixties for X-rated theaters, strip clubs, porn shops, and quasilegal prostitution. I hadn't been here in over two years, and coming back felt a little strange. It wasn't exactly like visiting the old neighborhood, but I did feel a twinge of something. Mostly, I was startled to see how dramatic the decline, how absolute the transformation brought on by VCRs and AIDS and surging real-estate values. The Zone hadn't changed so much as it had . . . well, disappeared. What remained of it had an air of obsolescence, almost of antiquity. I half expected to see anthropologists poking around, hoping to discover the secrets of an earlier age.

I had exited the T beneath Filene's and walked down past the buildings on lower Washington Street, two city blocks at some preliminary stage of transition from tenderloin district to urban shopping mall. A couple of strip clubs were still open for business, and even at this time of morning a few men were going in, their faces grim and careworn.

One thing hadn't changed: the grimness. There'd always been a certain joylessness among the pleasure-seekers in the Zone, a moroseness that sometimes puzzled me. I finally decided that the burden was New England itself, the twin

7

strains of Puritan and Yankee surfacing even here in a pervasive melancholia. The Puritan unable to enjoy sin, and the Yankee unable to enjoy anything that didn't represent a good value for the dollar.

LaGrange was a narrow, dirty side street, and when I turned the corner, Emma Pierce's telephone call began to make more sense. About fifteen women were picketing the sidewalk in front of the First Amendment, carrying signs and handing out leaflets in support of Proposition Six. PORN TERRORIZES WOMEN. PORN = HATE. VOTE YES ON #6. COALITION OF WOMEN AGAINST PORNOGRAPHY.

I paused on the curb across the street. The sight of an unshaven man squinting expectantly in their direction caused a couple of protestors to pause, eyeing me warily. I must have looked as if I harbored some plot to duck past them, slip through the door, and buy the latest issue of *Big Bottom*.

"Hello! Thomas!" Emma called out when she spotted me. "It was good of you to come on such short notice. I hope my call didn't offend you."

"That's the good thing about slummers, Professor Pierce. We're not easily offended."

She clasped my hand warmly and insisted that I call her Emma. She couldn't have been much taller than five feet, or much younger than sixty, but she radiated energy. Brisk, full of purpose, conspicuously in charge. She was wearing beige corduroy slacks and a strawberry crewneck sweater. Her face was open, friendly, deeply lined, and deeply tanned. She possessed the most intense blue eyes I'd ever seen.

"So," I said, "Proposition Six. You're picketing the First Amendment."

"You're damn right we are."

"Does this mean I'll have to cancel my subscription to *Corsets and Trusses*?"

"My, my, our cynical young professor. I've heard about that. Some of your colleagues told me not to bother. They warned me that I wouldn't be able to enlist your help." She laughed with a kind of gruff pleasure, and her eyes sparkled. "They said your idea of a pressing civic issue is whether or not to register to vote."

"It's always gratifying," I said, "to enjoy the esteem of one's colleagues."

"Well, you're here, and I'm glad. I was hoping you might give us the benefit of your expertise. Volunteer work, you might say."

"On the phone you mentioned something about, ah, dirty movies?"

She'd been carrying a padded manila envelope under her arm, which she now held up before me. "I'd like you to take a look at something I received in the mail. It's a video-cassette, and"—a nod toward the door of the porn shop—"there're two more inside."

I frowned and lit a cigarette in cupped hands, aware that my head once again had begun to pound. "Emma, I don't want to disappoint you. All false modesty aside, I'm not an expert on pornography. Reports of my moral death have been greatly exaggerated."

She smiled patiently. I rambled on.

"I've spent a certain amount of time in the seedier parts of Boston, yes—call it slumming, whatever—but that was a long time ago, at least it seems like a long time—"

"Relax, Thomas," she soothed. "Just come inside and have a look. Hear me out. You may be intrigued."

A young woman wearing a Gertrude Stein T-shirt stepped between us and spoke to Emma. Something about the Channel Four News unit not showing up until later in the day.

Emma turned back to me, somber now, her eyes betraying a hint of resignation, but her voice determined. "We've set up picket lines here because the news media will always run another story on the Combat Zone, and we need every bit of publicity we can get. People have no idea how bad things are. They hear that the Zone is dead, so they think that maybe pornography isn't a problem anymore. Well, the

Combat Zone may be dying, but what's taking its place is infinitely worse. We're being saturated. There's a miniature Combat Zone in every neighborhood video rental store in the country. Aisles of movies, action adventures, comedies, mysteries, dramas, and in the back, women getting fucked. What if there were an aisle where the Ku Klux Klan could rent movies about humiliating black men, or Nazis could rent movies depicting the torturing of Jews? No one would stand for it, and we're not going to stand for this either. This isn't a free-speech issue. Proposition Six isn't about sex. What it's about is the wholesale promotion of hatred of women, hatred that promotes violence.''

I'd been following the story in the papers, and judging by what I'd read, she was facing an uphill battle. Proposition Six was an antipornography ordinance, one of several city ordinances scheduled for an upcoming citywide election, and by far the most controversial. Designed to evade the futility of defining obscenity, the ordinance attacked pornography in civil rather than criminal court. Plaintiffs would be obliged to prove only that they had been harmed by pornography, not to define the precise nature of what had harmed them. The prospect of sympathetic juries and huge monetary awards against the producers of pornography, supporters argued, would have a chilling effect on the porn industry far beyond the city limits of Boston. Such a law promised dramatic results never achieved by the old obscenity laws. Opponents insisted that it was unconstitutional; a similar ordinance had passed in Madison, Wisconsin, only to be struck down in the courts.

The issue had polarized Boston's large community of activists. Bizarre political alliances had been forged, and traditional alliances broken. On one side, clergymen attended rallies with radical lesbians; on the other, civil-rights veterans planned legal strategy with the Adult Video Association. Adding to the political confusion, nearly a dozen national organizations and societies had descended upon the city, each with an ax to grind, plus a multitude of more obscure sects with more obscure agendas. Thus far, the only clear winners were the local tabloids and TV stations. Emma was right; the media always could be counted on to run another story on the Zone, especially if the topic was pornography. Porn sold newspapers, and it boosted Neilsons. Even though the referendum was still several weeks away, stories about the "Porn Prop" or "Proposition Sex" were appearing daily.

A lot of talk, but not all talk. Beneath the political exchange, subterranean passions had bubbled to the surface. In the past two months, firebombs had gutted two X-rated movie houses and a strip club, all within four blocks of where we were now standing. There were no injuries—the buildings were boarded up, abandoned—and there were no claims of responsibility. In a sense, the expression of violence seemed largely symbolic, a case of beating a dead horse. Many of the huge old movie houses and clubs of the Zone were now vacant, offering relatively innocuous targets for protest; torching them simply hastened the demise of the Zone, destroying buildings doomed to be razed anyway. But arson, like porn, was prime media turf, and the papers played the story to the hilt, sounding the obligatory alarms. TERRORIST BOMBINGS MAR PROPOSITION SIX DEBATE! COMBAT ZONE: NO LONGER A FIGURE OF SPEECH! "Not for the first time in its history," a dour columnist wrote, "Boston has become a stage for a volatile psycho-politico-sexual drama of censorship."

Emma and I remained at the curb, looking up at the facade of the First Amendment. An arrangement of stroboscopic lights pulsed huge triple X's in the bleak morning light. She placed the manila envelope under her arm, crossed the sidewalk to the entrance, and held open the door for me.

"So, Thomas, how would you feel about a brief dalliance with social action?"

Smiling, wrinkling my shoulders diffidently, I went inside. "You may be in luck," I said. "Brief dalliances are my specialty."

• • •

There is something unnerving about aisle after aisle of pornographic magazines at ten o'clock in the morning. To find yourself—hung over, without benefit of coffee— confronted by glossy photographs of sexual couplings, the poses relentlessly acrobatic, the focuses sharp enough to make you wince. And worse, neatly displayed along the walls, latex reproductions of human genitalia, lewdly disembodied, price tags dangling. And like it or not, you are suddenly reminded of your own biological existence, conscious of the animal living inside you, the beast who forced you to embrace your lover in the darkness, to assume strange postures, to emit strange noises, secreting.

Well, if you were lucky.

The interior of the First Amendment was cavernous. Magazines, paperbacks, and sexual accessories were arrayed up front, and an arched passage led to a large second room of peep booths and videocassettes.

A fat man with a buzz crewcut and huge, sloping shoulders presided over the front cash register. A *Racing Form* was spread out before him on the counter, and a radio blasted country music from behind his head. He was keeping time to the music by drumming a penile prosthesis on the counter.

He shifted his eyes from Emma to me. He said, "You with her?"

I nodded.

He said, "You here to give me some shit?"

I shook my head.

He said, "You here to buy something?"

"My apartment's too small," I replied amiably. "I don't have a place to hide it."

He didn't smile. He lumbered from behind the counter and stood in front of me. Large in the ass, even larger in the belly, he spread his feet in a military pose, wielding the dildo like a billy club, slapping it against his open palm. *Thwop. Thwop. Thwop.*

"You must be feeling brave this morning," he said,

sticking his face up close to mine. The enzymic odors of fried eggs and whiskey wafted under my nose. He tilted his head toward Emma and said, "Case you haven't noticed, her and her ladies' club been harassing all of my customers. She's too little to hit. You're not."

I wanted to tell him if he stepped back out of my face, I'd look a lot smaller, but of course I didn't. I just watched him slap the dildo against his palm. A scene was playing out in my mind, a little drama in which I attempted to explain to my boss, the chairman of the Am. civ. department, why I'd been pounded into unconsciousness by a rubber phallus. Just then Emma wedged herself between us and stuck her forefinger in the fat man's belly.

"Step aside, pissmonger. This cesspool happens to be a free place of business."

"Take my advice, lady—"

"Don't 'lady' me, you filthy misogynist."

He blinked. "What'd she call me?"

"Misogynist," I said. "Someone who gives massages."

His eyes gleamed with dumb, animal insight. "Massages? Tell this little old broad she ought to get her facts straight. You want a massage parlor, you got to go over to Chinatown. We got peep shows, buddy, not—"

"Don't talk to him," Emma said, "talk to me. I'm the one who's going to put your rancid carcass in jail."

"Yeah? You gonna throw ol' Wally in jail? Well, lemme tell you something. You better grow some balls first."

He turned and slapped the dildo savagely against the top of the counter. *Thwack!*

"If that were real," Emma observed with cold menace, "I'd make you eat it."

The fat man grimaced, as if he had received a blow. There was a silent pause which gradually lengthened and filled with tension. One thing was certain: no matter how emasculating Emma's insults, the fat man was going to pummel me, not her. I was about to say something idiotic, something like, Why don't we put away the dildos and talk this out? when the fat man surprised me. Offering no more than a sullen curse, he retreated to his post behind the cash register.

"Maybe you fucked up, lady," he said. "Maybe you come in here one time too many."

But Emma was already halfway down the center aisle, oblivious to his threats, the manila envelope under her arm, walking briskly toward the rear of the store.

The Dewey Decimal System of Desire. Everything in the shop had been arranged according to taste, women categorized by sexual activity or physical attribute, then divided and subdivided, again and again, until every permutation of lust had been addressed. Magazines devoted to women with large breasts (*Jugs*), hanging breasts (*Floppers*), cylindrical breasts (*Torpedoes*), lactating breasts (*Milkers*); magazines devoted to women engaged in oral, anal, interracial, or mammary sex; women who masturbated; obese women; black women; blond women; pregnant women; women dressed to appear prepubescent; women with shaved pubic hair, abundant pubic hair, abundant anal hair; large buttocks, boyish buttocks. It was unsettling to contemplate what confluence of genes or experience might provoke such minutely specific expressions of desire.

Maybe I should mention it to Elizabeth, I thought. My ex-wife was a psychologist, and it occurred to me that a session here might yield a rich psychic harvest. Who could withstand the challenge of walking these aisles? Aha, Mr. Zumwalt, I see that your face is flushed. Your breath quickens. So this is how it is? These particular photographs make your blood boil? Your heart's desire is a good spanking? Now we're getting somewhere.

Emma led me into a large second room where banks of private peep booths hugged both walls. The air was gamy and suffused with disinfectant. The center of the room was crisscrossed with tall display racks of videocassettes.

"This," she said finally, "is what I wanted you to see."

She removed a videocassette from the manila envelope and handed it to me. It was encased in a brightly colored promotional carton, cellophane wrapped. The cover photograph featured a young, pouting blonde, nearly nude, posing next to a large, painted cardboard object intended to represent a spaceship. In the crook of her right arm, the girl carried a space helmet. Title: *The Right Stiff.*

I said, "Is this the erotic film of high artistic value and emotional maturity that the world's been waiting for?"

"Don't laugh. You may be holding in your hands the future of Proposition Six. That video may help us win hundreds of votes. Maybe thousands."

I said, "You're joking."

I waited while she searched the rows of movies, walking back and forth among the aisles, methodically scanning the titles. A minute later and she had pulled down two more cassettes from the shelves. One was called *Lip Service,* and its cover hinted at a variation on the "naughty librarian" theme. The other was *Rear Admiral,* apparently an account of the sexual possibilities of the new coed navy: "It's not just a hand job, it's an adventure."

Who said the Age of Wit had ended?

The same actress, Sheena Sands, starred in all three videos, the young, pouting blonde posed variously as an astronaut, a librarian, and a sailor. The cover copy touted her as "the hot hot star taking the porn world by storm." I'd never heard of her, but then again I had a vague sense that some new starlet took the porn world by storm about once every three minutes. An identical tag line unfurled at the bottom of each carton: "Another Hard-core Classic from Venture Productions."

"I received the first one in the mail last week," Emma explained, "from a friend. She's convinced that it will help us. The note mentioned the other two movies, which were produced by the same company, Venture Productions. My friend thinks they'll cause a furor. According to her, these videos may stir things up enough to give Proposition Six a chance of passing."

I shuffled through the three cassettes again, studying them with new interest. What had I missed? Judging by the outside, they seemed routine, indistinguishable from the hundreds of videos that remained behind on the rack. Not much set them apart, at least not much that I could see. Same actress, I thought. Same production company. Probably the same three-year-old thought up the titles.

"I give. Why the fuss?"

For a moment Emma didn't answer. And then she said she didn't know.

"Beg pardon?"

"I don't know why they're important."

I just stood there, looking puzzled. "Wait, the friend who sent this to you, she didn't say?"

Emma shook her head. "Not in the note. She just said that they were important, and they would help. Her note said she'd call in a day or two to set up a time to meet. I've waited almost a week now, and I haven't heard from her. I have no idea how to get in touch with her."

"So you just *assume* that they're important?"

"Not really. This woman knows what she's talking about. She's a former student of mine. I have confidence in her."

"Student?" I said. "Emma, I don't know about your students, but mine aren't always pillars of trustworthiness. The only thing you can really depend on them for is BYOB."

"I understand," she said, sighing, "and ordinarily I'd agree with you. But Grace is different. I believe her. And her note mentioned a couple of things that persuaded me."

I said, "Such as?"

And then it happened.

A shock wave reverberated in my gut. A concussive noise brutalized my eardrums. I found myself on the floor, chin pressed to the sour carpet. For the briefest instant it occurred to me that the fat man had crept up behind me, then launched a preemptive attack upon my head. But then I was aware of being showered by videocassettes. I heard someone yelling; I listened with an odd detachment until I realized that the sounds were coming from my own mouth.

For the next few seconds debris settled. A jagged piece of Sheetrock fell next to my head. Thick, chalky dust hung in the air. Then there was utter silence.

Did I smell smoke?

I couldn't see Emma. I turned my head as far as I could in order to look behind me. I tried to get up. Nothing happened. It was an odd sensation; I couldn't tell if I was really trying to get up or merely pretending to try.

There was no pain. My brain must have been manufacturing generous quantities of some natural narcotic, because I was in a remarkably good mood. My mind filled with random thoughts, mostly inappropriate. I noticed that my hangover was gone. So here was the long-awaited cure: severe trauma.

I thought about *Helpless Laughter*, the reason I'd been hung over in the first place. I'd spent my entire sabbatical finishing the novel, and I'd been collecting nothing but rejection slips. Maybe things weren't so bad after all, I thought giddily. Maybe my death would help get it published. Better still, why not the more congenial publicity of a mere brush with death? Was there such a thing as a semi-posthumous novel? I giggled.

I saw Emma. She was very near to me. I hadn't seen her before because she was buried beneath a mound of videocassettes. I was able to see her now because her arm pushed out from beneath the cartons. With a slow, graceful movement, she gently folded her arm across her face, as if she were shielding her eyes. Her right forearm was bathed in blood.

Definitely smoke, and much heavier now. My lungs burned.

The silence broke. I was aware of the sound of voices coming ever closer, a chaotic shouting, crying, screaming. I was aware of a siren in the distance. I turned my head toward the commotion.

There, just two inches away from my eyes, was the manila envelope, and a videocassette on top of it. Sheena Sands pouted at me from the cover of *The Right Stiff*. Her naked breasts almost touched my nose. I reached out and clutched her to me.

I felt heat. Then I saw blackness. Then I felt nothing.

3

The following morning I discovered another set of breasts almost touching my nose. These breasts were large and matronly and belonged to a heavyset nurse who hovered above me, fluffing my pillows.

"How's that?" she said. "Better?"

I directed toward her a contented, heavy-lidded gaze. I said, "Mmmmmm."

I was in room 546 of Boston City Hospital, watching "Love Connection" on TV and entertaining myself by manipulating the panel of buttons that controlled my hospital bed. *Brrrrrr* . . . Slowly, very slowly, raising my upper torso, bending forward at the waist. *Brrrrrrrr*. . . . Slowly, very slowly, lowering myself until I again lay flat on my back.

The nurse remained by my bed, her expression bemused. She said, "Having fun?"

"Sit-ups. Got to keep in shape. I can only do about one a minute. I figure by the turn of the century my stomach will be hard as a rock."

To tell the truth, I was feeling not only well, but better than I had in years. I'd been given to the care of a disheveled, somewhat wild-eyed internist whose strategies for managing pain didn't include grinning and bearing it. His approach to dispensing prescription drugs wasn't so much "just say no" as "just say when." I'd been here almost twenty-four hours, and I hadn't yet been able to tell him where it hurt. It didn't hurt anywhere.

As far as I could tell, other than a seven-stitch gash where my chin had hit the floor, a general body ache, and some small bruises, I'd escaped any injury of consequence. I'd inhaled some smoke, and my lungs hurt, but my lungs always hurt; I probably inhaled more smoke on a voluntary basis every day. Occasionally I heard a faint ringing sound—not in my ears, but disconcertingly above my head and to the left. A few precautionary tests, another day of convalescence, and then home. "All things considered"— the internist winked—"not bad. Nice trick to walk away from a bombing with a cut on your chin, a few splinters in your butt. I'd call it a damned good result."

Except . . .

Something in his expression must have worried me. I stared at him uneasily. I said, "Is Emma going to be okay?"

"Her official status is critical but stable. Her doctors tell me she's lucky to be alive. We're hoping her luck holds out."

I gingerly fingered the bandage on my chin. "She was covered with blood."

"The bomb exploded inside one of the peep booths not far from where she was standing. Actually, the police said the booth helped contain the fire, kept it from spreading quickly. But the explosion itself splintered part of the door, which caused a sort of shrapnel effect. She suffered lots of tiny wounds, which account for the blood. Those are relatively minor; they're not our primary concern at the moment. She's very badly concussed."

I said, "Can I see her?"

He shook his head. "She's in intensive care. For now we just sit tight, wait, hope we don't find evidence of further internal injury. With this kind of trauma you never know. Just keep your fingers crossed."

For the next few seconds he carefully cleaned his steel-rimmed glasses. "She was simply standing in the wrong place," he said. "You, my friend, were standing in the right place. Her body seems to have shielded you. She took the brunt of it. If it weren't for her, Professor Theron, you'd be . . ."

His speculation dangled grimly. I wondered if I should remind him that laughter, not guilt, was the best medicine.

A team of very frustrated BPD detectives interviewed me for most of the morning. They seemed desperate to generate leads. Their spirits didn't improve as I rehearsed the little that I knew. One officer, a gaunt man with pitted cheeks, seemed intent on catching me in some inconsistency.

"Run this past me again," he said. "You said you didn't know Emma Pierce all that well. So why'd she call you?"

Relying on whatever powers of euphemism I possessed, I described to him the history of my slumming activities, my forays into the city, presenting myself as an acute observer of human behavior, a serious investigator of social and moral boundaries.

A gleam of triumph appeared in the detective's eyes. "She called you because you're a scuzzball?"

The hours passed, and more and more reporters clamored to interview me. The hospital staff refused to divulge my room or phone number and barred unauthorized visitors beyond the nurses' station down the hall from my room. I passed the time sleeping, watching soaps, and rereading the news stories that lay around me in the hospital bed.

A local tabloid exploited its customary formula of crass alliteration with the headline PORN PROP BLAST: FEMME FATALITY? The account in the *Boston Globe*, typically subdued, appeared at the bottom of the front page.

FEMINIST INJURED AS BOMB TRIGGERS FIRE
IN ADULT BOOKSTORE

Emma Pierce, a feminist historian recently appointed professor at Wesley College, was critically injured yesterday when an explosion caused a fire in the First Amendment Bookshop at 23 LaGrange Street. Professor Pierce is a member of the Coalition of

Women Against Pornography, a pro–Proposition Six group that had been picketing the Combat Zone bookstore at the time of the explosion.

A spokesman for Boston City Hospital said that Ms. Pierce was in critical condition, and as soon as she improved would undergo emergency surgery to clean her wounds. In addition to a severe concussion, the spokesman said, Ms. Pierce suffered internal injuries, received numerous burns and embedded fragments of metal on her torso, arms, and legs, and has multiple lacerations.

Thomas Theron of Cambridge, another Wesley professor injured in the blast, is being held for observation and was listed in good condition. Wallace Belcher, a resident of South Boston and an employee of the First Amendment, was unharmed.

Fire fighters worked quickly to bring yesterday's blaze under control. Police evacuated and searched other adult-entertainment establishments in the area, fearing more explosives might have been planted at other locations. None was found. Authorities refused to speculate whether the incident is linked to three arsons that destroyed vacant adult theaters in recent weeks. One source close to the investigation alluded to that possibility, saying, "If there's a connection, the stakes have been raised. This wasn't some boarded-up building waiting for the wrecker's ball. This was a working business, and we may have a casualty." A police spokesman said that further information would not be released until the physical evidence had been thoroughly examined.

Day two, and I was still in semi-isolation. By early afternoon, I found myself in the grip of a sentimental urge to call Elizabeth. Mistake, Thomas, big mistake. You've gone cold turkey for almost a year and a half, so why ruin it? I listed mentally all of the reasons I shouldn't call my ex-wife—it was an emotional crutch, it was a shameless play for sympathy, it probably wouldn't work—but I dialed her number anyway. If I was looking for a good excuse to call, would I ever have a better one than now? Would events ever again cast me in such a potentially sympathetic, even heroic light? Hadn't I just been wounded on the front? Hadn't I just fallen in the battle to throw off the unholy purveyors of porn? Thomas Theron, *mujahadeen*.

Two, three, four rings. No answer.

Rumor had it she'd rented a beach house on the Vineyard for the summer. I imagined her there on this late-summer day, spending her nights drinking and dancing at the Hot Tin Roof, her days cavorting on the nude beaches in Chilmark. I imagined her gorging herself on oysters. I imagined her . . .

In the middle of a particularly graphic image, Elizabeth answered. The impatience in her voice told me immediately that I'd made a mistake.

"Thomas? Why on earth . . . ?" Pause. "I'm very busy right now. What do you want?"

"I was just lying here thinking—"

"It's two o'clock in the afternoon. You're still in bed?"

"Haven't you heard? Haven't you read the newspapers?"

"I work for a living, Thomas. I have a lot of paperwork. Most professions aren't like teaching. Most people don't get twelve months off at full pay to sit around and read newspapers, go to the track, barhop, fiddle with a novel—"

"My sabbatical wasn't really like—"

"Who said anything about a sabbatical?"

"Amusing," I said. "Extremely amusing."

"What's in the papers?" she said. "I'm almost afraid to ask, but what am I going to find?"

"I got bombed."

"That's *news*?"

"No, I mean literally bombed. Not as in bars, as in Beirut."

This was greeted by a skeptical silence. She seemed to be

making an obvious effort not to say something inappropriate in the unlikely event I was telling the truth. Take your time, I told myself. Explain it step by step.

"I was in the Combat Zone," I began, "in a porn shop—"

Click.

Later that afternoon a hospital administrator stopped by my room. A grim little man with the unyielding aspect of a bill collector, he caught me standing by the open window, vigorously fanning the smoke from a cigarette. He clucked his tongue and stared glumly at his clipboard, then laid out some paperwork on the table beside the bed. I was being discharged. I proceeded to sign enough releases and legal waivers to prevent me from joking about the hospital, much less suing it.

Afterward, he lingered at the door, acting a little funny. I said, "Is everything okay, Mr. . . . ?"

"Rivets," he said, "Dr. Rivets." He frowned ambiguously.

I remembered the X rays and blood tests that had been ordered for me. A precaution, the internist said, strictly routine. But in the back of my mind, there existed a small worry that the lab might find something unexpected, something much worse than what they'd been looking for. No, Mr. Theron, your X rays are fine. No problem there. Pause. But you do seem to have a little touch of leukemia.

Dr. Rivets said, "So, the mysterious Peeper Prof. You're free to return to your life of iniquity."

"Beg pardon?"

"The mysterious Peeper Prof," he repeated.

"I'm afraid I'm not following you."

"Don't tell me you didn't see it? Professor, I'm afraid that you're a minor celebrity. Get ready for your fifteen minutes of fame."

Dr. Rivets reached over and slowly turned the pages of the *Boston Herald* that still lay unopened on my bed. He stopped on page eleven and pointed. I couldn't believe it. There was a picture of me, an old photo from the dust jacket of my widely unread volume of literary criticism, accompanied by a large column of type. I cursed and slumped back against my pillows. Thank God I already had tenure.

MYSTERY PEEPER PROF: BROWSING OR BOMBING?

Thomas Theron, professor of American civilization at Wesley, was also rushed to Boston City Hospital after Saturday's Combat Zone bombing. The extent of Professor Theron's injuries is not yet known, although they are not believed to be serious.

For now, his presence at the First Amendment remains a mystery, although there is growing speculation that his role in the episode may prove to be other than passive victim. Wally Belcher, an employee of the First Amendment uninjured in the blast, said that Theron entered the Combat Zone business "acting suspicious."

"I was being careful who came into the store because of the protesters outside," Mr. Belcher added. "I remember asking [Theron] if I could help him. Him and the lady were both acting hostile. Acting like real jerks. I had a feeling they were up to something, I just didn't know what."

Although police deny that Theron is a suspect in the bombing, reporters have learned that as an undergraduate at Wesley College he was a member of Students for a Democratic Society. During the late sixties and early seventies, the SDS was a radical student organization repeatedly linked to bombings and arsons of ROTC facilities on college campuses throughout the nation.

A check of the Wesley College library card catalog revealed that Professor Theron is the author of *Voyeurism and the American Novel*. Cambridge psychiatrist Dr. Irwin Hirsch said, "I have no way of knowing, of course, but it's within the realm of possibility that the author of an entire book on voyeurism might have some obsessive relationship to pornography." When pressed, Dr. Hirsch elaborated, "Without putting too fine a point on it, I'd simply observe that someone who tries to destroy a pornography bookstore might symbolically be trying to destroy a part of himself that he hated." Dr. Hirsch again insisted that he was speaking in general terms and intended no commentary on Professor Theron's situation.

Despite growing speculation, most observers at Wesley College remained skeptical that Theron had aligned himself with the antipornography forces. According to one colleague of Theron's, who requested anonymity, "When it comes to smut, Thomas Theron is generally regarded as part of the problem, not part of the solution."

Dr. Rivets looked hard at me. "Remind me not to send my daughter to Wesley."

4

Maybe ten feet outside the hospital entrance, a young man blocked my path. He possessed the cartoonish jaw and vacuous good looks of a male model, and he was wearing an expensive trench coat. He stuck a microphone in my face.

"Ray Hayes, Channel Four News. Professor Thomas Theron?"

Another man was standing behind him. This man was homelier and not so well dressed. He was wearing blue jeans and a lumberjack shirt, and he was carrying a video camera on his right shoulder. The video camera was aimed at me.

"Tell us, Professor," the reporter said, "what was your precise role in the bombing?"

I turned and headed off in the other direction. A young blond woman immediately cut me off. She, too, was good-looking and perfectly groomed; she, too, was trailed by a homely man aiming a video camera at me.

"Charlotte Davies, Eyewitness News," she said. She peered into my face with theatrical seriousness. "Professor, do you personally own or use pornography?"

"Wha—?"

I ducked and spun around and tried to make my way back into the hospital. By now two men wearing heavy necklaces of cameras were blocking the entrance, snapping off photographs of me with 35mm's. Automatic advancers whirred. Strobe flashes creased the darkening light.

No matter where I sought refuge in the gathering throng, teams of reporters thwarted me. They seemed to work in unison, herding me about the pavement in an awkward circle. My chin ached. All the soreness and pain I hadn't felt in the hospital now surfaced with a vengeance, strangely on cue once I'd cleared the hospital doors, as if my body had been on warranty. I sensed myself lurching, limping back and forth among the representatives of the press with a halting Quasimodo gait.

Questions were shouted at my back. Strangers gawked. Of all the thoughts that might reasonably have been on my mind, there was only one. My clothes. I was wearing the same white cotton shirt and jeans I'd worn to the First Amendment. They were covered with blood. Which probably explained why passersby were jumping so quickly out of my path.

"What is your relationship with Emma Pierce?"

"Were you involved in any arsons when you were a member of Students for a Democratic Society?"

I spied a taxi maybe twenty yards away, approaching along the street that passed in front of the hospital. I turned abruptly and headed for it. The crowd parted quickly, giving way to the desperate, bloodied man and the cameras in hot pursuit. Suddenly I found myself unencumbered. Ahead of me lay a clear path to the street. The taxi drew near. I put my thumb and middle finger to my teeth and whistled. A few more steps and home free.

Goddamn! Goddamn it! A large red Buick glided up to the curb at the passenger drop-off and parked right in front of me. My escape blocked, I watched helplessly as the taxi cruised by and out of sight.

The reporters surged forward, trapping me against the passenger door of the Buick. I turned to confront them.

"The blood on your clothes, Professor Theron, is that yours or Emma Pierce's?"

At least four microphones were thrust into my face. I

recalled the one sure technique for rendering videotape unfit for broadcast. Calmly and without inflection I began to utter obscenities.

Just then a voice interrupted me from behind.

"Need a lift?"

I turned and looked down. The driver of the Buick was leaning across the front seat looking up at me through the open window. A young man, grinning crazily.

He said, "You want to stand there with your dick in your hand, or you want a ride?"

At last, I thought, a question I could answer.

"You get them fucking reporters on your ass, man, you might as well give it up. Chasing some poor fucker up and down the street with a bunch of cameras, who the hell they think they are? Morley fucking Safer? They want, they can make the pope look like a rapist."

My benefactor drove with his arms resting comfortably in his lap, the forefinger of his left hand lightly touching the steering wheel at six o'clock. Mid-twenties, muscular, wearing white linen pants, a black T-shirt, and a small gold earring. His features were regular enough, but his complexion was something out of a nightmare. On his cheeks and forehead were dozens of tiny scrapes which had merged into one enormous, angry, superficial wound that virtually covered his face. A dermabrasion, I realized, an old-fashioned acne treatment; literally, a skin sanding. It looked like someone had tried to erase the center line on the highway using his face.

We'd traveled maybe a quarter mile down Massachusetts Avenue when I said, "Anywhere along here will be fine. Thanks, I really appreciate it. I can catch a cab from here."

He said, "You ever get arrested, man, exact same thing. Happened to me a couple of times in New York. Reporters shove those cameras right up in your face, you standing there handcuffed between two cops, knowing sure as fuck you're gonna be a big hit on the six o'clock news. What can you do? Pull your jacket up over your head? Squirm, bend down, hide your face? Maybe you don't care. Maybe you look straight at the camera like you're out for a stroll and say, Hi Mom. No matter what, man, your ass is in a sling. On TV you're gonna look like a mass murderer."

I said, "Here would be just fine."

He lowered his window and spat. His voice was indignant.

"What if the charges turn out to be bullshit, completely ungrounded, then what? They report that? They get back on TV and say, You remember that dude trying to pull the blue jacket over his head? Well, folks, he didn't do it. He didn't kill his entire motherfucking family like we said he did. It was this motherfucker we're showing you now, the dude pulling the *red* jacket over his head."

He hit the gas to make a yellow light. We were on Washington, and through the window I watched the streets signs fly past. Savoy. Perry. Laconia. Kneeland Street. Heading downtown.

I said, "Seriously, if you wouldn't mind dropping me off along here, I'd be grateful. Thanks for the help. I owe you one, Mr. . . . ?"

He said, "Teddy."

"Thanks, Teddy, but I can catch a cab from here. I need to get to Cambridge."

"Cambridge!" he said, slapping the steering wheel. "Man, ever since I got to Boston, I been hearing how great Cambridge is. All these little coeds, hot to trot. I'm from New York, and you ask me, Boston's this shitty little backwater, but maybe I ought to check out Cambridge. Why don't I give you a ride? I have to run an errand first, that's all. Just give me a minute. Won't take but a jiffy."

I was beginning to wish I'd stayed behind and faced the cameras. We kept heading downtown. Soon the Boston skyline rose up before us, the office buildings stark against the low, washed-out sky. We crossed onto Atlantic Avenue and then onto Commercial Street, heading out along the wharves. Sea gulls now, and fewer cars.

My benefactor said, "What you need is Era Plus."

"Excuse me?"

"Era Plus will get most of that blood out of your clothes. It takes a couple of times, maybe three times through the heavy cycle, hot and hot, but it will come out pretty good." He winked and lowered his voice conspiratorially. "That's nothing. I've had to clean up a lot more than that."

I shifted uneasily in my seat and tried to get a better look at him. He didn't especially look like someone who read "Hints from Heloise." Above his ravaged cheeks, his eyes were hard, opaque, unreadable. The more I looked at him, the more he unnerved me.

By now we were on the waterfront. We'd already passed the seafood palaces on the wharves, Anthony's Pier Four and Jimmy's Harborside, and soon we turned onto a deserted wharf paved with cobblestones. We bumped along toward the water. On either side of us were rows of abandoned warehouses.

"You said you have to run an errand?"

"Yeah, I need to have a serious talk with this guy. Ask him a few questions. See what his story is."

As far as I could tell, the place we'd driven to was one where there weren't any guys around and probably wouldn't be any time soon.

I said, "What guy?"

Maybe twenty yards from the water, my benefactor stopped the Buick, shifted into park, and turned off the ignition. Gulls were bobbing in the wind over the black water. Pilings creaked. Farther out, an empty barge stood at anchor, high in the water, showing a lot of rust.

He took a newspaper off the dashboard and handed it to me. It was a copy of the *Boston Herald*, folded to the Peeper Prof article. The photograph of me had been circled.

He turned and faced me. He smiled contentedly. He said, "This guy."

I just stared at him.

"Lucky for you I showed up at the hospital." He raised his palm, as if I were about to contradict him. "Of course, I'm not denying it was lucky for me, too. I'd been parked out front since maybe two this afternoon. I was getting a little antsy. And then what happens? You come bebopping out the front door. Those asshole reporters start harassing you. I pull up to the rescue. Mean, on the scene. Presto. You hop in my car.''

"You were waiting for me?"

"Funny how things work out sometimes."

For a moment he fell silent, occupying himself with a cigarette, tamping it on the back of his hand, hanging it at his lip, waiting for the dashboard lighter, finally taking a couple of leisurely drags. Then he reached over, opened the glove compartment, and began searching inside of it. This activity held my attention primarily because I had a good view of the compartment and of the only object he was likely to find: a pistol.

My heart raced, and chemicals surged in my blood. It was getting to be a familiar sensation. At the First Amendment when the bomb exploded. At the hospital, too, whenever the nurse had delivered to me that small white paper cup with the single multicolored capsule. And now, sitting here with the young man reaching for a gun. A young man named Teddy from New York who was an authority on removing bloodstains from clothes.

His hand came out of the glove compartment and the pistol was in it.

I edged nearer the door and slowly placed my fingers on the door handle.

"Hey, Professor, relax. You think I'm gonna whip out a gun, shoot you? Unh-uh. I ever have to shoot somebody, I make it so they never know what hit 'em." He balanced the pistol in his lap and reached back into the glove compartment. A moment later he withdrew his hand again. He was holding a paper napkin, offering it to me.

I just stared at it.

"Here," he said. "Back at the hospital, getting interviewed by the press started your chin bleeding. You get blood all over my seat covers, Professor, maybe I *will* shoot you."

I held the napkin to my chin. My benefactor was watching me and laughing. He seemed to be having a much better time than I was.

"Like I been saying, Professor, I just want to ask you a few questions, see what your story is. The other morning, when you met the lady professor, remember? Well, I was just down the street in my car, watching. I was sort of wondering what she wanted with you, what she said. I was wondering if maybe she gave you something"—he cast his eyes upward, as if he were trying to think of a random example—"maybe a videotape, something like that."

Was *that* what was happening to me? He wanted the videotape?

"You see, Professor, I don't know you. Maybe you're just what you look like, Caspar Milquetoast College Professor. Then again, maybe you and that lady professor are up to your ears in some kind of bullshit. The newspapers are saying all kinds of things. These are screwy times. Who knows what to believe?"

I tried to keep my voice steady. "Now wait, if you think . . . Wait a minute. The stuff about me in the *Herald*, that's strictly to sell newspapers. I didn't have anything to do with the bomb. You're crazy if you believe that—"

My benefactor leaned toward me and put his red, scabby face close to mine. It wasn't a pleasant experience. He spoke in a whisper. What he said confused me more than ever.

"Oh, I know that. I know you didn't plant the goddamn bomb. I've known that all along. I'll let you in on a little secret." He winked. "I know who did."

I didn't leave anything out. For the next half hour I gave him an even more detailed account of that morning with Emma than I'd given the police. He listened, smoking a cigarette, idly sifting through the contents of my wallet, which he'd spread on the seat between us: curled receipts from twenty-four-hour bank machines, crumpled scraps of paper bearing ancient scribblings, a small stack of ID's and plastic cards through which I achieved intercourse with the world.

"Wesley College faculty card," he said. "Mass. driver's license . . . a World Wrestling Federation membership?"

I laughed nervously. "It comes in handy. Some department stores require three ID's."

He ignored me. He paused over a snapshot of Elizabeth and said, "Tasty, very tasty. Anything else?"

I rummaged around in my pockets and pulled out a slim blue envelope I'd received in yesterday's mail.

He said, "Letter from Mom?"

"It's a rejection slip."

"A what?"

"Publishers send them to you when they decide not to publish your manuscript. Actually, a computer sends it. They're all pretty much the same. Thanks, but no thanks."

"You wanna read it for me?"

I removed the slip from the envelope and read, " 'Dear Author: Many thanks for giving Ogden Books an opportunity to review your manuscript; we assure you that it received our most careful attention. We regret to inform you, however, that we will not be able to publish it at this time. Best of luck, blah, blah.' "

"Aww," he said, "that's too bad." He stubbed his cigarette in the ashtray and sighed. "So, Professor, what you're telling me is, you don't know nothing about nothing. You don't know shit from Shinola. This lady professor calls you, but you don't know why, and she takes you to the back of the First Amendment and shows this videotape she got in the mail, but you don't know why that, either. She's about to tell you what's what, but then—*kaboom!*—and you're on your belly like a snake. You sort of remember reaching for the cassette, but you passed out. Far as you know, it's still back there, burned to a crisp."

I nodded.

He smiled placidly. "You want to make any last-minute changes to your statement? That's what the police always ask me."

I shook my head, and he flipped my wallet toward me across the seat. He returned the jumble of papers, holding back only the rejection slip, which he folded and stuffed into his pocket. "You don't mind, do you? It's got your address on it. That way, I ever find out you've been bullshitting me, I know where you live. Makes things a lot easier for me . . ."

The sentence drifted ominously. I was about to speak when he ordered me out of the car. He wasn't through with me. A sea breeze engulfed me as I opened the door, making me aware for the first time that I was soaked with sweat. I watched as my benefactor opened the rear door of the Buick, leaned down, and removed something from the floor of the backseat. It was a small wire cage covered with a yellow towel. He took the cage around to the front of the car, set it on the hood, and pulled away the towel. Inside the cage were two gray pigeons, perched docilely.

"I want you to help me let one of these go," he said. "You know anything about pigeons?"

I shook my head.

"You musta heard of homing pigeons? These are kind of like that, except in reverse. You let one of these go, you don't ever see it again." He removed one of the birds from the cage, handling it carefully, but holding it away from him, saying, "Don't get the wrong idea. I'm not some retard from Brooklyn who keeps a bunch of nasty-ass pigeons on the roof. Pigeons aren't my thing. I'm more into electronics. That's my hobby. See that little collar? I made it out of a beeper. It's a work of art."

Encircling the pigeon's neck was a collar which held a small metal device about the size of a matchbox. A homing device?

He moved away from the Buick, holding the pigeon with both hands, carrying it to the edge of the wharf, as if he expected the pigeon to set out for England. Just as he coiled and drew it back, preparing to release it, he paused. "I usually don't, but maybe we ought to give this one a name. Why don't we call him Professor? Let's say Professor's been a bad pigeon. Let's say he's been bullshitting his new friend who was nice enough to give him a ride from the hospital. Now let's see what happens to him. Ready?''

He threw the pigeon up, and it rose into the air, flapping powerfully. It started out over the water, then turned back. It stayed low, out of the sea breeze. But gradually it began to fly upward, easing up in tight circles, orienting itself.

My benefactor said, ''Why don't you take a shot at it?''

''What?''

''Shoot it,'' he repeated.

''Shoot it?''

''With your finger. Pretend. You know, just for fun. Don't let it get too far away.''

I watched the pigeon circling above us, its trajectory taking it in ever larger circles. Who was I to argue? I raised my forefinger and took halfhearted aim.

I said, ''Pow.''

The pigeon exploded in midair. An abrupt report, the sound of a single firework, muffled in the open space. A poof of feathers, windblown. A tiny clump of gray matter fell straight down, landing on the cobblestones maybe fifteen yards from where we stood. I couldn't take my eyes off the spot where it had been. There was nothing there. When I finally looked back at my benefactor, he was holding in his hand a small plastic device that resembled a TV remote control.

''Helluva shot, Professor,'' he said, patting me on the back, grinning. ''You fuckin' dusted it.''

5

Nick's Beef and Brew is a popular hangout for Wesley Law School students, four blocks west of my apartment in Cambridge. The decor at Nick's is amiably tacky, and the kitchen offers huge mounds of decent, cheap food. I usually ate here during off-peak hours, when the crowd was pleasantly bereft of youthful ambition. But now it was early evening, and the tables teemed with apprentice lawyers engaged in loud, intense debate. I overheard a few arguments about the First Amendment—both the original and its namesake—but the most animated discussions addressed questions of more immediate concern to young careerists: how much the big New York firms were paying first-year associates, how to switch from public-interest law to the corporate realm without losing face.

Three news vans had been parked round-the-clock at the curb in front of my apartment building, which is why I'd spent most of the last two days encamped here. I'd bought a change of clothes at the Wesley Coop, slept in my office at Talbot House, but otherwise I'd been lying low at Nick's. The mysterious Peeper Prof was in no mood for another episode of "Meet the Press." He needed time to think, and he needed a drink.

About eight o'clock, just as I lifted another Molson to my lips, a hand gripped my shoulder. I jumped.

"Whoa, Thomas," Elizabeth said, "it's just me."

I took a couple of deep breaths and composed myself. The bartender came over and mopped up the beer that I'd spilled on the bar.

"You okay?" she said. "I saw the news vans at your place. I figured you might come here. How're you feeling?"

"Shitty," I said. "Shitty and paranoid. It's hard to convalesce when you're being hounded by the Channel Four News team and a maniac bomber."

She didn't ask for an explanation, which is probably why our marriage had lasted almost two years rather than two weeks. She slid onto the barstool next to me and touched my arm. "I wanted to apologize for the other day, hanging up on you. It's been a bad week for me. That's no excuse, but you have to admit, you were saying some pretty strange things on the phone."

"I admit it."

"I finally read the papers. I tried to call you back, but the nurses wouldn't give out your phone number. I had no idea you were in the hospital—"

I raised my hand. "No apologies necessary. It's good to see you. Let me buy you a drink."

During the year and a half since our divorce, I'd made every effort to imagine Elizabeth in moderation: moderately beautiful, moderately happy, and in moderately good health. After all, wasn't it a classic delusion of solitude to fantasize an ex-wife or ex-lover inhabiting some realm of being vastly superior to your own? But not me. Not Thomas Theron, master of emotional perspective. I wasn't about to make that mistake.

Now, sitting face to face, barstool to barstool, my worst fears were confirmed. She looked even more achingly beautiful than I remembered, her eyes larger and brighter, her mouth more sensuous, her jawline more elegant, her hair blonder and thicker, her skin more luminous, and her teeth, so help me God, whiter. She was wearing jeans and an

oversize tweed herringbone jacket, pushed up at the sleeves.
"You look great," I said.

"Health club." She flexed a bicep. "Nautilus. You
should try it."

"I manage a few sit-ups when I get a chance."

"So tell me," she said, "what in God's name's going
on? That piece in the *Herald,* 'browsing or bombing'? Jesus." She smiled slyly, adding, "I don't know what you've
gotten yourself into, Thomas, but I know you better than
that. You may dress like a degenerate, you may hang out
with degenerates, you may even act like a degenerate, but
you're not a degenerate."

I said, "Thank you. Thank you so much."

Again a sly smile. "SDS? You never told me you were in
the SDS."

"I was a freshman. It was the late sixties. I kept hearing
these stories about wild, uninhibited leftist girls. So I joined.
It was more of a hormonal than a political decision."

"So you never set fire to the ROTC building?"

"The only fires were in my loins."

Before we knew it, I'd switched to bourbon, Beth was
nursing her second glass of wine, and we'd drifted into the
gentle dialogue of ex's on friendly terms, a considerate
exchange of lies. No matter how happy you were in the
months following a divorce, no matter how much business
boomed or love blossomed, you must take care to protect
the other's feelings. Be modest about your victories. Well,
as a matter of fact, Thomas, the day after our divorce was
final I won the Massachusetts lottery, but you know, they
spread out the payments over twenty years, and with Uncle
Sam taking his cut——*psseeesh!*——ten million's not that
much money.

And then Beth was quietly telling me of her admiration,
even reverence for Emma Pierce. "God, she's an amazing
woman. Her books have meant a lot to me. *Phallacies*
verbalized the anger of an entire generation of women.
Without Emma we might not know how to articulate the

issues, much less fight for them. . . . Goddamn it! Whenever I think about the hundreds of jerks who went in that porn shop. Damn it, why did she have to be there when it happened?''

I didn't remind her that I'd been there, too. I was spending a lot of energy trying not to stare at her. I invited her to join me for dinner. She made a counterproposal. She offered to fix something at her place and let me have her couch for the night. She said, ''I'm assuming, of course, that you don't want to go home and run a gauntlet of reporters. How's that sound?''

''Too good to be true. What's the catch?''

''You tell me everything. Emma Pierce, you, the First Amendment. I happen to believe in Proposition Six. I want to know what's going on. I want to help.''

I didn't need to be asked twice.

A little more than two hours later we'd eaten and were comfortably settled in Beth's new condominium on Marlborough Street, a renovated brownstone floor-through that she'd bought a few months back. Living room and small bedroom at the front, kitchen and bath in the middle, master bedroom and small balcony at the rear. A wall of exposed red brick ran the length of the apartment. Very pricey, at least in Boston's inflated real-estate market. Apparently her private practice was off to a running start. Mental illness must have been reaching epidemic proportions within the Hub.

I was feeling a lot better now, well fed, padding around Beth's place in sweats and stockingfeet, cradling a large snifter of bourbon as if it were a Fabergé egg. We'd found the sweat suit high up in a closet, old Wesley sweats of mine that Beth had kept; before dinner I'd showered and changed behind closed doors, reverting to a modesty we hadn't observed since our second date. Later, over dinner, I'd kept my promise to rehearse the events of the last four days. Four days? It seemed like four weeks.

Beth was saying, "You actually killed the pigeon?"

"No, no, he was jerking me around. He had a remote-control switch, something that might open a garage door, only he had it rigged to blow the pigeon to smithereens. Hell, maybe I should report him to the Audubon Society. I think it was a visual aid, to show what might happen if I lied to him."

"So what did he want?"

"The videotape. He said he was watching from across the street when I met Emma. He wanted to know why she called me."

"You never really said. Just why *did* she call you?"

"For the same reason you divorced me. I know my way around the Combat Zone."

"Come again?"

Why was it so difficult to imagine Emma stooping to soliciting my help? "I just know what she told me, Beth. She said she wanted to take advantage of—her words—my expertise. She was looking for someone familiar with the world beyond the ivory tower. Whatever she had in mind, she believed the video would win votes for Proposition Six."

Before long Beth had opened a second bottle of the wine we'd drunk with dinner, an old favorite of ours, Trakia cabernet, three dollars a bottle, direct from the estimable Suhindol region of Bulgaria. She was in the middle of a grim account of the women she treated at the clinic, of how often their histories included some warping episode with pornography. "It may not always be the primary factor, Thomas, but I hear it over and over again. You wouldn't believe how many victims of incest say the same thing. Porn was the icebreaker, they tell me, the catalyst. It was the instruction manual. The father or the uncle or the stepfather or whoever would bring some pictures in the bedroom and say, 'Now here's what we're going to do.' "

As if to buffer herself from the import of her words, Beth

reached for my snifter of bourbon, tilted it back, and shivered. She changed the subject.

"So did you watch them?"

I said, "The videos? Never had a chance."

"And you still don't know why they're important?"

"I don't think even Emma knew. The whole story sounds a little cockeyed to me. A friend of hers sent the video in the mail, along with a note that mentioned two other movies produced by the same company. The friend was a former student—I think Emma said her name was Grace—and she's the one who thinks the movies are so important. She said she'd call and set up a time to meet, but Emma never heard from her. So Emma never found out what she was talking about, except that the movies are supposed to really stir things up. Emma apparently believes her. Why, I don't know."

She said, "Maybe the videos are so violent and hateful and gruesome that simply exposing them might win votes for Proposition Six. Wouldn't that stir things up?"

"I don't want to disillusion you, Beth, but if no one's stirred up now, a few more dirty movies aren't going to matter."

"But maybe these aren't just three more dirty movies. Maybe this company is producing something really sordid and horrible, even illegal—"

"If the videos are already illegal, then how will they help Proposition Six? Look, Beth, I just don't think anyone cares. Maybe you should take a quick tour of the adult section of your local video store. The only people getting worked up are the guys standing back there trying to decide which movie to take home for the weekend." I paused thoughtfully, and before I knew it I found myself saying, "Look, if the video stores had a section where the Ku Klux Klan could rent movies about humiliating black men, or Nazis could rent movies about torturing Jews, maybe then people would get angry. But if it's women being humiliated, well, that's just business as usual."

She looked at me. "You're still capable of surprising me,

Thomas. I don't know many men who see things in that light.''

I dipped my head modestly. It'd been so long since I'd said anything that pleased her that I couldn't bring myself to tell her I'd only been quoting Emma Pierce.

Before long we cleared the table and carried our drinks to the sofa. From time to time I'd sneaked glances around Beth's apartment, looking for signs of a new romance. About the time of our divorce, she'd just ended a courtship with a Boston Symphony Orchestra violinist. But there was no copy of *Pro Musica* on the coffee table. No jockstrap hanging on the doorknob of the bathroom, for that matter. No strange brands of bourbon or scotch in the liquor cabinet. Nothing.

"So," I asked casually, "seeing anyone?"

"Who has time? I'm carrying a full load of clients at Booker and trying to build a private practice. Remember how I sounded on the phone? I think potential suitors find that a little hard to take." She ran a hand through her hair and smiled wistfully. "In a way it's a relief. Things are getting scary out there. News from the sexual front isn't good."

"So I've heard."

When she asked about me, I laid it on so thick that she started to laugh, saying, "It can't be as bad as all that."

"You haven't seen my ad in the personals? 'Self-deprecating, self-destructive, chain-smoking academic seeks beautiful woman for vulgar pleasure.' " I affected astonishment. "What, no takers? I know it's hard to believe, but nihilism isn't as sexy as it was a few years ago. On the bright side, I haven't been obliged to master the subtleties of condom etiquette."

Before long I was leaning back on the sofa with my feet up, watching Beth as she moved about the room. I couldn't take my eyes off her. The perfect curve defined by her rear end made my heart flutter with lust and nostalgia. I'd always felt a pang of sympathy for her male clients. Did the sight of those legs, dramatically long and wonderfully fit, cause as many problems as she herself solved, her mind and body working at cross-purposes?

I balanced the snifter on my stomach. I was beginning to feel warm and comfortable and happily inebriated. Relaxing on Beth's sofa in Beth's living room in Beth's new condominium no longer seemed unusual to me. I was having trouble remembering why we'd ever wanted a divorce in the first place. I was starting to get ideas.

Beth said, "So, what should we do about them?"

"Do?" I replied with dull contentment. "Them?"

"The videos Emma showed you. What should we do about them?"

"Do about them?"

"Come on, Thomas. Emma asked for your help. Whatever this is about, it was important to her. If she believed the videos would stir things up, then the least we can do is make some small effort to find out why."

So Beth was getting ideas, too. Different ideas. An edge had appeared in her voice. She was standing at the kitchen counter, rummaging through her purse. Then she placed a telephone call. I was watching her and thinking: I don't want to stir things up. I want things to lie there quietly, maybe gather a layer of dust. When she came back to the sofa, she handed me a membership card to a club called the Video Connection.

"I called them," she announced. "One of the videos is rented. One doesn't show up on their computer, so they don't have it. But the one Emma got in the mail"—I could tell that she didn't want to say the title—"the astronaut parody, or whatever it is, is right there. They're holding it for us."

"You realize," I said, "that just watching it may not tell us anything."

"What can it hurt?"

"Maybe a copy won't do. Maybe we need the actual cassette Emma got in the mail."

"Are you going to sit there and think of all the reasons we shouldn't do anything?"

Context, I thought. Everything is context. Had Elizabeth invited me over for dirty movies a week ago, I would have jumped at the chance.

"Don't look so glum," she said. "It'll be just like old times. Dinner and a movie."

6

It's not the easiest thing in the world to watch porn videos with your ex-wife. Nevertheless, by eleven o'clock we'd sat through *The Right Stiff* twice. Seventy-eight minutes running time. Five fully choreographed scenes of athletic sex. Times two.

Despite what I'd told Elizabeth, somewhere in the back of my mind I really had been expecting a black-market video, some unimaginable perversity masked by the cassette's routine cover. On the outside Sheena Sands the naughty astronaut, yes, but on the inside? By reflex my mind seized upon the morbid clichés of sexual depravity. Bestiality? Pederasty? Incest? Extreme S and M? The apocryphal snuff film?

Wrong. No forbidden images. Unless I was badly out of touch, *The Right Stiff* was pretty much standard fare. More lavishly produced than I was expecting, relentlessly explicit, but routine.

As it happened, the character played by Sheena Sands wasn't an astronaut, but a beautiful space alien who had traveled from her own galaxy in search of the perfect penis. To wit, the right stiff. Her standard for judging male genitalia ran counter to earth propaganda of the last two decades: strictly size. In her own words, she was "out to find a real whopper." The principal advantage of this "quest" motif—surprise—was to increase the number and diversity of sexual vignettes while decreasing the need for narrative exposition.

Every few minutes I heard Beth say, "I had no idea."

I finally asked, "No idea what?"

She said, "I'm not completely naïve about this sort of thing, but the camera shots, my God, they're so invasive. It's all so"—she laughed nervously—"I don't know how else to put it. Invasive. Graphic. And the girl, Sheena . . ." Her voice withered, and she looked over at me. "I just had no idea. Christ, Thomas, what do men get out of this?"

"It's a cheap date."

"What if they already have a date? Don't couples rent these, too?"

"Don't look at me. Dirty movies were never part of my romantic strategy."

If there was anything remarkable about the film, it was Sheena Sands herself. She was remarkably young, remarkably pretty, and remarkably flexible. She moved, spoke, and displayed herself with wanton glee. Her performance was so utterly without inhibition that it wasn't all that difficult to imagine her being from another planet.

Part sci-fi, part costume drama, part farce, the script was self-consciously jokey. Transported to earth from her spaceship (Starship *Intercourse*), Sheena suddenly finds herself in the presence of a hapless, bumbling accountant named George Dufus, who affects the mannerisms of Rodney Dangerfield with one exception—the frenetic collar tug has been replaced by a frenetic crotch tug. They meet on a rooftop; George works in an office below, and he has come to the roof preparing to jump, to put an end to his miserable accountant's life, when Sheena materializes. After a minute or two of goofy dialogue, she imperiously commands him to list the five most famous lovers on earth, past or present. His suicide temporarily postponed, nervously clutching himself all the while, George finally musters a list: Casanova, Valentino, Don Juan, Mata Hari, and somewhat inexplicably, Zorro.

The sex scenes then unfold predictably. Not limited by

time or space, Sheena transports herself to the bedrooms of the famous lovers, who exhibit their prowess in a sequence of torrid auditions. The goal, of course, is to provide a sort of sexual sampler. Mata Hari provides the obligatory lesbian scene. Zorro is black.

Toward the end of the video, Sheena's quest seems doomed. None of the lovers of legend, however skilled, proves to be the lucky possessor of the right stiff. She is on the rooftop again, preparing to return to her spaceship, and nerdy George Dufus is there, too, again suicidal, now having fallen hopelessly in love with the promiscuous visitor from outer space. At the last moment, however, as he stands on the ledge ready to leap, George shyly advances his own candidacy. He does so bashfully, more or less by dropping his pants. Printed across his bikini underwear is the logo ''Home of the Whopper.''

Ah, I thought, the genitalia of adults, the minds of children.

The actor who played George possessed the verbal skills of a fence post. What suited him for the role, however, was an accident of birth. He had been endowed with a sexual organ that would not have seemed out of proportion on a prize bull.

Another thing that inspired Beth to say she had no idea.

At eleven-thirty I rewound the tape, having spent much of the last two hours in danger of a perpetual erection, a circumstance inspired not so much by the movie as by Beth, who sat curled on the sofa next to me amazed and diligent and sexy, unaware of the sexual tension that was oppressing me. But my tumescent stage eventually passed. Boredom and fatigue set in. I kept nodding off. Once, twice . . .

Beth made a pot of coffee. We started in for a third time. Inured to the visual pull of naked bodies, we now determined to focus on stray details, to examine items at the edge of the frame, to concentrate on minutia, however unpromising. Beth warmed to the task, tucking her legs up under her on the sofa, cradling a mug of coffee, notepad in her lap.

Nodding off . . .

I woke with a start. I felt Beth poking me in the ribs, saying, "Thomas, do you see that?" It seemed very late. The TV screen seemed very bright. She poked me again. "Do you see it?"

I passed both hands through my hair, blinked, and squinted in the direction of the TV. Beth manipulated the remote control; the images scurried backward, then stopped, reversed, and scurried forward. I was aware of a high-speed-coupling, a pelvis pumping frenetically, of legs splayed in the air, the impression of a bronco being spurred. A figure stood beside a bed, dressing. Clothes seemed to leap onto it. Then the shadows brightened. Change of scene.

The image froze.

"There," Beth said. "Look."

What I saw was a still-frame shot, one of two exterior scenes in the movie. This one, I remembered, came at movie's end, with George again on the rooftop ledge, and Sheena preparing to beam up, her mission a failure. George, his hand frozen in the act of tugging at his crotch, peers over the ledge. The narrative would soon require that he turn back and win Sheena's love, in the process displaying the entire sum of his thespian skills.

"Yes, Beth," I said groggily. "I know, I know, he's amazing. But I don't think you should fixate—"

"Not his damn pecker, Thomas. Wake up. Look down. Look past him. Below."

Look at what? I wondered. She advanced the film and stopped it at a brief over-the-ledge-shot, offering a glimpse of the street below from George's point of view, the tips of his shoes hanging off the ledge. A sense of a modest height, no more than three or four stories. An urban street, a hint of a park. Lots of leaves.

"Ah," I said, "treetops. For a second I thought you woke me up for nothing."

"In the lower left corner of the frame," she said, ignoring me, "through the branches. There's a sign."

Which was true. Most of the sign was obscured—a street

sign? a storefront? a portion of a billboard?—but it was still possible to distinguish letters. Portions of three words were visible.

BO

PU

LI

Beth said, "Make anything of it?"

"An obscure Chinese poet?" I said.

"I'm serious," she said. "The letters are the beginnings of words. It's a phrase."

"Bob's Pub Liquors?" I suggested. "Bohemians Purchase Lithuania?"

She ignored me and advanced the tape some more. "Now watch this. While he's still looking down, the camera pans slightly and the angle changes. You still see the sign, but different letters appear. Look."

She advanced the tape frame by frame, and sure enough, at the left bottom corner of the frame, different letters on the sign could be read.

STO

BLI

BRA

I said, "Can I buy another vowel?"

Copying the letters onto a legal pad, she said, "You have to combine these letters with the other ones."

"Put them all together they spell *mother*?"

"Would you stop it! You don't see, do you? I always thought it was weird that you never had any aptitude for crossword puzzles." She studied the pad for a few seconds more and then began to rearrange the letters and fill in the blank spaces. With a triumphant flourish she faced the pad toward me and displayed what she'd written.

She said, "Ta-da."

On the legal pad were the words:

BOSTON
PUBLIC
LIBRARY

As revelations go, it wasn't on the order of, say, discovering that the Mona Lisa was Leonardo's self-portrait, but it wasn't a complete dud, either.

I said, "I'll be damned."

Venture Productions was filming porn videos in Boston, apparently not very far from the public library. Filming porn videos, come to think of it, not very far from where Elizabeth and I were sitting at this very moment.

Who would have thought?

7

Early the next week I reached into my letter box, took a deep breath, and pulled out yet another rejection slip for *Helpless Laughter*. A grand total of fourteen, minus the one Teddy had confiscated. But who was counting?

After three years of starting, quitting, starting, quitting, I'd finally finished the manuscript during sabbatical. Another small act of rebellion, of course, a thumbing of my nose at academics. Everyone at Wesley, including the bestowers of a fair-size Whiting research grant, assumed I was laboring on a long-overdue biography of the early-twentieth-century essayist Edmund Lowell.

The irony of my chosen escape was soon obvious. Running away, I found, took a lot more energy than my customary jog-in-place. Visions of leisurely days at the racetrack gave way to a reality of ten-hour stints at the typewriter. Very shrewd, Thomas. Nice escape.

But I surprised myself and persevered. And barely ten weeks ago . . . *finis*. I'd celebrated with a midnight raid on the English department photocopying machines, consuming two bottles of champagne while making copies of the manuscript, then sending *Helpless Laughter* to every publisher in Boston and half those in New York.

And now, rejection slips, a part of the process I hadn't anticipated. Oh, I'd expected rejection, of course; I just hadn't expected total indifference. All form letters, computer generated, which I'd been thumbtacking to the wall above my desk. The expressions of regret always rang a little hollow, as if the salutation had been, "Dear Self-deluded . . ." At some point I began to harbor suspicions that no one—editors? subeditors? sub-subeditors?—had bothered to read the first page. What writer hasn't heard horror stories of manuscripts, unsolicited and unread, consigned to the oblivion of "slush" piles?

If nothing else, today's rejection dispelled that fear. The note was accompanied by a brief, handwritten addendum in an elegant, almost genteel script, the obvious result of an expensive ink pen. Harbington Press, Park Avenue, New York City. I imagined mahogany-paneled offices, pipe smoke, worn leather chairs.

Mr. Theron: Did I miss something? A protagonist who doesn't speak? Should you decide at some future date to submit this manuscript to another publisher, I recommend mailing it in a plastic, zippered container. Anything that so closely resembles Death should be kept in a body bag.

The note was signed Arthur Berenson.

I stuffed the envelope, half-crumpled, into the side pocket of my jacket. After a moment, I retrieved the note and read it again.

I thought: yes, Arthur, but did you like it?

The bombing of the First Amendment soon spawned a host of accusations, prank calls, anonymous tips, and new threats of violence. On Monday a woman representing a sect of radical feminists telephoned Eyewitness News to claim responsibility for the Combat Zone bombings. "The real violence in this country," she declared, "is the violence perpetrated every day against women by pornography. Bombs are simply our way of saying no." She labeled

Emma Pierce an "impotent liberal, unwittingly supporting her male oppressors by trying to work within a legal system that enslaves her."

A local radio talk show received a call from a young man who confessed in a high-pitched voice, insisting that he was a member of a group of anarchist lesbians called the DD CUPS, Demented Dykes for Cutting Up Peckers. . . .

The police were quick to discredit such calls, but otherwise seemed to be making little progress. A Hollywood investigation, some said, long on press conferences and optimism, short on leads or evidence.

The air grew thick with charges and countercharges. Virtually every political faction opposing or supporting Proposition Six expressed revulsion at the violence, circulated the usual we-do-not-condone-terrorism statements, and promptly implicated a rival group. With so many players aggressively seeking the stage, my moment of celebrity didn't extend beyond the usual fifteen minutes. My curtain call took the form of a photograph in last Monday's *Herald*, an action shot of my departure from the hospital. Wild-eyed, disheveled, forearm shielding my face, looking like the latest deranged perpetrator of an unspeakable crime. Caption: "Educator of Our Youth?"

Amid the flood of press coverage, only one item managed to catch my eye. The owner of the First Amendment issued the following statement to the press:

> This act of terrorism demonstrates in the clearest manner possible the low esteem in which the forces of censorship hold the civil rights they claim to support. From this day forward there can be no doubt that this unholy league of so-called feminists and so-called Christians will not be satisfied with a mere abridgment of our freedom of expression. The penalty for disagreement, it seems, is death.

Officious, self-important prose, I thought, even for a lowly pornographer. I scanned the article again. The statement had been issued by the law firm Barrows, White & Abbott on behalf of a client named Byron Choate. I'd never heard of him.

Officious, self-important law firm, I thought, even for a lowly pornographer.

Whoever Byron Choate was, at least he was consistent.

On Wednesday Beth and I had lunch at an old bar-and-grill hangout of mine in the South End. She moved restlessly across from me in the booth; frustration had set her voice at a higher pitch.

"I don't understand it. How could it not be there? We saw it."

I said, "Maybe Bo Pu Li was an obscure Chinese poet after all."

"No, damn it, the sign said Boston Public Library. Why couldn't we find it? It just doesn't make sense."

Beth's plan was simple. Locate the sign, then work backward until we pinpointed the particular building and the particular roof on which the scene from *The Right Stiff* had been videotaped. Easy enough, right? A snap. Piece of cake. If we found the rooftop, of course, there were no guarantees that the rest of the movie had been filmed in the building below, but at least we'd have something. At least we'd have a place to start asking questions, and if we asked enough questions, maybe we'd get lucky. And then we'd have something to tell Emma. Emma was still in intensive care, but when her condition improved enough for her to see us, we'd have more to offer her than just a bouquet of roses. This was the sort of optimistic scenario Beth described to me as we began the search.

I'd tagged along, thinking maybe I might help with the angles and sight lines, something like a surveyor's helper. Of course, I was thinking, too, there are worse things in life than following Beth around on a Wednesday morning when she's wearing her old jeans. I considered it a pilgrimage, gazing upon the altar at which I'd so often worshiped.

Problem was, after spending the entire morning methodically walking the streets circling the Boston Public Library, we couldn't find the sign. We covered every square foot of sidewalk and street and alley, observed the building from every conceivable angle, and there was no sign. Beth was right. It didn't make sense. The sign didn't exist. It was as simple as that.

At one point it occurred to me that the sign might have been an aid to tourists, posted in another part of the city altogether, with an arrow pointing the way to the library. But we asked inside, and no one connected with the library thought such a sign existed.

At a quarter past noon, we stopped for lunch. The Rainbow Rib Room featured the only jukebox north of New Orleans with Professor Longhair, and the only menu in the world with a lunch combo of ribs, white bread, and chocolate milk. Beth wasn't all that happy about my choice of eateries, but I insisted. I was still pampering myself for having been blown up.

Beth surprised me by ordering a scotch. I surprised no one by ordering a double bourbon. The bartender soon brought me a half rack of pork ribs, dripping with a red peppery sauce, half-hidden beneath three slices of Wonder bread. All on a Styrofoam plate. With an expression of horror, Beth watched him position the meal in front of me.

She said, "You're actually going to eat that?"

"I'm taking your advice. I'm starting a new fitness program. Harden my biceps, harden my abdominals, harden my arteries . . ."

I gnawed on a rib bone, and Beth drummed her fingers on the table. In the background, Professor Longhair sang a bluesy number about women losing their minds and men eating wienies for lunch.

I said, "Before you get too worked up about this, tell me one thing. Suppose we do find the movie set—hell, suppose we catch Sheena Sands bare assed with the cameras rolling—how is that going to help Proposition Six?"

"Are you serious? Pornographers across the street from the public library? It's a lot easier to talk about free speech when this excreta is being produced in New York or California. Local TV will go nuts. They'll splash it all over the six o'clock news from now until the referendum. On one side of the street pornographers hiding their faces from the TV cameras, then cut to a shot of the library, a small child on the steps with an armful of books. You don't think that will generate outrage? You don't think that will get out the vote? You don't think that will stir things up?"

I regarded her skeptically. For the past few days she'd been meeting with members of the Coalition of Women Against Pornography, following up her discovery about *The Right Stiff*. Her eyes glowed with conviction. She held her hands in front of her eyes, thumbs inward, as if envisioning a headline. She said, "LA PORNSTERS INVADE BEANTOWN."

I said, "So?"

"The tabloids will have a field day."

"That's where you lose me. The tabloids are *already* having a field day. What's going to change?"

"Not a damn thing if we sit on our asses. It would be great if we could just walk in and ask Emma what's going on, but we can't. So we need to get a line on Venture Productions. Right now, for all we know, Venture Productions doesn't exist. It's just a name on the carton of a dirty movie. The only thing that ties that movie to Boston is a partially obscured sign of the public library. That's all we have."

"I hate to keep putting a damper on things, Elizabeth, but we don't even have that."

Twice in the same week, I thought. After so many months out of touch, we were together twice in the same week. Today I was having a much easier time remembering why we'd divorced. The primary reason was in Beth's eyes right now, a look of frustrated impatience. Beth was a compulsive doer, and I was just as compulsive an observer, and Beth could never quite consider observation a legitimate activity. I'd resisted her calls to action all through our marriage, and now, just as we seemed to be getting on some kind of new footing, I was resisting her again.

I said, "So you think I should try to infiltrate a nest of pornographers?"

"There's no need to be melodramatic, Thomas. No one said 'infiltrate.' Just ask a few questions, see what you can find out about Venture Productions. You know people. That must be why Emma called you."

I leaned back in the booth, blew a lungful of smoke toward the ceiling, and grimaced.

"Aren't you the least bit curious?" she persisted. "This is right up your alley. It's like a moral dispensation to go looking under rocks."

As a matter of fact, I was curious, but I was also feeling a little skittish. Images of hands had begun to haunt my dreams. Emma's bloodied hand, groping up from a clutter of pornographic cassettes. My benefactor's hand, holding the remote-control switch amid a poof of feathers. And weirdly enough my own hand, moving of its own accord, slowly engaging my own neck in a death grip.

"While you're visualizing tabloid headlines," I said, "try this one: PEEPER PROF HITS DAILY DOUBLE: ASS BLOWN OFF IN SECOND BOMBING."

Beth rolled her eyes. "Are you serious? What are the chances of that happening?"

"Virtually nil," I said, "if I mind my own business."

We finished eating in silence. A few minutes later we paid the bill and slipped out of the booth. As we left the bar the construction workers surreptitiously ogled Beth, and Professor Longhair crooned still another song ripe with misery and betrayal.

We crossed Memorial Bridge into Cambridge, drove along Mem. Drive, turned onto Chauncy Street, and crossed over to Mass. Ave. We parked in front of my building and sat there maybe five minutes without speaking. The gutter was still littered with cigarette butts, the residue of the media stakeout for the Peeper Prof.

I could sense Beth studying me, thinking: Emma Pierce virtually saved his damned life and he won't get off his ass and ask a few questions. But what she said was, "I know what's stopping you. It's that damn manuscript you're sending around. You think Proposition Six is censorship, and you think Emma is the leader of a bunch of bluestockings. Every writer in Cambridge is against Proposition Six, so now that you've finished that damn novel you think you have to be against it, too. Well, that's bullshit."

"Come on, Beth, you know me better than that. I never act on principle."

"Then what's the problem? I'm starting to get a weird feeling here, like maybe I'm missing the obvious. Maybe you just like pornography. Maybe you like knowing it's there just in case you ever get a hankering for it."

A note of tension crept into her voice; a nerve had been touched. I felt as though we'd been playing a friendly game of poker, and without our noticing the pot had grown to enormous size, and suddenly we were forced to play for keeps.

"Even if Proposition Six passes, what makes you think it will stop porn?" I asked. "They found pornography on the dining-room walls of Pompeii, for Crissakes. It's existed for centuries, for millennia."

"So there was pornography on the dining-room walls. There were also slaves in the dining-room serving dinner. You think that's a good idea, too?"

"I'm just saying, as long as there's a demand for it, it will continue to exist. Even if it's horrible, there's not a damn thing you or I can do about it. That's all I'm saying."

"Even if it's horrible? Even? That's the goddamn problem, Theron, men really don't think pornography is horrible—"

"Of course it is. I didn't say it was good—"

"You didn't say it's wrong, either. But if it's wrong, shouldn't the law at least say so? I don't care whether Proposition Six stops it or not. At least we should say it's wrong. Free speech my ass. Every moronic congressman in Washington wants to push through a bill to stop protestors from degrading the flag. So what we're going to have is a country where you can't piss on the flag, but you can piss on women all you want."

I got out of the car and crouched by the open window. I tried to speak with a calmness I didn't really feel. I said, "Even if I agreed with everything you say, what do you expect me to do about it? Remember this morning? We couldn't even find a damn sign in front of the damn public library. That should've been the easy part—I presume the sign is out there somewhere on a signpost, stuck in concrete—and we couldn't even do that. Well, pornographers not only move around, but they probably don't want to be found. What makes you think I'm suddenly going to develop a gift for this sort of thing?"

Which was more or less how we left it. A minidivorce.

I ran upstairs, changed, and pressed the button beneath the blinking red light on my answering machine. Professor Braithewaite, the chairman of Am. civ., had called to inform me of a departmental lunch meeting in the small dining room at Talbot House, a week from Thursday. For what purpose, he didn't say. There was something vaguely ominous in the way he ended the message with, "Your attendance is obligatory," but I didn't dwell on it.

I pulled on a pair of shorts, an old cotton shirt, and sandals, and headed for my office in Talbot House. Classes started in three weeks and I needed to prepare. Preparation involved taking the course syllabus I'd used the past three years, changing the date at the top, and photocopying it. No use tampering with a good thing. Should take, oh, about half an hour. Then I'd mosey on over to the bar at Grendel's.

The postman was standing downstairs in the foyer, opening the bank of letter boxes. He gave me a thumbs-down sign and handed me a small bundle of mail.

He said, "This is no fun for me, either."

I pulled out two skimpy envelopes, rejection slips number fifteen and sixteen. "Don't worry, Albert, I'm not a shoot-the-messenger kind of guy."

He grinned. "It's the stiff-the-messenger-at-Christmas guys that worry me."

Folded in with the bulkier pieces proclaiming GRAND PRIZES for MR. T. THERON, I came upon a beige business letter. A little heft to it, I noticed. Rag paper. Embossed letterhead.

I said, "Wait a minute."

I opened the letter and just stood there. It was from Adage Press, the oldest and most prestigious publishing house in Boston.

We here at Adage Press are impressed by your novel, *Helpless Laughter*. We would be most interested in publishing it. Please make an appointment at your earliest convenience to discuss our offer. We congratulate you on your achievement and look forward to welcoming you to our company of distinguished authors. Best wishes,

Samuel Dodds

I read it again.

I found myself suddenly in that rarest of moments. The past ceased to exist. The present became engorged with simple, unqualified joy. The future opened before me as a reservoir of pure possibility. My mind floated, carried on a crest of uncomplicated emotion, unencumbered by doubt or fresh longings or even by coherent thought. I'd hardened myself for so long against bad news that the surge of happiness startled me.

The moment almost seemed to me like that other well-known moment of bliss, similarly liberating and climactic.

And that's just about how long it lasted.

I didn't even make it to a cash machine, much less to a bar. Three blocks outside of Wesley Square, I stopped in my tracks, midwhistle. Something on the opposite side of Mass. Ave. caught my eye.

There, in the window of an electronics store, a dozen television sets were on display, each of them transmitting an image of Emma Pierce. There'd been a flood of TV stories about Emma all week, of course, and the media had been using this very same dust-jacket photograph. In multiples, though, the image was a little disconcerting. The portrait was quaintly posed, maybe two decades old, and didn't do Emma justice.

At this distance, on the largest of the TVs, I could discern a series of numbers superimposed beneath Emma's photo at the bottom of the screen.

Something about the numbers bothered me.

I hurried across the street, weaving through traffic, squinting at the numbers, still fuzzy and indistinct, and thinking: No. No way. A telephone number, I told myself. Maybe an address for get well cards and flowers. Nothing more.

I stepped up to the store window. The photo of Emma lingered on the TV screens. The numbers came into focus. My stomach began to churn; a sour taste rose in my throat. Not a telephone number, not an address, but dates: 1931–1990.

Hurrying inside, I listened to the news bulletin. Carried by a dozen TVs at low volume, the voice-over sounded eerily stereophonic. The announcer read the end of the story, his tone solemn but without dignity.

". . . funeral will be restricted to members of the immediate family. A memorial service has been scheduled for Friday, August 31, at Wesley's Elliot Chapel. A spokesperson for the family has requested that in lieu of flowers, contributions be made to the Coalition of Women Against Pornography."

A salesman stood a few feet away from me, looking idly

in the direction of the screen, grooming himself by wiggling a forefinger in his ear. I asked him what had happened. He took his finger out of his ear and slapped his belly.

"They don't know for sure. They say she was getting better. Then all of a sudden she just croaked. Heart gave out or something. Sounds like to me she just took a real serious turn for the worse."

Part II

The Pornographer

8

8

At a little past noon on Thursday, I was back in the Incredible Shrinking Combat Zone, standing across the street from the Pink Lady, an abandoned strip club now gutted by fire. The Pink Lady had been the target of the first Combat Zone arson, but the club's marquee survived, a local landmark still presiding over lower Washington Street in all its brazen glory. ALL COLLEGE GIRLS. ALL NAKED. ALL THE TIME.

In front of the scorched entrance, a beggar had set up shop, a forlorn-looking dwarf who was working the lunchtime traffic. I stood on the opposite corner and watched him for maybe fifteen minutes. In his face it was possible to find the embodiment of need: cheeks dirty and streaked with tears, beard grizzled, eyes solicitous and dulled by a piteous expression of defeat. His manner was completely devoid of defiance or resentment; regardless of contributions, he politely thanked and God-blessed everyone within earshot.

He was raking it in. As the perimeter of the Combat Zone receded, the traffic passing through had become increasingly upscale; a lot of well-heeled pedestrians were dropping dollars into a small box at his feet. Every few minutes I observed him surreptitiously stash a fistful of bills.

I crossed the street and stood a couple of yards away from him. I said, "Your shoe box runneth over."

He didn't look up.

I said, "Tell me something. Those streaks on your face, are those tears?"

He still didn't look up.

"The reason I ask is, you're so low to the ground, I thought maybe a dog had pissed on you."

That got him to look at me. He squinted and shielded his eyes against the sun. "You get a kick outta that, mister, harassing a dwarf?"

"Could be," I said, "have you seen a dwarf anywhere?"

Giggy Slater was almost as tall as I was, and he'd been running scams in the Zone for at least a decade. This particular routine was simple and embarrassingly lucrative; Giggy kneeled on his empty sneakers, covered the bottoms of his legs with a tattered overcoat, and affected a pose of profound defeat. The ruse was detectable only upon a second or third look, and most pedestrians were uncomfortable with more than a glance. I'd even donated a few times before I caught on. Actually, I didn't catch on; I just spotted him one day standing in line at a nearby liquor store, buying a fifth of Glenlivet.

Giggy kept looking at me until he finally grinned, exposing a row of teeth no larger than kernels of corn. "Shit, the professor. I thought maybe you moved to Mars. Where you been?"

"Keeping to the straight and narrow," I said. "How about you, Giggy? How's life at sea level?"

His voice was a raspy growl. "The air is rich."

We reminisced for a few minutes before I got around to telling him what I was after.

"Hump movies? What you want to know shit like that for?"

"I have a naturally curious mind."

"You want a naturally dead body to go with it? I wouldn't fuck with pornographers, Tommy. People say it's a nasty business."

"No harm in asking a few questions," I said. "I'm just making a few discreet inquiries."

Which is how I'd been justifying it to myself. Tracking

down Venture Productions might not advance the cause of Proposition Six, but what choice did I have? Willing or not, no matter how tenuous my moral obligation, Emma's death had rendered further discussion irrelevant. What had been a favor now assumed the authority of a deathbed request.

The problem was, I was getting nowhere. No one had ever heard of Venture Productions, and no one knew anything about skin flicks being shot in Boston. I'd just spent two days prowling around what was left of my old haunts, and the experience had been a little humbling. Might as well face it, Thomas, I told myself. You're just not the lowlife you're cracked up to be.

"So, Giggy," I said, "what's in store for the Pink Lady?"

"Probably be a shoe boutique this time next year," he said with a snort. "Some of these clubs will hold on for a while, but the peep shows? The all-night movies? They're just flophouses, anyway. You kidding me? Medical center squeezing in from the north, retail district from the south. A lot's changed since Mr. Cuillo died."

Chew-low, I thought. It wasn't a name that inspired a lot of fond memories. Vincent Cuillo had been an aging patriarch of the Boston underworld, former owner of the Pink Lady, and the sort of man who would've made it his business to know about Venture Productions. He also happened to be an amateur poet, a fervent admirer of Ezra Pound, and—not unlike the Combat Zone itself—something of an anachronism. A couple of years back our lives had briefly and curiously intertwined. In his own peculiar way, Cuillo had befriended me. It was a little hard to explain, but one time he'd actually given me a Mercedes-Benz, an automobile I enjoyed for all of two months before someone hot-wired it.

And last fall I'd come across his obituary.

"Keeled over right back there in his office," Giggy said. "Doctors said he wasn't getting enough oxygen to his brain. Lay there for maybe two hours until Gerald found him. You remember Gerald, right, his bodyguard? There's that emergency room on Barker, so Gerald lugged him all the way over there, cradling him with one arm, pushing through all the drunks with the other. It wasn't a lot of fun to watch.''

The flood of dollar bills into Giggy's shoe box had slowed to a trickle. My presence seemed to have disturbed the delicate ecology of charity.

''Why don't we grab us a beer,'' he said. ''Most of my regulars already been by. Man, this ain't the greatest way to make a living. I bought some kneepads off a kid on a skateboard. They help some, but—''

A young woman had paused next to me. Digging in her purse for money, she looked up in time to see Giggy rising to full height, groaning, and rubbing his knees.

''Growth hormone,'' he explained solemnly.

We walked down lower Washington Street, Giggy pointing out the latest signs of demise and sighing nostalgically. ''Zone's never gonna be the same. Property's getting too valuable around here. Real estate's booming.''

''Literally.'' I smiled. ''Booming. Going sky high.''

Giggy erupted in a wheezing laugh that sounded almost as if he were choking. ''Yeah, every coupla weeks, *boom, boom, boom*. I heard that bomb last week went off in the First Amendment. Didn't sound like much from here, not even a backfire. Somebody told me that lady finally bought the farm. I guess that guy was with her, that other professor, he's okay. For a while people were saying he's the one who did it.''

I stared at him. ''Giggy, that was me.''

''What was you?''

''The professor who was there when it happened.'' I touched my forefinger to the small bandage on my chin. ''See, wounded in action.''

''Wait a minute, you're really a professor? I mean, like a teacher?''

''What'd you think?''

''Shit, I don't know, you're always carrying a *Racing Form*. I thought you were a gambler, you know, 'the professor.' '' He was regarding me with something akin to dumb wonderment. He narrowed his eyes. "So whatdaya teach?"

"Literature."

"You mean like poetry?"

I nodded gravely, as a police officer conceding that he'd shot someone in the line of duty. I said, "It's part of the job."

Giggy silently pondered the revelation. "It's kinda weird, Tommy. It's kinda like hearing that Doctor J, you know, that Doctor J is just a doctor."

We ducked into a small bar off Tremont and stood alongside a dozen or so construction workers who were leaning over bottles of Budweiser and watching soap operas on the bar TV. A few men were playing nine ball. The pool table was two-thirds regulation size, covered with orange felt, and tilted. If you could get the object ball in the southeast quadrant, I recalled, gravity did the rest.

Giggy was still in a sentimental mood. "Everything's moving out to the suburbs. With the sex business, it's like squishing the air in a tube, man. Squish it here and it pops up someplace else. A couple of clubs are already out there, out along that stretch of Route One near Revere. A big club called Manray's opened maybe a year ago. Big, fancy club, almost like Atlantic City. All the girls used to strip around here are dying to catch on there. People say it's something to see. But I guess you knew that."

Manray's? I'd never heard of it.

"You got to give Mr. Choate credit. He did all right for himself. He bought up everything around here at the right time, and now he's gettin' out while the gettin's good. Got himself set up at Manray's. I'd say he's got it covered."

"Mr. Choate?" I said. "You mean Byron Choate?"

"Yeah, the last couple of years, he bought up most of Cuillo's holdings. Hell, he owns the Pink Lady. He owns most of the parcels around here. Now he's just sitting back while the yuppie developers make offers."

The same man, I recalled, who owned the First Amendment. The man with the expensive law firm. The man with the gift for self-important prose. The lowly pornographer.

"He don't really look the type, but you never can tell. Young guy, kind of pale, keeps his hair tied back in a little ponytail. I've only seen him around here a couple of times. Doesn't really stand out. When Teddy's with him, you hardly notice him."

I stopped short. "Teddy?"

"Yeah, the guy that works for Mr. Choate. Teddy."

I thought, Oh, shit. Could it be?

"What does Teddy look like?"

Giggy's eyes brightened. "Like fucking death. He got here from New York about six months ago, just another ugly guy. But the last time I saw him, his face was a fucking mess. Gruesome. Looked like he tried to shave with a cheese grater."

I said, "That's a treatment for acne."

"You know him?"

"Not really. I know who he is."

Giggy cackled. "A treatment for acne? Yeah, well, you ask me, ol' Teddy needs a treatment for his treatment. He's bad news. I know it sounds crazy," he added, lowering his voice to a whisper, "and I haven't seen it myself, but people say he does this little thing with a pigeon you wouldn't believe."

"Oh," I said, "I'd believe it."

Later that night I sat alone at the faculty club bar, trying to absorb what Giggy told me. So Ugly Teddy worked for Byron Choate, who owned not just the First Amendment, but a sizable portion of the Zone and a new suburban club called Manray's. Teddy wanted the videotape, which probably meant Byron Choate wanted the videotape, which meant . . . I had no idea what it meant. And what did any of it have to do with Venture Productions? I'd been poking around for two days now, and I felt like I was going in reverse; the more questions I asked, the dumber I got.

Around ten o'clock, I spotted Rolland Palmer at the other end of the bar, and since he was here, I figured it couldn't hurt to ask him, either. Rollie was an associate professor at Wesley Business School, and my working premise was that pornography had a lot more to do with free enterprise than free speech.

"Skin flicks?" he said. "In Boston?"

Rollie held a match over his pipe bowl and studied me through the puffs of blue smoke. He was wearing a paisley bow tie and an oxford-cloth shirt, his navy blazer draped over the back of his barstool. His expression was playfully abashed.

"I suppose it's not altogether a surprise, Thomas. Videotape has brought radical change to the porn industry. Compared to shooting sixteen millimeter, there are virtually no start-up costs, you need very little in the way of technical expertise, and the overhead is negligible. That probably tempts a lot of new people to try to break in, to become players. As a business market, porn has opened up all over again. It's frontier days."

I looked at him. "Did I miss an article in the *Wall Street Journal*?"

"Someone ought to cover it. There's an occasional article in *Variety,* that's all. Porn's an eight-billion-dollar-a-year industry. *Billion.* That's bigger than most of the feature-film companies put together."

He warmed to the subject, and I listened, pleasantly surprised that his knowledge of the business world extended beyond the conventional markets. "We live in curious times, Thomas. The sexual revolution may be over, but the cat's out of the bag. We're not returning en masse to chastity. Real sex may take it on the chin, but fantasy sex is on the rise. A lot of sexually active people are converting from doing to looking"—he shrugged—"and that gives pornography an impressive upside."

"No safer sex than that," I said, "a man and his TV."

"Or his telephone. Who would have believed that Dialing for Dolores would fly? It's the ultimate dry hustle. Vicarious sex, all forms of solitary sex are going to be big business in the next few years."

"A brave new world of voyeurs, eavesdroppers, and masturbators?"

"Consumers, Thomas, consumers."

"With the business world poised to meet the demands of a changing age?"

"No one ever claimed the marketplace is pretty."

I said, "So you're saying just about anybody could start a company like Venture Productions?"

"No, no, I said just about anybody could *produce* a skin flick. That's the easy part, creating the product. What would it take? A video camera, a dirty mind, and some people willing to copulate in front of a camera. But if you're telling me Venture Productions already has videos out there in the stores, ready to be rented, that's another story. Being a pervert is easy. Distribution and sales, that's the hard part. That takes money, organization, clout."

I said, "So that would shut out the little guys, the basement entrepreneurs."

He nodded. "Probably. When you come down to it, the essential difference between Hugh Hefner and some guy in Peoria taking Polaroids of his wife is distribution and sales."

I had an uneasy feeling that when the product was hardcore videos, things got a lot trickier. More dangerous. In the world of pornography, wasn't distribution and sales merely a euphemism for organized crime?

"That's what it used to mean," Rollie agreed. "Now, I honestly don't know. I'm just making a few educated guesses. It's pretty obvious that whatever the porn industry used to be, it's not that anymore. Everything revolves around video rental. There are thousands upon thousands of video stores, and most of them carry an adult list. I'm telling you, it boggles the mind how much money that means. And for all intents and purposes, it's legal. Somebody's getting rich off it. I'm not sure who, but somebody."

Soon the bartender was wiping down the bar and storing the garnishes and perishables in a small refrigerator. The faculty club closed at eleven-thirty, which was one of its primary shortcomings. This blow was softened by the fact that members were entitled to run tabs. I received two bills a year, both about the size of two weeks' pay.

Rollie and I paused outside on Quincy Street, watching a group of students pass by. Laughing, walking on unsteady legs, they appeared to be doing precisely what Rollie and I were doing, returning home from a bar. Ah, professors and students pursuing shared interests. Was that what people meant by "academic community"?

"You mind telling me what the hell you're up to, Thomas?"

"Oh, to this point, I'd say what I'm up to is killing time."

"Well, I'd be careful if I were you. For a humble scholar, your name seems to be popping up in the news with alarming frequency. I read what happened at the First Amendment." He smiled. "As a general rule, people who get blown up say once is enough."

"I won't argue with that."

"Care for a bit of advice?"

"Always."

"If you're going to do this, whatever it is, keep your eye on the money. Any business enterprise as marginal as porn will be something like a shell game. You can't let the sleaze or the skin distract you. The pea is money. Everything else is just subterfuge. Keep your eye on the money."

I thanked him and we shook hands and he headed off into the night. A moment later he called back to me, his voice disembodied in the darkness.

"Remember," he said, "don't think sex, think money."

A half hour later I lay sprawled on my bed, staring at the ceiling, contemplating my next move. "Don't think sex," I repeated aloud, "think money." The words didn't exactly float off my tongue. It wasn't going to be easy reversing a mental habit of a lifetime.

9

Early the next morning I arrived at Beth's to file another lack-of-progress report. On impulse I'd stopped by a street vendor's and bought her a small bouquet of late-summer flowers.

"We have an anniversary coming up," I explained.

She eyed my offering dubiously, as if the flowers were the initial gambit in an elaborate scheme to render her emotionally vulnerable. She looked beautiful, just leaving for work, wearing a black-and-white-checked jacket with padded shoulders, black skirt, white blouse with a high collar, and pearls. She may have been right about the flowers.

"Anniversary?" she said. "We do not."

"Not precisely an anniversary," I said. "We're about to cross a significant temporal boundary. Starting Sunday we'll have been divorced longer than we were married."

"Ah," she said, "you remembered."

"That's one of the problems with being jaded. Right beneath the jaded part is a mass of unexamined sentimental goo."

She half turned as she held a vase under the kitchen tap. "How do you manage it? I don't know anyone else who can make 'jaded' sound preferable to normal emotion."

We sat at her kitchen table and drank coffee. Beth wasn't having any better luck with Venture Productions than I was.

She'd spent hours on the phone to Barnard College in New York, where Emma Pierce had taught for almost three decades before coming to Wesley. She was trying to track down the woman Emma had mentioned to me that morning at the First Amendment—the friend named Grace, the former student who started it all, mailing *The Right Stiff* to Emma, insisting it would stir things up, saying she would call later and then . . . nothing.

"It took about two dozen calls, but I finally got someone to listen to me," Elizabeth said, "a young woman in the registrar's office who's a fan of Emma's. Once she understood what I was after she was very eager to help. But it's still a long shot. The name Grace isn't much to go on, and former student could mean just about anyone in any of Emma's classes for the last twenty-five years."

"Could be a list of thousands."

"If we had a last name, this would be a snap."

I said, "Like finding the public library sign, that kind of snap?" Silence. "Beth, I'm not even positive her name was Grace."

"You're having second thoughts?"

"I barely had first thoughts."

Whatever her name was, finding her would be almost too good to be true, a quick, clean escape from the confusing muck I'd been dredging up around me. No more pigeon murderers, no more pornographers with ponytails and preppie-sounding names.

"Emma called her a friend," Beth said. "To me at least, that suggests someone older. But referring to her as a former student sounds more formal, as if it might be someone younger, so who knows? Care to speculate, Professor?"

"Don't look at me. In the literature department, we mostly refer to our former students as unemployed."

I looked at the vase of flowers between us, and then I watched her jotting notes on a legal pad, planning. Beth could happily lose herself in the task at hand, but these domestic encounters were beginning to threaten my equilibrium, leaving my sentimental goo dangerously exposed. I felt a compensatory surge of cynicism. I waggled my eyebrows impishly.

"No one said this was going to be easy," I said, "but we'll keep plugging. I have a pretty good track record, remember? This isn't my first mission of an X-rated nature to the Zone. Ring a bell?"

Beth frowned. "What's so funny?"

I said, "Think back. Remember what you used to hide in the bottom drawer of your dresser?" I let that sink in a little. I said, "Under your sweaters?"

A look of puzzlement. Then slowly her cheeks began to redden.

I said, "Right. Now remember when that particular item malfunctioned, and you were too embarrassed to buy a replacement? Remember who came to the rescue?"

"Thomas, that was a back massager."

"I've heard it called that, yes. 'For all those hard-to-reach places.' "

"Damn you, Theron," she said, increasingly flustered. "Am I doomed to have that held over my head for the rest of my life?"

An imaginary cigar perched in my fingers, I executed a fair impression of W. C. Fields. I was my old jaded self again. "If you're holding it over your head," I said, "you're doing it wrong."

At a little past ten, I found Monkey Poussin in the Lounge Fifteen, handicapping the afternoon's program at Suffolk Downs. He was working on his speed figures, and he'd taken most of the bar for himself, spreading out his *Racing Form*, along with several heavy notebooks stuffed with stray papers, a couple of legal pads, a thick book of charts and mimeographed past performances. He was pacing back and forth along the bar, lost in concentration. There were a couple of empty bottles of Rolling Rock in front of him, a cigarette hanging on his lip, and two more lit cigarettes balanced on ashtrays along the bar. If you didn't know better, you'd think he was some crackbrained alcoholic ex–MIT professor whose hobby was calculating the trajectories of NASA spaceflights.

I said, "So, Monkey, what looks good?"

Monkey was a tiny, jittery man. He spun toward me with worried eyes, his chin tilting upward, as if he were a very small dog offering his neck to a rottweiler.

"Jeez-us! What . . . hey, Thomas. Hey!" His features expressed several subtle stages of relief as he gradually realized that I wasn't a creditor. He possessed large, wet eyes and a mouthful of big, nicotine-stained teeth. On occasion he had reason to be nervous.

Monkey's appetite for betting action was prodigious, and his losses legendary. He always needed money and sometimes I defied common sense by lending it to him. At Suffolk Downs he'd achieved a status roughly comparable to a small debtor nation. If you hung around him long enough, he'd make you feel like a small midwestern bank with poor judgment.

But Monkey knew almost as much about the marketplace as Rolland Palmer, although not from a business-school perspective. Monkey had taught himself finance for the same reason convicts teach themselves criminal law: he was hoping that knowledge would give him power over the thing that tormented him.

So I was more than a little discouraged when Monkey drew a blank. Venture Productions didn't mean a thing to him. I sat there at the bar, staring morosely at the beer I'd just ordered. I glanced at my watch. I wasn't particularly in the mood to start nursing beers at ten in the morning. At this rate, I was going to get alcohol poisoning long before I got anywhere near Venture Productions.

"That stuff these reporters come up with is crazy," Monkey was saying, happy for the interruption. "All that about lesbians and religious fanatics and terrorist bombings is pure horseshit."

I nodded glumly, not really listening. Monkey seemed as preoccupied with the Combat Zone bombings as everyone else.

"You believe the newspapers, you might as well hang it up. Maybe that political terrorist crap happens somewhere, but it's not happening here. It's no secret what's going on. Everyone around here knows. The police know, too, they just have a hard time proving it."

"I suppose you know who the mad bomber is?"

He paused to take a gulp of beer. "Yeah, I know. Except I wouldn't say he's mad. I'd say what he's doing is kind of fucking smart."

I said, "He?"

"Forget the politics, Tommy. What's happening is real estate. Flipping buildings."

I was slowly tuning in. I'd begun to swivel my barstool slightly, tracking the homunculus as he paced back and forth along the bar. For his part, Monkey was not unaware of my reviving interest. He could be a little like a drug dealer when it came to information. He'd give it to you free until you got interested and wanted more. Then he'd make you pay for it.

He stopped pacing and stood in front of me. He leaned in and whispered confidentially, "Where are you, Tommy?"

I just looked at him.

He said, "Come on, just tell me. Where are you right now? Where are you?"

I had no idea what he was talking about.

I said, "In a crummy bar with a compulsive gambler having beer for breakfast?"

"Ooo, touchy, aren't we? Look, what I'm getting at, we're in Boston, Tommy. Boston, don't you see?"

I'd had this kind of dialogue with Monkey before. The experience was a little like trying to float on water. The trick was to relax and let yourself go; struggling only made things worse.

No doubt about it, I agreed, Boston was where we were. Yep, Boston.

Monkey said, "Now tell me, what's the first thing you think of when you think of Boston?"

I said, "The Celtics."

He rolled his eyes. "Come on."

"The Freedom Trail."

Eyes squinted closed, he pinched the bridge of his nose and slowly shook his head. I'd often used a similar pose of resignation and disappointment to motivate some of my slower students.

I said, "Baked beans?"

"Christ, Tommy don't be such a fucking tourist! Arson, okay? Arson is what you think of when you think of Boston."

"Arson," I said. "That's what I was going to say next."

"Come on, you knew that! Boston is the arson capital of the whole country, of the whole fucking world for all I know!"

Monkey was watching me expectantly, as if I were about to express profound gratitude for the insight he had just bestowed upon me.

I said, "So?"

He began pacing more rapidly than ever, sighing and shaking his head, saying, "Tommy, Tommy, Tommy," but I could tell he was enjoying himself. At Suffolk Downs, whenever he was privy to some inside tip, he would act similarly put-upon. His goal was to increase his economic leverage. The next landmark of a conversational journey with Monkey, I sensed, was close at hand. Money was about to change hands.

He said, "You're gonna want me to spell this out, aren't ya?"

I brought out a twenty-dollar bill. I had to bring out another one before he stopped pacing, palmed the bills, and perched on the barstool next to me.

"All right, I'm going to tell you a story, just like one of those little stories in the Bible, you know, a parable. Verily, verily, I say unto you. Except this parable is about real estate, okay?" He moved closer and spoke in a low voice.

"Now listen up. Let's say in the last year or so you've acquired a group of buildings in this depressed area, okay? Thing is, your depressed area is surrounded by lots of pretty good areas—whatever the opposite of depressed is—so a lot of yuppie developers are starting to line up at your door, waving their checkbooks. So you're sitting pretty, right? You're thinking serious profit."

"For the record," I said, "we're talking about the Combat Zone, right? About a man named Byron Choate?"

Monkey was shaking his head furiously. "This is a parable, remember? For forty bucks you don't get names. When Jesus told the meek they was gonna inherit the earth, you think he named names? Unh-uh. Not on your fucking life. See, he was protecting himself. That way the meek couldn't get lawyers and sue."

Don't struggle, I thought. Relax. Float.

"Okay," he said, "all these buildings you've acquired have no real value themselves, they're just waiting for the wrecker's ball. First thing a developer's going to do is level 'em, make way for his condos, hotel complex, office complex, two dozen Benettons, designer popcorn outlets, whatever. The point is, the buildings are a liability. No developer's gonna give you good money for buildings that have to come down. All you're really selling is land and location. You with me?"

I smiled patiently.

Monkey ordered another Rolling Rock and paid for it out of my pile of change on the bar. He took a swig of beer and said, "Okay, let's say maybe you're a little greedy. Maybe you want to get paid for the buildings and the land. So you start considering your options. All of a sudden a light bulb goes off in your head. You remember where you are."

He began encouraging me with little inward flicks of his fingers, as if he were on the sidewalk helping me to parallel park.

"Come on, Tommy, where are you?"

"Boston," I recited dutifully, "the arson capital of the world."

"Riiiight. Give the man a Kewpie doll. If every one of your buildings burned to a crisp, shit, that's the best of all possible worlds. You cry all the way to the bank. You collect insurance for the buildings, and you still have all these el primo lots to sell to the yuppie developer."

I was beginning to get the drift. The point of Monkey's parable seemed to be that Byron Choate had torched his own buildings. Had acquired the services of Ugly Teddy from New York. What surprised me more than anything else was that the story made sense.

Monkey took a couple of quick, impatient drags on his cigarette. "And one day God smiles on you. You get lucky. Things get even better. You wake up and find all these women are parading in front of your buildings. You ask somebody, what the hell is all this? Somebody tells you these women are plenty pissed off. These buildings you own have businesses that piss these women off. They're mad as wet hens. They're so mad that some of them might do something crazy. They make threats." Monkey looked at me and pretended to flip through an enormous, imaginary bankroll. "And that's when you break into a big, shit-eating, money-making grin."

Was it possible? I wondered. Could the antiporn terrorist bomber be the pornographer himself? Rollie Palmer was right. Don't think sex, think money.

I finished the Rolling Rock and sat there a moment, trying to digest what he'd told me. "Byron Choate is not only bombing his own buildings," I said, "he's blaming it on the antipornography groups?"

Monkey dipped his head and threw up his hands, as if to defend against a blow. "I never said that. No names. I just told you this story." But after a couple of seconds, a look of pure wonder appeared on his face.

"Blame?" he said. "Nobody has to blame nobody. It's beautiful, made to fucking order. Every reporter in town is falling all over each other trying to stick it to the lunatics, religious freaks, lesbians. And all the lunatics are trying to stick it to each other. No matter how off-the-wall something is, people believe it.''

Peeper Prof, I recalled. Browser or bomber.

Just before I left, Monkey added a final wrinkle. ''You know what the kicker is? You don't just take all these profits and insurance money and hide it under the mattress. You invest. You take all this money and maybe you start your own Combat Zone out in the 'burbs. You open a new club out on Route One, a big spiffy place, all shiny and brand-new.''

''A club called Manray's?''

He didn't answer.

I said, ''Manray's is Byron Choate's place.''

Monkey smiled. ''I never said that. You hear me say that?''

Early afternoon I stopped for lunch at a hole-in-the-wall hot dog joint on Rowe Street called Hershel's Hot Dog Haven. No lunch counter, no tables or chairs, just a small window open to the street through which Hershel turned a brisk business in hot dogs, coffee, and soda.

I leaned down and peered through the window. Hershel was a slim, sinewy man wearing a filthy apron. With a single motion of his spatula, he gave about twenty franks a quarter turn on the grill.

I said, ''Give me two with mustard and relish. Easy on the rat hairs.''

''Fuck you, buddy,'' he muttered.

I waited until he turned around and eyed me. He slid two hot dogs across the sill between us. He said, ''Hello, Thomas, since when you got something against rat hairs?''

I stood there eating and contemplating what Monkey had told me. The scenario sounded plausible, even compelling, but so did a lot of things that weren't true. The source was Monkey Poussin, I kept reminding myself, not Carl Bernstein. At Suffolk Downs Monkey trafficked in precisely that same kind of inside information. A lot of those hot tips sounded plausible, too. Which was small consolation when your horse finished last.

And even if it was true, just where did it get me?

I'd been lifting up rocks, and small, slimy creatures were crawling out from under; they just happened to be the wrong slimy creatures. I'd learned more than I cared to about the economics of pornography, arson, and real-estate scams, but I still knew virtually nothing about Venture Productions.

Maybe I was asking the wrong questions.

The more I thought about it, the more absurd my strategy seemed. Why would anyone know about Venture Productions, any more than they would know about, say, Lorimar Productions or MTM? The analogy was simple. You didn't ask people if they had heard of Lorimar Productions; you asked them if they had heard of Joan Collins.

I said, "Hey, Hershel."

"Yeah?"

"Let me ask you something."

"Yeah."

Point-blank, I decided, no preliminaries. "Have you ever heard of Sheena Sands?"

He didn't miss a beat.

"Sure, yeah. Sheena Sands. Yeah. She's got a body that'll make you weep. I see her in a lot of the skin mags now, those X-rated movie magazines. Whatsis, you know, stuff like *Erotic Cinema Review*. She's getting a big rep. She's a star."

A change of questions, I thought, works wonders.

Hershel said, "Funny, I got in an argument with a customer of mine just a couple of weeks ago. He kept swearing he'd seen her before anybody'd ever heard of her. He said Sheena Sands might be making movies now, but not even a year ago she was just a young girl stripping. I thought he was lying—I mean, who remembers a stripper's *face*—but he swore it was her."

"A customer of yours saw Sheena Sands stripping?"

"Yeah, said she was pretty good. That's why he remembered her when she showed up in the movies."

"Did he say where she was stripping?"

He frowned and cast his eyes upward. "What's it called? Nice place, supposed to be very nice. Not around here, out in Revere. They haven't been open even a year yet. I've been thinking I ought to check it out, except who wants to go way the hell out in the sticks? You know, out there on that stretch of Route One that's starting to get funky. Shit, what's it called?"

I repeated the name that I'd been hearing more and more as each day passed. The new club that had opened on Route One. The big glitzy club that represented the latest incarnation of the Combat Zone. The club that Byron Choate built.

I said, "Manray's?"

He snapped his fingers and pointed at me. "Manray's, that's it."

10

Herman Melville, Ralph Waldo Emerson, Walt Whitman, Henry David Thoreau . . . Thomas Carlyle Theron?

The receptionist at Adage Press peered at me over a pair of half glasses and frowned. When I displayed the letter with Samuel Dodd's signature and mentioned my appointment with Percy Hotchkiss, she frowned again. I didn't blame her. I couldn't believe Adage wanted to publish me either.

Adage Press occupied an elegant five-story town house just off the Public Garden; the outer office was almost a caricature of what I'd imagined, an ornate but comfortable nineteenth-century reading room. High ceilings, mahogany-paneled walls, chesterfield sofas, and wing chairs scattered about on antique Tabriz rugs. Portraits of the literary gods hung everywhere; large oils on canvas, spare pencil profiles, early photographs of wizened men with penetrating gazes. What nooks remained teemed with prizes and memorabilia: American Academy of Arts Awards, National Book Awards, a few Pulitzers, a letter from Samuel Clemens. A bust of Emerson occupied a bay-window pedestal, yet even the sober transcendentalist was subdued by familiarity; someone had used his head to support a battered tweed walking hat.

The only nod to modernity was an elaborate security system. While the receptionist conferred quietly on the telephone, I studied the buzzered inner door, hoping it wasn't designed to bar authors who'd been sent "yes" letters by mistake. The receptionist nodded begrudgingly toward a nearby chair and told me that Mr. Hotchkiss would be out shortly.

I waited. It was eerie, I was thinking, very strange. Once again my life was intersecting with public events. Six months ago Adage Press had been in the news, too, though with nothing approaching the sensationalism of Proposition Six. In this room, I knew, the pervasive sense of calm and insularity was deceptive. Even here, behind the staid facade and the impression of glacial movement, there had been change, even upheaval. Adage Press had achieved headlines on the business page.

Adage, the last great name in publishing to remain independent, had finally succumbed to the economic imperatives that had determined the fates of the other great publishing houses, forcing them into the secure paternal embraces of large corporations. Six months ago the press had been sold for $300 million to a communications conglomerate owned by Samuel Dodds (dubbed the "empire builder" by the press), who counted among his holdings two national magazines, a textbook publisher, a chain of bookstores and theaters, and who was now in the process of completing a package deal for a half dozen TV stations.

The sale of the prestigious house unnerved a lot of book lovers and publishing purists. The literati bristled; brows were knit; tongues were clucked. When a publisher has to answer to the bottom line, some feared, quality inevitably suffers. Serious books go unprinted, while the blandest of commercial appeals crowd the shelves of bookstores. Publishing was a calling—huff, huff—a sacred trust, not a business.

Much of the uneasiness was generated by Samuel Dodds himself. Dodds was a self-made man with a self-made fortune, an unpretentious but gifted salesman blessed with a knack for beating corporate executives in their own boardrooms—or such was the face he presented to the world. Whether or not his public image derived from the efforts of a New York public relations firm, Dodds seemed to relish it. At the time of the sale, I remembered, the new owner of the most revered publishing house in Boston had boasted in an interview that he hadn't read a book in ten years.

The interview caused a minor tempest. A local book reviewer had dryly questioned Dodds's intellectual capacity, calling him a "rude man without redeeming qualities of spirit or soul, at home in the world of getting and spending, perhaps, but not in the world of letters. In short," the reviewer concluded with exquisite condescension, "a master of business administration."

I held in my hand the letter with Dodd's signature, crumpled and slightly smudged from rereading. Let's not be too hasty, I thought, let's not rush to judgment. Ten years is quite a dry spell, yes, quite a gap between books, but why not give him the benefit of the doubt? Maybe he was simply waiting for the right book.

"Professor Theron?"

A rumpled man of maybe sixty years approached me with his hand extended, smiling affably. "My name's Percy Hotchkiss. As I mentioned to you on the phone, I'll be editing *Helpless Laughter* once we get your name on a contract. I'm happy to have the assignment. I just finished the manuscript last night. Congratulations."

His blue eyes were piercing and alert; the rest of him was a mess. His beige sweater vest was dotted with pills of wool, his shirt collar was badly frayed, and his baggy corduroy trousers were about to give way at the seat and knees. If he crossed this room enough times with his hand extended, sooner or later someone was going to slip a quarter into his palm.

I said, "To tell you the truth, I was beginning to worry. Publishers haven't exactly been beating a path to my door."

He smiled. "A novel with a speechless hero? That's a tough sell."

"It didn't bother you?"

"When you lug home as many manuscripts as I do," he said, winking, "you begin to wish more authors would try it. I especially enjoyed the racetrack scenes. I used to play the ponies a bit myself. It really struck a chord when your hero bet his entire savings on a filly named Jesus Saves."

"I wasn't sure readers would swallow that."

Before the receptionist buzzed us through the door, Percy Hotchkiss paused at the bust of Emerson, retrieved the battered tweed hat, and patted Emerson on the head, saying, "Heel, boy, that's a good Waldo."

I followed him up two flights of stairs and along a row of small cubicles that reminded me of my own office in Talbot House at Wesley. The air in the hallways was seasoned with pipe, cigar, and cigarette smoke. Proof, I thought, of the centrality of nicotine to the creative process. No cigarette police here.

Along the way Percy introduced me to some of his colleagues, young men and women eccentrically attired, chatting and joking with an easy rhythm born of years of comradeship.

Here, too, I observed evidence of turmoil. Two dour young men squeezed by in the narrow hallway without speaking. A chilly silence descended upon Percy Hotchkiss and his group as they watched the men pass. Expensively tailored gray suits. Yellow power ties. The tension was palpable, as if two armies were encamped here, each with different uniforms and different allegiances, uneasily coexisting.

"It's no secret," Percy sighed, "the waters around here have been roiled. Anytime there's a takeover you always hear a lot of cheerful talk from new management about staying the course, blah, blah, blah. You know, the reason we bought your company in the first place is that we like the way you do business—that sort of thing. But heads always roll."

Two more men with purposeful strides squeezed by without speaking.

"Fresh troops," Percy said. "MBAs, otherwise known

as squeaks.'' He cocked his ear toward the noisy footfalls of the young men. "Hear that? Wing tips.''

The question in my mind must have been obvious, because Percy laughed and gave my shoulder an avuncular pat. "Oh, don't worry about me,'' he said. "I'm too old to be sent packing. And most of the younger men and women will land on their feet. My only concern is for those who stay on and tough it out. What kind of projects will they be taking on? If you've just edited a book nominated for a Pulitzer Prize, how are you going to get pumped up for a ghostwritten autobiography of Robin Leach?''

Percy's tiny office overflowed with books—books stacked two deep on shelves that rose to the ceiling, books jammed sideways into the crevices between shelves, books balanced in knee-high piles on the floor—leaving room only for two chairs pressed up to either side of a desk. We slipped through the door one at a time, as if we were fighter pilots easing into a cockpit.

"Which brings me to a happier topic,'' he announced after he'd settled in. "When your manuscript appeared on my desk the other day with a note from Mr. Dodds, I had misgivings. But now, I couldn't be more pleased. I consider his decision to publish your novel a wonderful omen.''

My face flushed with pleasure. Samuel Dodds was proving himself a man of uncommon intelligence and perception.

"An omen?''

"I finished *Helpless Laughter* just last night,'' he reported happily. "You can't imagine how excited I was to discover that your novel has no commercial appeal whatsoever.''

I cleared my throat. "Thank you, uh . . . that's great news.''

"I'm teasing, of course, but something's afoot. I don't think you truly appreciate the significance of the letter you received. Samuel Dodds signed it. Dodds himself! Not only that, he's here, upstairs, at this very moment!''

"Dodds?''

"He was already in town tying up some TV deal, and he decided to stop by and sign up your book personally. I just got word this morning. I tell you, everyone here feels very good about it. It bodes well for the future."

"I'm not sure I'm following you."

"What it means," he explained, "is there's still room at Adage Press for quirky little novels, books for which there's no ready-made market, books such as yours. I think Dodds is using your novel to send a signal to all of us, allaying our fears. We've been worried that the future of Adage might be one relentless stream of glitzy, commercial projects. Hell, maybe all that bad press finally got to him."

I was a guinea pig? I wondered. Me and my . . . what did he say? Quirky little novel?

"Don't get your feathers ruffled. All I'm saying is, commercially speaking, yours isn't a safe book. You didn't write it with one eye on the market. It takes a little nerve to write a book these days with no sex in it."

"And with a protagonist who doesn't speak," I added.

"Who doesn't have a name for that matter."

"Who only gambles and laughs."

It felt peculiar, sitting here and assisting my new editor as he compiled a list of everything that would doom my book to commercial failure.

Percy smiled reassuringly. "You don't know what a relief it is to read something that tries to be different. It has flaws, to be sure, but in its own way, it's ambitious. It creates an interesting world . . . actually an underworld." He pointed to a stack of manuscripts on his desk and flicked his fingers dismissively. "If I read one more lamebrain mystery," he said, "I'm going to puke."

Another editor popped his head in the doorway to ask Percy's advice on some bit of esoterica. They seemed to speak back and forth in a publishing code, exchanging knowing looks and knowing laughs. A minute later Percy turned back to me. "Now," he said, "about the title."

"What about it?"

"Before you go up to meet him, Mr. Dodds wanted me

to discuss a revision that he seems to feel strongly about. A compromise may be necessary.''

''I was sort of attached to *Helpless Laughter*,'' I said. ''It's second nature.''

''Just hear me out. The title he has in mind requires only a minor emendation. In a sense it achieves precisely the same tone as *Helpless Laughter*. Vulnerability, isolation, with a small undercurrent of defiance.''

''Okay, let me have it.''

He said, *''Naked Laughter.''*

I said, *''Naked Laughter?''*

''Give it a chance,'' he said, ''let it sink in. You have to admit, *Naked Laughter* does resonate in much the same way.''

I let it sink in.

''I don't want to seem argumentative, but if it's the same, why change it?'' I asked.

''One-third of books are sold on the basis of the title. That's a fact of life. Like it or not, *Naked Laughter* is catchier. It will strike a browser as sexier.''

''An image of a naked person laughing is sexy?''

He was carefully tamping his pipe, nodding sympathetically. ''I understand how this might throw you for a moment. Let me put things in a different perspective. Any strategy designed to broaden your audience and increase sales isn't necessarily a bad thing. You care about the book, so why not ensure that as many people as possible read it? And there's certainly nothing wrong with making Samuel Dodds happy, the man who's footing the bill. He paid a truckload of money for this house, so you may have to humor him a bit. If you balk on this, who knows? Nothing's been signed.''

I said, ''The old good publisher, bad publisher routine.''

''Why not consider it a compliment? Hell, an honor. Sure, it may just be a whimsical exercise of authority, but at least he's showing interest. At least he's taking a few minutes to meet you. If I were you, I'd be relieved ol' Sam didn't come up with something really funky.''

"*Naked Laughter,*" I said. "It sort of grows on you, doesn't it?"

"Give me this one, and I think I can hold the line against other changes. *Naked Laughter* isn't so bad. I guarantee, this will help us market the book."

Everything he said possessed a certain logic, but I couldn't really tell if Percy Hotchkiss believed any of it. Did I detect a certain weariness behind all his words of encouragement, as if he was merely being brave in the face of impending doom? It occurred to me that I might have been witnessing the final throes of his relentless optimism.

Before long Percy escorted me upstairs and through a network of corridors and on into the suite of offices that Dodds had taken for his temporary use. He wished me good luck and hoped he'd be seeing me soon. I rocked back on my heels nervously. I told him I hadn't really dressed to meet an empire builder–media mogul.

"Relax, how bad could it be? The man doesn't read books, remember?"

A secretary ushered me into Dodds's office and left me there. Dodds—I guess it was Dodds—had his back to me, engulfed in an enormous executive chair of black leather. For the next ten minutes, he kept me waiting as he fielded a nonstop series of telephone calls. With his chair swiveled away from me, I couldn't make out much of what he was saying, but judging by the frequency with which he referred to the stock ticker beside the desk, I guessed he wasn't swapping old literary ancedotes.

Corner office, picturesque view of the Public Garden. Inside, there wasn't a book in sight. Whichever exec normally occupied the space, I supposed, knew who signed the checks. He wanted his boss to feel right at home. If illiteracy's good enough for Mr. Dodds, yessir, it's good enough for me.

Finally the chair swiveled toward me.

"Your first novel, Professor?"

I nodded.

"Good, that's good."

"It is?"

"Yes. It gives us, as your publisher, an opportunity to present you as an exciting new voice in fiction, before you've had an opportunity to provide evidence to the contrary."

"Oh."

He didn't talk like the rube he'd been pictured as in the press, and he didn't look like one either. A small, immaculate man—mid-forties?—he possessed a huge, photogenic, exquisitely groomed head, which made his small body seem puppetlike. His hands were tiny and delicate and always in motion, gesturing as he spoke. Young face, old eyes. Thin lips. The knot on his yellow tie was so small and perfect and tight that I couldn't help wondering how he secured it without causing the veins on his neck to protrude.

Dodds glanced at his watch and bared his large, white, bonded teeth in something supposed to resemble a smile. His eyes held me with frank confidence, as if I were an object brought to him for appraisal. He suggested we get down to business. He pronounced "business" so that it possessed almost a sensual quality.

"Don't take this the wrong way, Mr. Theron, but I'm going to be blunt. I haven't read your book and I don't intend to. To be perfectly honest, I couldn't give a fuck whether Adage publishes it or not."

"Seriously," I said, "speak your mind. Don't hold back on my account."

Again the impersonation of a smile. "Yes, well, as a matter of fact, I don't intend to hold back. I have a responsibility to this organization. I assure you, my indifference to your book has a sound business purpose. It tends to give me an edge in negotiating your contract, don't you think?"

There may have been people in the world who could have articulated this view and appeared charmingly frank rather than merely brutal. Samuel Dodds wasn't one of them.

"Listen, Mr. Dodds—"

Damn! Why didn't I call him Sam? Sammy?

"—I'm not expecting much. I've heard that there's very

little money in fiction, but I'm a little at sea. I'm going to have to give some thought to what my negotiating posture should be."

"I can save you some time. During my brief reign here at Adage, I've learned one crucial fact. All first novelists have the same negotiating posture. It's called bending over."

He punctuated his speech again with his odd impersonation of a smile. It finally occurred to me what was so unsettling about it. It wasn't a smile at all, but a gesture of aggression. Samuel Dodds was simply baring his teeth, like a dog or a shark.

I wondered what would happen if I reached over and pulled the knot on his power tie just a little bit tighter. Would he bite me? An assortment of belligerent rejoinders were popping into my mind, the little verbal assaults that surfaced whenever I felt threatened. I reviewed them one by one, then looked at him and said, "Okay, Sam, where do I sign?"

11

Manray's was a big, expensive-looking club fronted by a parking lot full of big, expensive-looking cars. A large neon sign had been erected on stilts high above the club—the word *Manray's* in curvy red neon script under a royal blue palm tree—a beacon to the travelers on Route 1. The architecture was supposed to be soaring and airy with a tropical signature, but the club bore an uncanny resemblance to an oversize International House of Pancakes.

I weaved between the parked cars near the entrance, thinking, So here's what happens when flesh peddlers flee the decaying inner city for the suburbs. From inside I heard a muffled roar and a few catcalls, which sounded curiously high-pitched. Lively crowd, I thought. In the Zone, it was all the patrons could do to keep from passing out into their beer.

At the door a bulky young man wearing a tuxedo blocked my path. College football lineman, I guessed, all bull neck and baby fat. His head was massive, but his eyes, nose, and mouth were bunched efficiently at the center of it.

He said, "Sorry, sir."

I stopped. "Yes?"

He said, "It's Tuesday."

I said, "Ah, Tuesday. Of course. Thank you very much. I'll make a note of it." When he didn't move away from the door, I said, "You're not expecting a gratuity for that?"

He didn't smile. "Tuesday is ladies' night. We have an all-male revue this evening. No men allowed."

I said, "An all-male revue with no men?"

"No male patrons, sir," he explained. "We feel that the presence of male patrons might inhibit the ladies during the show. Sorry, it's policy."

By now it was painfully obvious. Small groups of women were beginning to emerge from the club. In twos and threes, mostly young, well dressed, laughing hysterically, and very drunk.

One of them passed me, giggling. "Miriam, I can't buh-LEEVE you did that!"

I looked at the doorman and said, "Maybe you can help me. I'm trying to locate a dancer who may have worked here. Female dancer. These days she's calling herself Sheena Sands. Ring a bell?"

Silent and bored, he gazed past me into the distance.

I said, "Any chance I could just slip inside for a few minutes? I promise to be as inconspicuous as possible. I'd just like to ask some of your fellow employees. It would be a big help."

He'd heard it all before. I was just the latest pathetic bozo trying to harass one of the strippers, probably in the name of love. I knew he was asking himself: Why couldn't some customers accept that whatever happened inside didn't extend beyond the front door?

"Sorry, sir, Manray's employees aren't allowed to give out personal information about the dancers."

"And that's that?"

He stood impassively. He reminded me a little of the robot in *The Day the Earth Stood Still*—Gord Whatever—who nobly guarded his master's spaceship, waiting for a call to action. Nothing fazed him, either.

Sighing and turning on my heel, I said I'd be back the following night.

"I'd advise you to bring a date, sir."

"A date?"

"On Wednesday nights Manray's is pleased to present

our famous Jack and Jill Revue," he recited. "Our stage show features the finest in both male and female striptease. Only couples, sir. No admittance without a date."

I didn't bother asking him if the club ever set aside an evening for dissolute old shitbags who drank too much and behaved like assholes.

I thought, Well, screw it. You've come this far, Thomas. Give it another shot. I didn't particularly want to cause a stink, insist on my right of entry to an all-male nude revue, so I opted for the bribe. I reached into my pocket, brought out a twenty, and gave him a glimpse of it.

"It's an hour's drive back to Boston," I said. "Just a few simple questions, nothing more. I'd be very grateful if . . ."

The money didn't tempt him in the slightest. He remained unswervingly polite.

I said, *"Klatu barato nictu."*

"Sir?"

"Never mind," I said, "wrong code," and headed back to my car.

Two women were weaving through the parking lot, laughing hysterically, swaying as they walked; they paused and steadied themselves against the fender of an Olds 88. Like the other women I'd seen coming out of the club, they were maybe late twenties, attractive, and very drunk. I passed by them no more than ten yards away, but they didn't notice me.

"I can't STAND it!" one of the women squealed. "It was HUGE!"

She was spreading her hands a couple of feet apart, the classic, hyperbolic measurement of the fishermen. "God, it musta been . . . what? How many inches?"

Her friend made a face as though she were swallowing cough medicine. "How would I know? In Newton they only taught us the metric system."

I thought they'd never recover from that one.

"You remember that little bikini he was wearing, the guy who did the nerd routine?"

The two women looked at each other, eyes wide, then shouted in breathless unison, " 'Home of the Whopper'!"

Elizabeth said, *"Naked Laughter?"*
I said, *"Naked Laughter."*
"Really? *Naked Laughter?"*
"Come on, what do you think? What does it bring to mind?"
She considered the title for a moment. "Our honeymoon?"
Our first signs of progress had put us both in a pretty good mood. I was giving Beth a ride home from her Brookline office and along the way telling her everything I'd learned—at least suspected—about Byron Choate. A shadowy pattern was beginning to emerge, the dimmest of outlines. The significance of the porn videos, I'd come to believe, wasn't their content so much as what they represented. I was only guessing, of course, perhaps guessing wildly, but I accepted my conjectures for the same reason some people accept the existence of God: If I was wrong, what did it matter?

One thing was clear. Whatever questions I asked, the answer I kept getting was Byron Choate. He'd parlayed his holdings in the Combat Zone for Manray's and a fresh start on Route One. Now, two dancers at Manray's turn out to be stars in Venture Productions videos. A coincidence, perhaps, but another explanation was far more intriguing: Wouldn't a club featuring male and female strippers offer a logical base from which to launch a video production company?

Just how high did Byron Choate's ambitions run? Was Manray's merely a toehold in some envisioned realm of porn, literally sprung from the ashes of the Combat Zone? Not a bad idea from a business point of view. Be the first on your block to adapt porn to the changing times. High-tech vice in the safe suburbs. What was Rollie's phrase? "The ultimate dry hustle"?

"If he hired that guy Teddy to commit arson," Beth

observed somberly, "then he murdered Emma. It's as simple as that."

"I know."

"Don't you think we should go to the police?"

"And tell them what? That my main clue is the logo on some guy's underwear? That my sources for these eccentric allegations are a beggar who pretends he's a dwarf, a gambler named Monkey, a guy who runs a hot dog stand? Do you know what the police would do—I mean, once they stopped laughing?"

Once we got to Beth's place, she began shucking her work clothes the moment she stepped inside the door—just as she had when we were married. She stepped out of her shoes and then out of her skirt as it fell into a heap on the floor; she touched the kitchen counter for balance; I watched raptly as she curled her panty hose down past each ankle and off. Funny, I thought, how the passage of time could restore suspense to such an innocent domestic ritual.

Elizabeth said, "I've got something to show you."

I smiled. "Don't tell me your underwear says 'Home of the Whopper' too? That ruins my whole theory."

She shot me a grow-up look, pulled on a hooded sweatshirt, and wiggled into a pair of faded jeans. She began rummaging through some papers on top of a small desk in the living room. She said, "You're not the only one who's been busy. I've had some luck, too."

I said, "You found Grace."

She shook her head. "Our friend in the registrar's office is still working on it. She'll call the moment she comes up with anything."

I said, "You found the library sign?"

She shook her head. "Don't remind me."

"Well?"

She handed me a copy of a paper called *Dirty Water*, an underground weekly that had flourished in Boston during the late sixties and early seventies, now reduced to lethargic sleaziness. The paper was opened to the classifieds, a page featuring escort services, full-body massages, and personal ads soliciting sex. Lots of "DWM seeks SF for discreet interludes, double-jointed a plus." Some of the codes were more exotic than I remembered. What the hell was a DBMC?

My eyes came to rest at the bottom right-hand corner of the page where Beth had circled an advertisement with a black felt marker.

She said, "People run ads for nude models in here all the time, so I asked myself, why not a casting call for a skin flick? Brilliant, huh?"

ACTRESSES, ACTORS NEEDED, FILM EXPERIENCE HELPFUL BUT NOT NECESSARY. CONTACT MS. LOFTON, VENTURE PRODUCTIONS, P. O. BOX 1035.

A casting call? Damn, why didn't I think of that?

"I came across it last week and got off a note to the box number. Ms. Lofton finally called back yesterday."

"Wait . . . you've already talked to her?"

"Well, she sounded a little bubbleheaded, but yes, we talked. I tried to pump her for information on the phone, but she wasn't very forthcoming. Basically she said enough with the questions, what can I do for you?"

"And?"

"I told her I needed a job. I told her I wanted to audition for a part."

"You what?"

"Look, Thomas, it's not as if we have dozens of hot leads. We don't have the luxury of picking and choosing. We have to follow what we get."

I wasn't sure what to say. I had a vision of myself suddenly old, befuddled by the willfulness of youth. No, young lady, you most certainly are not going to audition for one of these . . . one of these . . . *art* movies!

Passing my hand through my hair, I turned toward the liquor cabinet, pulled down a tumbler, and poured myself a generous bourbon. Poking around the periphery was one thing, but walking right in and sticking our noses in the middle of . . . well, I didn't know what. But if I was close to the mark on any of this, Byron Choate was not only a pornographer, but an arsonist and murderer. And at least one person who worked for him carried a gun.

"You can relax," Beth said, "the girl wouldn't give me an audition. She said thanks, but they didn't need any more actresses. She said if I wanted she'd give me a call as soon as they needed someone."

As I brought the tumbler of bourbon to my lips, I was aware of Beth standing close behind me. I felt her arms encircle my waist. She hugged me.

I said, "Mmmm."

She propped her chin on my shoulder and whispered, "Thomas?"

"Mmm-hmm?"

"Don't be upset."

"I'm not upset. I'm relieved. All I'm saying is, let's take things slowly. We're making progress, why push it?"

She said, "I'm afraid there's more. I haven't finished."

"Yes?"

"The reason the girl at Venture Productions wouldn't give me an audition was because they're not looking for women, they already have women. They need men. She said what they really needed was actors."

I set the bourbon on the sideboard and turned to face my ex-wife just as she was saying, "That's what I've been trying to tell you. I set up an audition for you."

12

It's the shirt, I thought. It must be the shirt.

When I closed the door behind me in the private dining room at Talbot House, a dozen or so of my colleagues stopped eating and stared up at me. I was a half hour late, yes, but strolling in late for Am. civ. lunch meetings wasn't the sort of offense that provoked stares. I slipped unobtrusively into my customary chair nearest the door and farthest from the bureaucratic action. At the far end of the gleaming cherry table the department chairman, Professor Gayle Braithewaite, observed me silently.

It's my shirt, I told myself again. Green palms; red, blue, and yellow parrots. Everyone's admiring my shirt.

Only a last-minute call from Braithewaite's secretary had kept me from missing the meeting altogether. I'd been on my way out the door when the phone rang, pausing one final time to contemplate a confession the Apostle Paul had made to the Romans almost two thousand years ago, which I'd typed and posted above my desk. It was a sinner's complaint, a dire commentary on the impossibility of free will, and lately, the guiding principle of my life.

THAT WHICH I WOULD DO, I DO NOT. THAT WHICH I HATE, I DO.

Today also happened to be the day Beth had scheduled my appointment—I couldn't bring myself to think "audition"—at Venture Productions. Hence, my spectacularly gaudy shirt. Last night she'd instructed me to search my closet for "something tacky, something a bachelor-of-the-month might wear." Which didn't exactly give me the clearest visual image. I found the polyester parrots wadded up at the bottom of my closet, worn once to a New Year's Eve party years ago.

Tink-tink-tink-tink. Braithewaite was tapping his water glass with a spoon and clearing his throat. His gaze again settled on me.

"I'm afraid we've been getting a barrage of letters, Thomas, complaints from alumni and parents. They see your photograph in the papers, they read about . . . pornography? voyeurism? terrorism? What must they think? That we've handed their children over to an anarchist? A sybarite?"

I thought: It's not the shirt.

"We have a responsibility to address these charges," Braithewaite continued, "to consider whether they merit further investigation. Frankly, from what I've heard about Proposition Six, I'm a little surprised that you've permitted yourself to become associated with it. Censorship of any kind undermines the very foundation of academia. I needn't remind you that the intellectual life of each of us in this room depends upon an open debate among controversial ideas."

I groaned inwardly and thought: Controversial ideas? The Am. civ. faculty—myself included—had as much experience with controversial ideas as we had with intercontinental ballistic missiles. But I didn't say that. I responded with deference and humility. I explained that my only sin had been to answer a call for help. I'd intended no political statement, although it was certainly my right to do so. "Professor Pierce asked for my help," I concluded mildly, "and I offered it. Any one of us would have done the same. What happened afterward was simply out of my control."

Professor Braithewaite was fluttering his fingers in front of his eyes as if he were being bothered by gnats. "Ah, yes, poor Emma," he said, frowning, "a tragedy, of course, a tragedy. . . ."

He reminded everyone of the memorial service the next day, then fell into a long digression, a rambling eulogy to Emma, which he interspersed with veiled swipes at the women's studies department. Braithewaite considered women's studies a craven pandering to women and minorities. Recent events only confirmed his worst fears: if you lower academic standards, it's only a matter of time before someone gets killed.

For the next few minutes there was a lot of vague, accusatory talk, some breast-beating about free speech, but things weren't all that bad. Gradually I began to relax. This was a faculty meeting, after all. I'd attended enough of them to know that whatever the goal—censure, praise, reordering secretarial supplies—it was rarely achieved. I doubted that my own appearance on the agenda would focus the wandering minds, would unite the disparate voices in anything resembling a chorus of condemnation. Another forty-five minutes or so, and I'd be home free.

Glancing around the table, I saw mostly distinguished, aging scholars who might have been on weekend pass from an elitist nursing home. Here and there sat young associates, beardless youths who solemnly hung on the words of their elders, learning the pecking order, busily identifying the seats of power in order more ardently to kiss them.

If there was an unknown, it was Stephen Kenan. Kenan's presence at such a small-potatoes gathering should have unnerved me, only I had a pretty good idea why he was here. Kenan was the great addled genius of American Puritan studies, professor emeritus, one-time patriarch of the department, who through a combination of advancing years and a weakness for crystal Methedrine had reverted to his earlier role as enfant terrible.

He'd come, I suspected, not as a participant or observer, but as a diner. Kenan compulsively attended free meals, and his special love was the all-you-can-eat institutional fare heaped before us. Oblivious to the proceedings, he noisily shoveled in huge mouthfuls of industrial-grade mashed potatoes. The chairs on either side of him remained vacant, accommodating his thrashing elbows.

Twenty minutes later and things were still looking good. I listened happily as hobbyhorses were ridden, grudges revived, axes ground—all to the background thunder of Kenan's energetic masticating and slurping. Professor Lutcavage offered a sheepish confession of complete ignorance of the topic at hand. "Excuse me, Gayle, precisely what is this Proposition Six to which we keep referring?"

And then:

A squeaky voice. A false note of self-deprecation.

"I'm the junior man here—this is all a bit new to me—so last evening I took a moment to acquaint myself with regulations relating to committee procedures. According to the bylaws, we are obliged to present any charge relating to moral conduct before the entire faculty, as well as before student representatives."

The voice belonged to Peter Van Buren, a young associate sitting to my immediate right; he'd been hired from Princeton while I was on sabbatical. Van Buren had a reputation as someone you shouldn't turn your back on. "I hate to make waves, but Professor Theron's case is precisely the sort that requires referral. If you ask me, it's damned irresponsible of anyone succored by this university to undermine the very ideals that nurture it."

No one asked you, you officious little shit.

"Excuse me, Peter, did you say 'succored by this university' or 'snookered'?"

"I've heard about you, Theron," he said, staring at my parrot shirt, his eyes cold and impersonal, like a predator's. "If you're attempting to trivialize this issue, I don't think you should get away with it."

"Are you saying that I should be put on trial?"

"Rules are rules."

I leaned toward him and whispered, "Don't screw

around. If you want to score a few points with the geezers,
fine, just don't do it at my expense.''

"Just what are you suggesting?"

"I'm suggesting that you pipe down, you little toad. I'm
suggesting that if you're looking for an ass to kiss, kiss
mine.''

"Wha . . . what the hell did you say?" he stammered.

"You heard me."

"Damn it, I want . . . I demand . . .''

At the other end of the table Braithewaite began plinking
his water glass and frowning. "Now, Peter, what's trou-
bling you? Please, everyone, we're having trouble hearing
you. Speak up.''

At that moment the room became very quiet. It reminded
me of that moment in old Tarzan movies when the hunter
notices the sudden hush of the jungle, and all the bearers
look around uneasily. Not quiet, but the absence of sound.

All eyes slowly turned toward Stephen Kenan. He had
stopped eating, which accounted for the queer silence. The
commotion had roused him. His eyes were ablaze.

"Whores!" he shouted suddenly. "Images of whores!"

His enormous head jutted forward like a turtle's, the withered skin of his neck dangling. He surveyed his fellow
diners as if for the first time.

"Yes, Stephen?" Braithewaite inquired meekly.

"πορυογραφς. Porno-graphia. Images of whores!" A
large curd of some unidentified vegetable rode the corner of
his mouth as he spoke. He directed toward his colleagues a
withering stare and demanded, "Tell me quickly! What was
the Victorian term for ejaculation? Anyone?"

The old professors around the table sat mute, avoiding
Kenan's gaze and fidgeting like freshmen.

"Are you deaf?" Kenan cried. "Quickly! What was the
Victorian term for ejaculation?"

I suppressed a smile, knowing that the god of chaos had
finally intervened on my behalf. Of course the god of chaos,
like every other god, helps those who help themselves.

"Spend?" I called out.

"Yes!" Kenan croaked, pounding the table. "Spend! Not come, spend! Don't you see? The eroticists, no less than the historians or poets, reveal the basic preoccupations of an age. Spend! A reduction of the world to material economics. Now tell me something else. Which sexual position fascinated the Victorians above all others? Which position of sexual congress appears most frequently in the illicit renderings of the age?"

I had no idea. I was about to hazard a guess—hell, say anything—when Van Buren beat me to it, eager to impress the great Kenan.

"The missionary position? That is, face to face?"

The disdain on Kenan's face would not have been greater had Van Buren positioned a huge turd at the center of the dining table.

"Imbecile! I'm not speaking of sexual practices, I'm speaking of the sexual imagination! What fascinated them?"

"Uh, well . . . perhaps some form of . . . autoeroticism?"

"Not what fascinates you, my young onanist, what fascinated them!" Kenan impatiently lit a cigarette, drew on it, and waved it about his head distractedly. "Sixty-nine, don't you see? Sixty-nine! If you took the time to look, you'd find images of mutual oral copulation everywhere in the literature. The oral-genital position represented to the Victorians a perfect cycle of expenditure and consumption. Spending and consuming, spending and consuming, spending and consuming. . . ."

As he repeated this last phrase, a violent fit of coughing took hold of him. Deep, shuddering, painful coughs. The gobbet of vegetable, which miraculously adhered to the corner of his mouth, was now propelled to the opposite side of the table, where it skidded beneath the rim of Van Buren's plate. The spasm eventually released him. Kenan sat silent and winded.

"Yes, Stephen," Braithewaite offered soothingly. "Yes, I see. How . . . interesting."

And that was that. Braithewaite took advantage of the lull to push the meeting toward an abrupt end; a moment later we were filing out of the room. Van Buren remained behind, trying to make amends with Kenan, who ignored him. At the door Braithewaite took me aside and offered a final, vague admonition "not to engage in conduct unbecoming a professor of the university." He smiled weakly.

I looked into Braithewaite's old, watery eyes and solemnly assured him that there was no need to worry. I didn't have the heart to tell him what I was about to do.

"Parrots?" Elizabeth stood in the doorway, appraising my shirt with bemused resignation.

"It suits me, huh?"

"I said *bachelor*-of-the-month, not bowler."

The address for Venture Productions was near the harbor on Duffy Street, an old factory district undergoing rehabilitation. I guessed that we'd find Venture Productions in the unrehabilitated part. As we drove closer, the adrenaline began to pump in my blood. I was feeling a strange combination of dread and exhilaration. Beth was giving me a pep talk, saying, "Relax, just go in and see what you can find out. What's the big deal? What have you got to lose?"

"Other than my self-esteem?"

She reached around to the backseat where she'd stowed a large leather shoulder bag.

"What's that?"

"No hip, unemployed actor would be without a rehearsal bag." Then she reached up and attached a small piece of silver jewelry to the rim of my right ear.

"If it's all the same to you, I'm not going in there wearing earrings, okay?"

"Not earrings," she said, "an ear cuff. Very chichi. Maybe it will give you an overall air of irony. Let everyone know you're just kidding about the shirt."

The building itself was a lot spiffier than I'd expected, a converted four-story warehouse of red brick, freshly sandblasted. Along the ground floor were a half dozen new storefronts and a couple of vacancies with real-estate signs in the windows.

I sighed heavily, got out of the car, and squatted by the open window. "I look like a complete asshole, right?"

She winked and handed me the issue of *Dirty Water* folded to the advertisement. "That's what we want. Only a complete asshole would answer this ad." She squeezed my forearm. "Come on, lighten up. Try to think of this as a wonderful opportunity. What if Proposition Six is successful? You won't simply be teaching American civilization, you'll be influencing it. You'll be affecting fundamental change in the way women are perceived in this country."

I said, "Be still, my heart."

I still couldn't believe what I was about to do. I headed up the sidewalk toward the storefronts, looking for number 29, and when I found it, the small sign on the oak door said TELE-TECHNIQUES, INC. I went inside anyway.

"May I help you?"

"Venture Productions? The sign on the door—"

"Old sign," the woman said, "come on in."

"I'm looking for a Ms. Lofton?"

"I'm Sandy Lofton."

She was sitting behind a glass desk, wearing a leather miniskirt, and showing a lot of leg. Older than I'd expected, skinny, and pale as a vampire. Her black hair was spiked high and there were big streaks of silver on either side of her head. Her breasts seemed wildly out of proportion to her small frame; beneath her black jersey, they appeared to be the size of small sofa cushions.

I said, "My girlfriend called you the other day and set up an appointment."

"Name?"

Shit. What name had Beth given her? My name? Shit.

"Come on, this is the easy part. Name?"

"Don Carter."

That didn't seem to cause a problem. Of course she probably didn't know that Don Carter was the greatest right-handed bowler of all time. So far, so good. The woman behind the desk didn't exactly jump up and down and shout "A star is born!" but she didn't laugh either. I don't know why not.

"So, Don, you want to be in pictures?"

Arch smile. "I guess show biz is in my blood."

"Anything else in your blood we should know about?"

She handed me a three-by-five card and I sat down and printed some phony information on it. I'd been trying to scan the paper on her desk, without much success, searching for . . . a production schedule? A convenient summary of locations and dates? There wasn't much to see. The office itself was small and neat, furnished with wicker chairs, glass tables, and corn plants. Nothing hinted at a darker purpose; if anything, the freshly painted white walls, the gleaming oak trim and floors suggested an antiseptic, almost Scandinavian fastidiousness. The only thing that looked promising was a door off to the side of us, and I wondered where it led. Maybe that's where they stored the K-Y jelly.

She read what I'd printed on the file card and said, "So tell me about yourself. Any experience?"

"To tell you the truth, I'm not too familiar with what kind of jobs are available. I was just hoping . . ."

"You need the money, right?"

I shrugged. "What I'd really like is something offscreen. I don't know, a desk job, maybe. Something like what you do."

"This isn't MGM. I don't do this full-time," she said. "During production, I'm the AD. Occasionally, I fill in as a fluffer."

Fluffer. It sounded like one of the many jobs of unclear purpose that I'd seen listed in the credits at the end of movies—gaffer, best boy, grip. "Sounds good to me," I said. "Could you use another fluffer?"

She peered at me over the rim of her glasses. "You don't know what a fluffer is."

"No, but I'm willing to learn."

"A fluffer," she began, and stopped. "How can I break this to you? A fluffer is a girl who keeps the male actors aroused between shots, at a peak of excitement, so to speak, while camera positions are being changed." She let me hang there a few seconds, relishing my discomfiture. "Are you looking to make film history?"

"No, no, I have enormous respect for cinematic tradition." Pause. "Just out of curiosity, who keeps the actresses excited?"

"The guy who brings 'em their paychecks."

I said, "Of course."

We quickly established that I had absolutely no experience related to film, not even high school plays. I didn't mention that I'd given a few memorable classroom performances.

"What I was thinking," I began, "is that I could work on scripts. I've never written a screenplay, but I'd like to try. I'm a writer."

"Writer." She pronounced the word as if I'd said duckbill platypus. "We're talking about adult videos, remember? We've already got people who can spell uh-uh-uh-uh."

"What about oooeee?" I suggested helpfully. "Eeeyyy-iii? Yippee-yi-ki-yay?"

"Cute," she said, "very cute, but no. Sorry, Mr. Carter, all we have for novices are bit parts, you know, a couple of new faces, new bodies." She appraised me matter-of-factly. "How big are you?"

"Six-one. A hundred and eighty the last time I weighed myself."

"No, no, no," she said. "How *big* are you?"

I sighed. I had a sinking feeling that I knew what she was really asking me. She waited for my answer, batting her eyelashes charmingly, and my mind began to drift. What was I doing here? Why was I standing in a pornographer's reception area, dressed like the bowler-of-the-month, using an alias, wearing an earring, fielding

questions about the size of my privates? Why? Because of
a dark, implacable curiosity? Because of lingering guilt
that the bomb had killed Emma Pierce and not me? Because I still cared for Beth and would do anything to
please her? Because I hadn't thought of a graceful way to
get out of it? Ah, Thomas, your chickens have come
home to roost. These are the problems you have when you
have no problems.

"Sorry," I said, "but I'll just be going now. Just doesn't
feel quite right, what would my parents say, all that. . . ."

I'd seen everything there was to see except what was
behind the inner door beside us, so maybe I'd take a quick
peek before I left.

She said, "That's not the—"

"There a bathroom around here?"

She was coming around the desk now, and I had the door
open, saying, "Don't bother, I'll find it," and looking inside. A small anteroom opened out into a large unfinished
space. No chance to dwell on it, because there was someone
on the other side, coming toward me. We recognized each
other at the same instant. I started backing up. He was
coming toward me, saying, "The fuck you doin'?" and
drawing back his fist, cocking his arm to punch me. I got
my hands up in front of my face. Nice, quick reaction, only
the punch landed right below my sternum. I doubled over
and sank to one knee, sucking air.

I heard the woman say, "Teddy, what, are you crazy?"

I was on all fours now, a classic puking position, looking
at Teddy's shoes.

He said, "You know who this is? This is the professor I
gave a lift from the hospital. Guy kept swearing to me that
he don't know nothing about nothing." He stooped down
and I caught a glimpse of a pistol. I felt the barrel of it up
under my chin, lifting my head, so he could look at me.
Yeah, it was Teddy. His tone was aggrieved, saying, "I
was nice to him. I believed him."

He kept lifting the gun barrel, forcing me to my feet, and
then lifting it farther still, until I was on tiptoe. He didn't

stop until my head was tilted back so far that I had to look down my nose to see his scabby face.

"What I want to know is, Professor, you're so fucking in the dark, what're you doing here?"

The gun barrel pressed up hard under my chin, I managed an inarticulate blubber.

"Exactly what is it you teach, Mr. Professor? A course in fucking with the wrong people?"

13

There is a quality of fear that obliges us at a moment's notice to forsake the cynicism cultivated in a lifetime. I spent the next half hour in a state of desperate sincerity, offering the usual silent prayers, making the usual promises to devote my life to the benefit of mankind should I get out alive. Theron the Repentant.

Teddy ushered me through the building to a rear exit, and to a small back lot where his red Buick Electra was parked. We pulled out of the lot onto a side street, and then onto Duffy, and as we sped away I glanced back to see Beth's car and her outside of it, leaning against the front fender, arms folded. I tried to stay calm. A moment later we were on Commercial Street, heading toward an unfamiliar section of the South End. No pedestrian traffic here; only an occasional truck on the avenue. We turned down a side street of abandoned buildings. Midblock, the Buick slowed and stopped.

I heard myself ask, "Where are we?"

Teddy lit a cigarette and made a show of dipping his ugly head and looking around with mock concern. "I don't know where we are. Shit, Mr. Professor, you think we're lost?" He grinned at me, shaking his head almost with resignation. "Man, I got to hand it to you. When you fuck up, you fuck up royally. You go all the way."

He flipped his cigarette butt out of the window, propped

his arm along the back of the front seat, and aimed the pistol directly at my head.

"Wait . . . wait! What the hell are you doing? I was just asking a couple of goddamn questions! I was just poking around!" My voice sounded high-pitched and creaky.

"Easy, Mr. Professor, don't bust a gut. Here, I got something for you. Put this on."

He tossed a piece of black canvas at me; it hit me in the face, then fell into my lap. I picked it up. I sat there holding it.

"It's a hood," he said. "Put it on, asshole."

My hands shivered uncontrollably. I fumbled at the opening until I managed to slip the canvas over my head.

"Good, good," he said. "See? No peeking. Okay, now feel those two little leather straps down by your throat there? Yeah, right, those. Feels like a dog collar, huh? Just buckle those up, nice and snug. Kind of seems backward, yeah, but you can do it. Take your time. There, that's it."

Pitch darkness now, and a sudden claustrophobia. Within the hood, my breathing sounded harsh and loud. But at least I didn't have to look at Teddy.

He said, "That's not just any hood you got on. Found it in a sex shop, something they sell to these guys want women to truss 'em up, I don't know, stick pins in their balls, something. Only I had a better idea. I added a few goodies, wired it up special. I call it a truth hood. I rigged it for pigeons who been bad, who been lying to me. Pigeons who keep sticking their little fucking beaks where they don't belong. Funny, I was gonna test it out last week on that lady professor. Gonna sneak up to her hospital room, slip the ol' truth hood on her, see what she had to say for herself. Maybe ask her some of the questions I asked you. But then I heard she went and croaked on me. I was thinking maybe the truth hood was gonna go to waste, a lot of trouble for nothing. Only now I got you."

I sensed him moving closer, stopping an inch or so from my nose. "Guess what I'm holding in my hand right now, Mr. Professor, in case you get some idea to fly away?"

I didn't answer.

"Let me put it this way. I pull this switch, you're gonna get a headache'll show up on the Richter scale."

I fought myself calm. No, not calm. I merely kept myself from screaming. "Listen, Teddy"—my voice was weirdly muffled—"you're making some kind of mistake. What we have here is a failure to communicate."

"*Cool Hand Luke*," I heard him say. "Yeah, Mr. Professor, I saw that flick, too. Paul Newman, George Kennedy, runs on TV every once in a while. That's the final scene, right? Now how does it go? Luke tells the sheriff about this communication problem and then . . . shit, Mr. Professor, you remember what happens then?"

I just sat there.

"Oh yeah," he said. "Luke gets blown away. He takes a serious one in the gut. Very tragic. Girl I was with couldn't stop crying."

The Buick began to move. The hood disoriented me. Panic disoriented me. Each movement of the car disoriented me. I began to feel nauseated each time we made a turn. The air within the hood grew increasingly hot and stale. An image appeared in my mind: the hood exploding, blowing out taut like a vacuum-cleaner bag, then sagging back on itself, going limp. Another image, worse: what had been my head inside the hood, an unidentifiable goo. I fought an urge to gag. Still another image: my head coexisting inside the hood with the undigested remains of my faculty club lunch.

Maybe fifteen minutes later we made what felt like a right turn, eased over a small bump, seemed for a moment to descend, and finally came to a stop. I heard a mechanical door close behind us. Teddy helped me out of the car, his palm on the back of my head, clearing the doorjamb, like a policeman manipulating a suspect. No, a prisoner being led to his execution. Our heels clicked on concrete. The air was close and cool. I sensed a subterranean darkness. I was hoping it wasn't a mausoleum. I was hoping it wasn't a place you could set off an explosion and no one would hear.

We mounted a stairway—one, two, three flights—
Teddy's hand gripping my elbow. Behooded and nauseated,
I ascended haltingly. My repentance began to take more
exotic forms. I forswore slumming, peeping, all general
forms of inquiry, holy wars, feminism. I pledged myself to
celibacy. I vowed to reexamine my tainted heart.

We passed through a door and Teddy stopped me,
reached up under my chin, unbuckled the hood. It came off,
and I looked around. I saw Teddy holding the hood in front
of my face, grinning.

"Wait a minute, this ain't the special truth hood I wired
up for bad pigeons. Whatdaya know? It's just a regular
hood. It's for stupid pigeons who'll believe anything. Had
you going there, huh?"

I found myself in a corridor which opened out into an
enormous loft converted to an apartment. Polished hard-
wood floors, expensive rugs, expensive furnishings. The
loft had been divided into various living spaces, although
nothing was completely hidden from view. At the far end of
the loft, beyond a living area, was an enormous unmade
bed.

Teddy laughed some more at his joke, told me to wait,
and then left through the door we'd just entered. I waited.

Nothing happened. After maybe five minutes passed, I
began to look around. The corridor in which I stood was
designed as a gallery, track lighting above. What I saw
displayed on the walls beneath didn't reassure me.

How to describe it. Art? Pornography? Erotica? Curios-
ities? Grotesques? An extensive collection of large, expensively framed photographs, plus an occasional painting,
each of them an attempt to communicate some physical or
spiritual extremity, as if the goal had been to achieve a
photographic or painterly equivalent to *Ripley's "Believe It
or Not."* A good many of them I recognized, some were
new to me, but all were bizarre, nightmarish. The murder
victims of WeeGee, the Halloween mongoloids of Diane
Arbus, the transvestites and transsexuals of Bertram Pon-
tellier, the medical freaks of Pyle and Gould, the circus

freaks of Roger Wolke, a host of other circus freaks that I
recognized: Jo-Jo the Dog-faced Boy, Krao the Missing
Link, Grace McDaniels the Mule Woman, Albert the Frog-
headed Boy, Koo-koo the Bird Girl, Lionel the Lion-faced
Man, the Nameless Alligator Boy, Julia Patrana the Ugliest
Woman Who Ever Lived, John Merrick the Elephant Man.

And finally there was a nude portrait of Sheena Sands,
beneath which had been attached a small, hand-printed label: SHEENA SANDS, SEX KITTEN. There was a dark joke in
the label—Sheena no less than the circus performers had
been put on display for her freakishly perfect tits and ass—
but I could only guess at what sort of mind could generate
such humor.

I began to feel the weight of someone's gaze on me. A
voice from somewhere inside the loft said, "Do you admire
my grotesques?"

I turned to see a short, young man coming down a stair-
case I hadn't noticed. Blond hair swept back from a patrician face, gathered into a short ponytail. He approached me
carrying a highball glass in each hand. His features, if anything, were overly fine, marred only by a small rippled
pouch of flesh under each eye. Late thirties, early forties,
his age was difficult to guess. Only the pouch beneath his
eyes suggested decline; otherwise his skin remained as bland
and fresh as an infant's. He wore eyeglasses with plastic
frames of deep burgundy, a white button-down shirt rolled
up at the sleeves, khaki pants, and white sneakers.

"The appeal of the grotesque," he said, "is identical to
the appeal of pornography, don't you think? What I mean
is, a man entering the carnival sideshow and a man entering
the adult theater both experience the same illicit, voluptuous
thrill. They expect to see some profound invasion of privacy, perhaps even some mystery solved."

Calm, cultivated, assured, not trying to persuade me of
anything. He offered me one of the highball glasses, scotch,
and as I gripped it we both noticed that my hands were still
trembling.

He said, "Teddy can get a little carried away. He's gifted

at what he does, but with Teddy, you have to take the good with the bad.''

I told him I was due for some of the good. The young man smiled and nodded, then turned back to the photographs, gesturing with his drink.

''Do you know what a therapist once told me about my gallery, about my collection of grotesques? She said that I was struggling against spiritual emptiness—that's how these people talk. She said that I was applying live wires to my soul. Freaks—*bzzzt!* . . . deviants—*bzzzt!* . . . sexual oddities—*bzzzt!* . . . erotica—*bzzzt! bzzzt!* Live wires, she said, just to see if my dead soul would twitch.''

He raised his hand to silence me, as if I were about to object to this analysis.

''An exaggeration, perhaps, but on the whole, not without a kernel of truth. Nothing shocks me, Professor Theron, nothing inspires wonder or awe or dread. Can you imagine what that's like? If a man isn't moved by life's mystery, how does he know he's alive? If he's impervious to shock, who knows what he is capable of?''

For starters, I thought, arson and murder.

He paused to sip his drink. ''I'm afraid I'm talking too much. If you don't mind my asking, Professor, what makes you feel alive?''

I said, ''A kidnapping usually works for me.''

''Kidnapping? That's far too strong a word. Teddy tells me that you've been inquiring about a company in which I have an interest. Let's just say we're assisting you in bringing your inquiry to fruition. I'm curious. How did you come to apply for a role in a pornographic video?''

''I have occasional lapses in judgment.''

''So that's what we have here, a case of poor judgment?''

''Honestly, I'm just feeling my way along. I don't know anything. If you're worried about Proposition Six, I really don't—''

''Proposition Six? Are you on some mission to rouse the public, inspire them to cast a vote for decency? Are you serious? Is that what you think this is about?''

"I know some women who do."

"Do them a favor. Tell them that any second-year law student could tie up Proposition Six in court for the next two decades."

"What about an arson rap and a murder charge, how long could a lawyer tie that up?"

He smiled at the little change-up. "I'm not aware of anyone pursuing such allegations"—looking at me—"are you?"

He picked up a remote control from a side table and aimed it at an enormous TV screen on the other side of the room. An image of human genitals appeared, a close-up of an energetic penetration.

"In the business we call this a piston shot. All this fuss about Proposition Six isn't about pornography at all. It's really about the power of visual images."

He removed from his pocket a slim blue envelope and handed it to me. My rejection slip, the one Teddy had taken from me.

"As a writer you especially should appreciate what I'm saying. If you were to commit to the page the lewdest scenario you could imagine, give an account of the absolute worst that is in you, who would care? Who would raise one word of protest?"

I said, "Other than my mother?"

"You'd do well to take me seriously, Professor Theron. We live in a world of invasive cameras. The power of the visual image has replaced the power of the word. The camera intrudes into every nook and cranny of the world around us. Just turn on public TV any evening and you'll find some little drama of reproduction and death. Tonight the birth of the pigmy salamander of South America, tomorrow the mating habits of the Sudanese tree frog, all in slo-mo and living color." He nodded toward the genitals copulating on the screen. "So why should we be surprised when someone finally turns the camera on us? Why should our own couplings be immune to scrutiny? Ah, but that's when the fun begins. Our own image threatens us. It makes us squirm."

His eyes never left the screen as he spoke. He turned toward me, his manner disarmingly cheerful, which encouraged me to say, "Do you mind if I ask you a question?"

"Not at all."

"You seem to know who I am. I'm only guessing about you."

"Excuse me," he said, executing a modest bow, "my name's Byron Choate. I'm your friendly neighborhood pornographer."

14

Teddy, would you have Sheena join us?''

Byron Choate leaned over a white desk at the far end of the gallery and spoke into an intercom. A muffled voice replied, and Choate said, "No, no, that's fine. She'll be fine," and turned to me. "I have a treat for you, someone I'd like for you to meet."

On the TV screen behind him the shot of the copulating genitals had been supplanted by a less dramatic image. A man standing in a room. Overhead view, without particular interest, just a man standing there, roughly my . . . wait. How many parrot shirts could there be in the world? I turned, looked up, and saw it. The camera was mounted high above the door behind me. I looked back at the TV and moved my right arm just to make sure. The arm on the TV moved.

I studied the screen. Funny, I don't look like I'm about to pee in my pants.

Byron Choate ushered me past a low partition to a massive sofa in the space arranged as a living area.

"Let me tell you about a dream I have, Professor Theron, a recurring dream that often jolts me upright, sweating in the night. Sometimes it hovers just within mind's reach, and I am able to retrieve bits of it before it is swallowed up beneath some dark pool of unconsciousness.

"A scene from a movie replays in my brain. *The Elephant Man*, perhaps you've seen it. The moment is dramatic. The disfigured hero, having suffered countless humiliations and degradations, is finally cornered by his tormentors. He lies shivering on the floor of a public latrine, where he has been trapped. 'I am not an ANIMAL,' he wails at them, 'I am a HUMAN BEING!'

"Except in my dream, it doesn't happen just that way. I have myself assumed the role of the Elephant Man. I know this because my vision is impeded on both sides by grotesque protuberances very close to my eyes, which I take to be knobs of flesh that have sprouted on my cheeks. I am looking up from a smelly floor, and I see among my tormentors people whom I vaguely recognize: two elderly persons who strongly resemble my parents, the therapist I mentioned to you before, and a woman who resembles my former wife.

"My voice reverberates in the dank room. 'I am not a DEGENERATE!' I shout at them. 'I am not a MORAL INFANT! I am not a SLEAZE!' Then there is a dramatic pause, which gradually lengthens to the point of tediousness. 'I am a . . . I am a . . .' the Elephant man stutters, unable to think of who or what he is. Eventually, my tormentors leave in embarrassment."

Byron Choate was looking at me as though he expected a meaningful reply, but all I could think of was, Why the fuck are you telling me this? I shifted uneasily on the sofa.

"As dreams go, I wouldn't put it up there with Martin Luther King's, but . . ."

I don't know whether he heard me. He'd moved beyond another small partition to the bedroom now, and I watched as he occupied himself unfolding a black tripod. He brought out a small aluminum case, opened it, and removed a video camera. As he worked, he spoke to me over his shoulder.

"Professor Theron, what do you think of pornography?"

"What do I think?"

"Yes, pornography, what do you think of it?"

"You brought me here to ask my opinion of skin flicks?"

He set the camera on top of the tripod and reached under the mounting to secure it.

"Judging from what's been written about you in the news, I have the impression that you're a scholar of the underlife. The Peeper Prof? I think we have something in common. At Cal I did my graduate work in the film department, but as an undergrad I studied Renaissance lit. So here we are, a couple of old English majors, trying to make it in an MBA world. Humor me. Pornography, erotica, smut—tell me what you think."

"Jesus, I don't know," I started, my mind racing. I didn't really know what I thought, but I knew what Beth and Emma thought, so I said that. "It's about power, it's a crutch . . . the creation of pathetic, impotent men who can only exert power over women vicariously."

As soon as the words left my mouth, I realized what I'd said. I cleared my throat. "Present company excepted, of course."

Nothing I said seemed to bother him. I was beginning to get the impression that he was pursuing a dialogue not with me, but with himself. He continued to fiddle with the camera, peering through the lens and reaching around to adjust the focus. He swiveled it on the tripod and stopped it when it was pointed at the bed.

He said, "Some men have argued that the source of all curiosity in life—philosophical curiosity, scientific curiosity, and so forth—is nothing more than the sexual curiosity of childhood. And that is how they account for the obsession with pornography. This early sexual curiosity refuses to evolve, to progress to adult forms."

"Oh," I said. "You mean some men spend their lives looking at women's vaginas, while others move on to other things, like discovering subatomic particles?"

He put his hands up and smiled. "Don't look at me. Look at Freud. But it's interesting, don't you think, to consider that all curiosity may ultimately be of a single cloth. The curiosity that compelled Einstein, that compelled Galileo and Edison, is the very same curiosity that compels Johnny to play doctor with the little girl next door.''

A vacant grin appeared on his lips, and he stood there entranced, as if his mind had settled upon some faraway memory that pleased him.

I said, ''The next time they award Nobel prizes, I'll keep that in mind.''

The door opened and Teddy appeared with his arm around Sheena Sands. By reflex I rose from the sofa, as if preparing for a formal introduction. What to say to her? Compliment her on her fellatio technique? Ask her how she achieved such an expressive range of moans? But then it was clear that I didn't have to say anything. As they crossed the room, she faltered once or twice, swooned against Teddy's arm as he supported her. She was barefoot and she wore only a silver slip.

Byron Choate said, ''Sheena's feeling a little relaxed right now. Sometimes she gets just a little too relaxed, don't you, darling? It's hard for us of lesser talent to understand the pressure of being at the top of one's profession.''

As they came closer, I tried without success to match this girl to the girl who'd given the wildly uninhibited performance in *The Right Stiff*. If I hadn't been expecting Sheena Sands, hadn't heard her name, I wouldn't have recognized her. Her eyes were glazed, and she didn't appear to know where she was. I would've felt sorry for her if I hadn't been so busy feeling sorry for myself.

''Sheena, I'd like you to meet someone. This is Professor Theron.''

''. . . Puh-fesher . . . ?''

''Yes, darling. He's very pleased to meet you. He's a big fan. He's seen all of your pictures. He even went to the trouble of trying for a role in one of our films. You should be flattered. I think he has a crush on you.''

Teddy half carried Sheena Sands to the bed and balanced her on the edge of it. He pulled the slip over her head. She submitted as a sleepy child submits, not resisting or helping. She looked even younger without the slip. There were small bruises on her thighs. She swayed and slouched back-ward. She lay there, horribly exposed. I looked away.

Byron Choate was observing her through the camera. "Sheena, darling, the professor wants to be in pictures. What do you think, darling? Do you think Professor Theron has star quality?"

She struggled to bring herself upright. She swayed slightly and then found her balance.

"Yesss," she said. "Oh yesssss."

"I think it's only fair we give him a screen test, don't you?"

She said, "Oh yess."

I said, "No. No way."

He looked at me and sighed. "I'm afraid you don't have a choice. This will be my little insurance policy. To put it simply, you're annoying me, and you're annoying friends of mine. I want you to stop poking around. I don't think you know anything. I don't think Emma Pierce knew anything. I think you're stumbling in the dark, with all your silly talk of arson and Proposition Six. But you've stumbled this far and I want to make sure you won't stumble any farther. Trust me, you'll be much happier that way."

He told me to remove my clothes.

I tensed my entire body and took a small step back. I glanced quickly from side to side, looking for what I don't know.

"Now there are a couple of ways we can proceed. Teddy has all sorts of little devices that I'm sure he'd love to try out on you. But I don't think you'd like that, and I wouldn't like it much, either. When given the option, I've always preferred sex to violence."

Again he told me to remove my clothes. I took another step back, and he nodded toward Teddy, who brought out a small collar like the one he'd used on the pigeon. He dis-played it on his extended finger.

Teddy grinned crazily. "This is a real small one, but it's got a lot of firepower. I got a good idea where we could strap it on you."

A hard knot pulled tight within my stomach. I felt dizzy. I looked at Teddy and the little leather strap he was holding. Slowly, I reached for the top button of my shirt.

Byron Choate was peering at me through the camera. He paused and raised his head. ''The power of the visual image,'' he said, ''that wasn't just so much idle talk. When the camera is directed toward us, Professor Theron, it threatens us. It makes us squirm.''

15

I stood on tiptoe in front of Wesley College's Elliot Chapel, trying to spot Elizabeth in the milling crowd. We'd arranged to meet a half hour before the memorial service, but scores of people arrived early, quickly filling the chapel seats, overflowing onto the steps outside. The mourners were mostly women, all thankful for the opportunity to pay their respects to Emma Pierce. A week earlier she'd been buried during a small private ceremony in New York City.

I followed the latecomers inside, still searching the faces around me for Elizabeth's. From the back of the hall, I listened to a series of eulogies delivered by Emma's colleagues and friends. Despite my usual immunity to any strategies of eloquence, and despite my impulse to distance myself from the emotional content of weddings, funerals, and births, a couple of the speakers got to me. I heard the same words again and again. *Passion. Commitment.* The legacy of Emma's life had been passion and commitment. To tell the truth, the words soon began to ring in my ears like a rebuke. After all, wasn't I the cool ironist, the man who'd spent most of his adult life trying to get out of things? And now I was just about to get out of something else.

In order not to think about myself, I thought about the police. I'd spent most of the morning at the station on South Everett with Lieutenant Cryder, one of the detectives who'd grilled me a couple of weeks ago back at the hospital. He listened to me for maybe fifteen minutes before he put down his notepad and uttered a noise that sounded like a bark.

I said, "I know this sounds a little screwy, but—"

"A little? Have you been listening to yourself? All I'm waiting for now is the part where the little green men take you for a ride in their spaceship." He calmed down and tried to gather his features into an expression resembling sympathy, but the best he could manage was a grimace. "Look, I'd like to help you, but come on! Listen to what you've told me so far."

He flipped back through his notes. "Okay. Your ex-wife finds this ad in the classifieds, so she convinces you to apply for this job screwing girls in front of a camera—"

I rolled my eyes.

"—and you wear this disguise—"

"It wasn't really a disguise."

"Okay, not a disguise, just these clothes you don't normally wear, so nobody'll recognize you. Earring, dumb shirt, purse—"

"An actor's bag. Listen, I wanted to—"

"Whatever. You use an alias . . . whoa, my mistake. Not an alias, just a name that's not yours. So, now, let me see . . . about midway through this audition this girl starts to get personal, wants to know if you measure up, and you get cold feet. But then this weird fucker pops out of nowhere, puts a bag over your head, and hauls you off to some preppie asshole who props you up next to a drugged-up porn queen"—by this time the lieutenant was beginning to enjoy himself, punctuating his account with little eruptions of laughter—"and films it! Shoots this five-minute clip of you and the girl, and she's about to pass out, and you're about to crap in your pants—except by now your're not wearing pants, right? And for what? Something to hold over your head, he says, so you'll quit nosing around. Hell, I thought that's why you went there in the first place, to get in the goddamn movies! Okay, Professor, now you tell me. You hear a story like that, what're you gonna think?"

"Would I make up something like that? I swear, if I were lying I could be a lot more convincing."

"A story as crazy as that has got to be true, right?"

I looked at him.

"Unh-uh, Professor. That's TV. That's 'Magnum, P.I.' Out here in real life things are a lot simpler: the nuttier the story, the nuttier the guy telling it."

Waiting for a cab outside the police station, I felt more numbness than anger. Why should I let it bother me? I was getting out.

The memorial service ended and once more I stationed myself on the steps outside and searched among the mourners for Elizabeth. Someone tapped me on the shoulder.

"How're you feeling?"

I turned and recognized the young internist who'd treated me after the bombing, the one who'd kept the nurse coming around every few hours with a dose of feel good, which was probably why I couldn't remember his name.

"Fine," I said, "a little sore, but okay. Doctor . . . ?"

"Kimball," he said. "I was hoping I'd see you here. You're a hard man to get hold of. I've been trying to call you, but you never seem to be around, and you didn't return any of my messages."

So that's who'd been calling. Someone from the hospital had been leaving his telephone number on my answering machine; I hadn't returned the calls, figuring that any follow-up inquiries from the hospital were more likely to be about my bill than about my health.

"Sorry, I guess my machine's on the blink."

"I wanted to give you this," he said, handing me a white, rectangular envelope, the type that comes with greeting cards. My name had been scrawled in pencil on the front. Through the thin paper it was possible to make out the words GET WELL SOON.

"Thanks, that's very thoughtful, but it's really not—"

"No, no, it's not from me. It's from Emma Pierce. She gave this to one of her doctors who gave it to me to give to you. When she, uh, you know, passed away, with all the commotion, it sort of slipped my mind.''

"I thought she'd survived the worst of it," I said.

"We all did. But with a trauma like hers, at her age . . . It happens.''

He handed me a brown paper sack. ''This turned up, too. I don't know if you want it now, but when they brought you in the ER that day, you were clutching it like the family jewels. I almost had to pry it out of your hands.''

I reached into the sack and brought out maybe the last thing in the world I expected to see. *The Right Stiff*, the copy Emma had shown me that morning. The very one she'd gotten in the mail. Sheena Sands on the cover, pouting. There were bloodstains on it.

"Someone in the ER must have seen the cassette lying there and I guess just borrowed it for a while. Actually, when it turned up the other day, that's what reminded me about the get well card from Ms. Pierce. Sorry I didn't get it to you sooner.''

He lingered, and for a moment we exchanged the usual banalities that death generates.

He said, ''The card was a nice thought. She was in a lot of pain.''

I said, ''You heard what her friends said inside. She was a nice person.''

He was waiting, I think, for me to explain or maybe to open the card and read it. I did neither. I thanked him again, put the cassette back into the sack, and slipped the card into the side pocket of my jacket.

Just as I was about to give up on her, Beth came out of the chapel. I stepped forward to give her a little hello peck on the cheek, but she hung back, awkwardly. If you were a woman, I suppose this wasn't really an occasion where you wanted to be seen kissing a man.

"What did the police say?" she asked.

"They were greatly amused, but not persuaded.''

With Beth was a stern-looking woman whom I recognized as one of the eulogists, a colleague of Emma's who also worked for the Coalition of Women Against Pornography. The three of us walked along a campus path choked with the stretch limousines that had delivered various dignitaries to the service. I handed Beth the brown sack with the cassette and told her how it had found its way back to me. We solemnly examined the bloodstains. I didn't ruin the moment by pointing out that the blood was probably mine.

Beth's friend, Agnes Wharton, was full of quiet purpose, describing the coalition's plan to mobilize against Byron Choate, to picket the building at 29 Duffy Street.

"That's where he produces his movies," she told me. "There's a soundstage in back. What you were about to walk in on the day you were there was a shoot in progress." She said, "It turns out that young Byron is a local boy, the only son of a wealthy mother in Milton. From what we can piece together, he wasted the last seven or eight years at film school in California, confronting a basic lack of talent. He came back east when his mother died, and I suppose porn was the way he hit upon to spend his inheritance. About a year ago he bought Tele-Techniques, a small video company in Concord making corporate training films, and that gave him all the hardware he needed to set up shop. We think he moved to the Duffy Street location because of the warehouse space behind the storefronts, more than enough to construct a soundstage." She concluded wryly, "He seems to be making a serious commitment to his new vocation and resolving an identity crisis at the same time."

Beth was looking at me funnily. "Maybe now's not the time to discuss it," she said, "but when you and the girl were there, and Choate put the camera on you . . ." She stopped. "You didn't actually . . . I mean, the two of you didn't—"

"You know me. I've never been able to perform under pressure," I said, both of us willing to let it go at that. I managed a smile and changed the subject. "So you found the infamous Boston Public Library sign."

"You mean it found me."

A final absurdist touch in an increasingly absurdist scenario. When I hadn't returned from the audition, Beth didn't
know what to think. Knowing me, she said later, she
thought maybe the audition had gone so well that I'd run off
to Hollywood with stars in my eyes. She knocked on the
Tele-Techniques door, and no one answered. She returned
to her car and began to drive around the building. There was
a small park on the north side—a new park, part of the
city's plan to support the new residential growth in still
another gentrifying area—and Beth stopped to ask a group
of parents and children who'd gathered there if maybe
they'd seen me. And that's when the Boston Public Library
sign came down the street and pulled over to the curb and
parked right in front of her.

A library on wheels, a van with BOSTON PUBLIC LIBRARY
painted on the side panel. The van serviced neighbor-
hoods without easy access to local branches, visiting this
particular park three afternoons a week, loaning books to
neighborhood children. The library van must have been
parked there when the roof scene from *The Right Stiff* was
filmed.

We stopped next to a Honda Prelude. Agnes Wharton got
in the driver's side, saying, "We intend to make sure everyone knows who else has moved into the neighborhood.
We intend to put Byron Choate's ass in a sling."

"Sure you don't want to join us for lunch?" Beth asked
me.

"Can't. I have an appointment at Adage at two."

Another time, Love, I'm off to meet my publisher. It was
the sort of thing I'd been hoping to say for a long time, but
right now it didn't do much for me.

Beth said, "I feel terrible we haven't had a chance to
celebrate the book. I owe you dinner and at least one bottle
of champagne. I'm really proud of you. It's wonderful."

"Right now," I said, "it's the only thing keeping my life
from turning into pure shit."

They drove off, and I hailed a cab, wondering if I should

have told them again that Byron Choate didn't give a damn. If he wasn't worried about being nailed for arson and murder, he certainly wasn't worried about the legal threat posed by some city ordinance of dubious constitutionality. Something was making him nervous, yes, but whatever it was, whatever fears gripped his perverted little heart, they had nothing to do with Proposition Six.

A couple of other things were bothering me, too. I'd been forcing myself to think money, not sex, and that had worked most of the way. The markers along the trail had dollar signs all over them, but when I got to the end of the line, what did I find? Not a sleazy guy obsessed with making a buck, but a sleazy guy obsessed with himself. A wealthy ex–film student with a therapist and Elephant Man nightmares and a Freudian view of the world that had been cribbed from a freshman primer. I didn't know what motivated Byron Choate, but it certainly wasn't money. Apparently he already had that.

And another thing. Why had someone with such an obvious yen for the bizarre—what had been his melodramatic phrase? live wires to make his dead soul twitch?—why had he produced such conspicuously bland films? Judging by *The Right Stiff*, the audience he seemed to have in mind was suburban couples trying to get themselves worked up after they'd put the kids to bed. It didn't make sense. Hell, maybe even pornographers compromised their vision, bowed to the leveling demands of popular taste.

The cab let me out in front of Adage Press. There were a lot of questions I couldn't answer, but I wasn't going to worry about them too much. Why should I? Everyone seemed happy. Beth knew what she wanted to know about Venture Productions; the coalition had a fresh target for protest; Byron Choate was probably happy because whatever he was really hiding would likely stay hidden. I was happy, too, maybe the happiest of all. I'd escaped Ugly Teddy with all my body parts intact, unexploded.

And I was out of it.

• • •

"Percy Hotchkiss," I said, "my editor. You remember, an older gentleman with pills all over his sweater."

When I asked the first time, the receptionist got a queer look in her eyes. If she was about to go into her snob routine—sorry, first novelists have to use the service entrance—she'd picked the wrong day. I wasn't in the mood.

"Percy Hotchkiss," I repeated. "He's only worked here about forty years."

This prompted an even stranger response. Her eyes welled with tears and she snuffled. She was trying not to cry.

"I'm afraid Mr. Hotchkiss no longer works here. I'm afraid he's been let go by Mr. Dodds."

"I . . . are you sure? Percy told me he wasn't worried. He said something about being too old to be put out to pasture."

"That's what a lot of us thought. I got my pink slip last week. I'm being replaced by some young . . . by a young . . ." She was tracing curvy lines in the air with her hands.

I said, "Bimbo?"

She nodded.

The man who'd replaced Percy Hotchkiss was named Benny Murphy, and when he finally came out to fetch me after a twenty-five-minute wait, he was wearing a green-and-yellow jacket that opened onto an enormous beer belly. He led me down the hallway, happily confiding that the editing job was just temporary. Just last week he'd been running ad accounts for one of Samuel Dodds's magazines in New York, and he was about to do the same in Boston, only for TV, as soon as Dodds finalized the deal for Channel Eight. I'd read about it, hadn't I? Mr. Dodds was in the middle of a monster deal, buying six TV stations from UrbanView and selling off the plum, Channel Eight, so he'd wind up paying an average of $125 million or so for the other five stations, which if you knew TV stations was a steal. Some deal, huh? Mr. Dodds was something, huh?

And since Mr. Dodds had already sent him here, waiting for
the deal to come through, why not keep busy? Try your
hand at editing, Mr. Dodds said. You know, in the meantime.

With all his books and bookcases gone, Percy Hotchkiss's office seemed a lot roomier now. Benny Murphy sat
down and the chair disappeared beneath him; he spread his
knees wide as if to make his balls available should it be
necessary to scratch them. He slapped my manuscript on his
desk, pulled open the front cover as if it were the hood of an
automobile, and squinted inside.

"*Naked Laughter*," he said, "great title. I like it. Great,
it's great."

When I told him that the title had been the brainchild of
Samuel Dodds, he was beside himself. That his very first
literary judgment had been unwittingly to approve the
taste of his boss, well, things just didn't get better than
that.

He turned the pages quickly—whatdaya say we roll up
our sleeves and edit this sucker?—and before long he was
frowning and scratching his chin.

"Okay, your main character, this guy . . . now what's
his name, I can't seem to—"

"He doesn't have a name."

"Yeah, yeah, I kind of thought that. Forget it." He emit-
ted a snorting laugh. "Hey, what's in a name, right? No,
the thing I'm getting at, this fella doesn't seem to have a
helluva lot to say, does he?"

"He doesn't say anything."

"Okay, that's sorta what I thought. I wasn't sure. I was
sort of skimming through there after a while. I thought
maybe he might've said something later in the book."

"No. He laughs."

"He laughs." Benny repeated the words haltingly, as if
he were unfamiliar with them.

I said, "Right."

"See, the problem I got with your book is, you're gonna
have this great title *Naked Laughter*, so the last thing you

want is for somebody to buy this book and take it home and maybe feel shortchanged. You see what I'm saying? You got *Naked* on the cover, so maybe you ought to put some naked on the inside too.''

Benny Murphy sat behind his desk brooding. After a couple of minutes he got up and paced back and forth in the small space where Percy Hotchkiss's bookcases had been. His brow was deeply furrowed and he seemed to be grappling with the riddle of the ages. Suddenly his eyes lit up; he snapped his fingers and pointed at me.

"Got it. If he doesn't say anything, maybe you could have him express himself in some other way, you know, nonverbally.''

Grinning madly, my new editor formed a circle with the thumb and forefinger of his left hand, and with the forefinger of his right hand vigorously penetrated the circle. What had Byron Choate called it? A piston shot.

"You know what I'm saying. A man of action, not words.'' He winked at me.

Before my very eyes, the one thing that was keeping my life from turning into shit was turning into shit itself. Easy, Thomas, I told myself, don't panic. He said he was just temporary. Ride it out.

I calmly explained that there was no sex in the book on purpose. I didn't just forget. I thought it was a good idea. Percy Hotchkiss agreed.

"That's why old Perceroo is in his backyard getting acquainted with his weed-eater. Mulching his gladiolas.''

"Listen, publishing is a business, I understand that. There are important commercial considerations. But fiction doesn't exist in a vacuum. The world has changed. Nowadays sex is a blood sport. People get killed.''

My editor looked at me as if I were a child. "It's a boooook,'' he said slowly. "You can write anything you want. This guy can dip his wick till the cows come home and—presto!—he's clean as a whistle. I mean, hell, you want to you can make his farts smell like perfume.''

This last notion seemed especially to please him, as if he

were just beginning to appreciate the power of the imagination.

I stood my ground. "All I'm saying is, the days of uninhibited, freewheeling sex are over. If I pretend they're not, the book just won't ring true."

Benny Murphy could barely conceal his shock. "True?" he said. "Excuse me, but I know lots of people still fucking their brains out. On the other hand, I don't know anybody who don't talk."

Actually, the worst thing was he had a point.

"Listen, Professor, no offense, but you got a great title like *Naked Laughter,* and we're hoping it will get some people to pull your book off the shelves and take it up to the cash register. You have any idea how many books are sold based on the title alone?"

"One-third," I said, dutifully reciting the statistic Percy Hotchkiss had recited to me.

"Damn right. All I'm saying is, people buy a book says *Naked* on the cover, they're going to want some naked on the inside. You wouldn't want to disappoint them, would you?"

I said, "It doesn't bother me if it doesn't bother you."

His expression suddenly turned menacing, as if to say he had spent enough time playing kiss ass to some geek author. "It bothers me," he said. "Write some sex scenes. Put old whassisname in the saddle a couple of times. Be back here Wednesday."

At about two o'clock that morning, I pushed away from my desk, lit another cigarette, and stared at what I'd just written. On my left was a pile of wadded paper and five empty bottles of Rolling Rock. On my right was a legal pad, upon which I had scrawled every bit of sexual slang I'd ever heard. Staring back from the typewriter was my very first humping scene. I didn't know if it was any good, but to give myself credit, nothing smelled like perfume. I'd only go so far.

Only later, just as I was about to fall asleep, did I remember the get well card from Emma. I got out of bed and fumbled for the light, found my jacket hanging on the back of my desk chair.

Once I got back in bed, I opened it slowly. Even if it was only a get well card, I knew that this would be as close as I'd ever come to communicating with the dead.

There was a note, a brief message scrawled in the same hand that appeared on the front of the envelope. Maybe in some part of my brain I'd been expecting it, but I experienced it as a surprise. It took me a few minutes to decipher the writing, and when I did, I felt a chill. I lay there a moment longer, shivering beneath the covers.

I picked up the phone, began dialing Beth's number, then hung up. Instead I got dressed, went out onto the deserted street, and waited for a cab. One finally came, and fifteen minutes later I was downstairs in Beth's foyer, ringing her buzzer. She answered groggily, then let me in, looking worried now, asking me if everything was okay. I gave her a moment to gather her wits. Then I told her about the note.

"So what does it say?"

"We can stop wondering about Grace," I said. "Emma wanted us to know who she is. Emma said if I knew who Grace was, then I'd know why Emma believed her."

"So who is she?"

I handed the card to her. "It doesn't exactly give her name—"

"What?"

"—only her stage name."

She was reading it now, in her robe on the sofa.

I said, "Grace is Sheena Sands."

Beth continued to read silently.

I said, "There's something else. Emma says that Sheena is in trouble. Someone may be trying to kill her."

I didn't return home that night. Once we'd said everything we knew to say, we went into the bedroom and reached for each other under the covers. News, even bad news, has a way of enlivening the senses. We didn't talk. We didn't think, for that matter. I don't know what was going on in Beth's mind, but for me sleeping with her was simply a part of a larger and consistent pattern. Every other part of my life was proceeding without regard for the consequences, so why should my emotional life be any different? So, in the early hours of morning, Beth and I joined together, her face beneath mine, the new face that remained curiously unfamiliar, superimposed on her other face, the face I'd been married to and that I knew better than my own. Oh yes, our senses were enlivened.

That was one thing about divorce, I thought. Your bodies didn't necessarily agree to it.

Part III

Sex
Scenes

16

Puritan Greyhound Park rose up in an enormous asphalt parking lot just off Route 10. As you came upon it from a distance, depending on your mood, its squat, spherical profile resembled either a spaceship or a toilet bowl.

We pulled into a parking space encrusted with the residue of countless oil pans, and Beth said, "Explain it to me again, what are we doing at a dog track?"

The last few days I'd begun to feel like the old vaudeville comedian who touches his fingers to flypaper: the more I flailed and tried to extricate myself, the more hopelessly I became entangled. Even from the grave Emma Pierce was still tugging at me, hauling me in at the end of an invisible line. I wasn't such an expert at getting out of things, after all.

One thing was clear: If I had any notion of helping Grace or Sheena or whatever name that pitiful girl was using, I was going to need a little help myself. I had the feeling that every time I poked my head out of my apartment, Ugly Teddy would be waiting there, ready to attach an explosive to my person. If I ventured out again, I wanted someone with me, someone who wouldn't be unduly concerned by the prospect of confronting Teddy. The only person I knew who fit that description was Gerald Valentin.

"And he's here?" Beth said.

"So I've been told."

"Who is he, anyway," Beth said, "the Equalizer?"

"Better," I said. "He'll give us a definite advantage."

Gerald Valentin was a former professional wrestler, a huge, unsightly man who for the past twenty years had been Vincent Cuillo's bodyguard. Like Cuillo, Gerald belonged to another age, and with the old man dead, I had trouble imagining Gerald's life. What came to mind was a soft cliché of movies, the passing of the Old West, with Gerald as the aging cowboy living beyond his usefulness, thrown into the modern world of pickup trucks, no spitting on the sidewalk, his spurs always ruining someone's oak parquet floors. But I had to keep reminding myself that Gerald wasn't an old broncobuster. He busted heads.

A lot had changed since I'd seen him last, and I had no idea where to look. So yesterday I'd returned to the Combat Zone to ask Giggy Slater. I found Giggy just where I'd left him, stationed across the street from the Pink Lady, begging dollars from the lunch crowd. He'd added a new wrinkle to his scam.

I said, "Giggy, I don't know what sort of ethical standards apply in your line of work, but you have to draw the line somewhere."

He shrugged. "I just drew it a little farther out."

Giggy's legs were hidden beneath the false seat of a wheelchair: no longer a dwarf, but a paraplegic. There must have been a pained expression on my face, because he said, "What's the big deal, Thomas? The dwarf thing was killing my knees. I figure the wheelchair will extend my career another five years, easy. It's like when the White Sox moved Pudge Fisk to the outfield."

I let it pass. Who was I to offer ethical instruction, anyway? The lines I'd been drawing for myself lately weren't models of consistency. Working with Beth and the Coalition Against Pornography by day, I retired to my desk at night, swigging Old Forester and plinking into my typewriter vignettes of sexual union as prurient and as lacking in redeeming social value as my heated brain could issue forth. The legal pad at my side now held an exhaustive glossary of lust, a word or phrase to evoke every conceivable debauchery. The nameless hero of *Helpless Laughter*—I smiled ruefully—or *Naked Laughter* or whatever title that pitiful book was using, wasn't laughing so much now. He was too busy prodding and poking and pronging, dorking and schtuping, grunting and rooting . . .

"Gerald?" Giggy was saying. "He was coming around here for a while after Mr. Cuillo died, wandering the streets like he didn't know what to do with himself. Haven't seen him for months. Funny, out of all that crowd, he's the only one I feel sorry for. Somebody told me he's living with his sister somewhere. You know, kind of retired."

I said, "I guess there's not much demand for aging ass kickers."

"Gerald's a piece of work, huh?"

"Any idea where I might find him?"

"A guy I know works at the dog track, said he sees him out there sometimes."

"Raynum Park?" I said. "Puritan?"

Giggy said, "Puritan. The guy I know tends bar in the lounge, called the Muzzle, I think. He said Gerald shows up a lot of weekends."

And so Sunday afternoon here we were, Beth and I, passing through the turnstiles at Puritan Greyhound Park. Inside, the air was overheated, recycled, and slightly rank, suggesting a history of excretory accidents. We weaved through a gauntlet of men who hawked tout sheets just inside the gates, then pushed into the grandstand crowd, the dregs of the gambling world: the compulsives, the semi-deranged, the pathologically optimistic, the terminally bored.

The crowd was close, and Beth was breathing into the crook of her arm. An elderly man swooned back into us. I helped him regain his balance; he turned toward us on tremulous legs.

Elizabeth said, "Oh my God."

Stuck to the center of his forehead was a paper napkin, adhering to his skin by virtue of the congealed blood from a small wound near his hairline. The area around his nose and mouth was fouled with a nameless crud. He thanked us and moved off toward the betting windows, listing radically. Only his right eye—the eye unobstructed by the napkin—remained steady, trained on the overhead tote board that flashed the odds for the first race.

The Muzzle Lounge was on the second floor, and we passed among a growing throng of bettors, bracing themselves for the day's action, grimacing over their first boilermakers. I didn't spot Gerald. We asked Giggy's friend, the bartender, and he said, yeah, Gerald showed up a lot of the time, but you never knew. Gerald didn't say much about himself. Come to think of it, the bartender said, he never said much about anything.

We waited at a table near the balcony, overlooking the races below. I ordered a Bloody Mary; Beth pointedly declined. She was still surveying the scene, slightly aghast. Her expression reminded me of the night we'd first viewed *The Right Stiff*.

"When we were married," she said, "*this* is where you used to come? Remember what I said the other night about your bad habits acquiring a certain charm? I take it back."

"These are the dogs, Beth. I don't play the dogs. I play the horses. There's a big difference."

"Such as?"

"Horse racing is the sport of kings," I said. "Dog racing is the sport of the mentally infirm."

Below us, a dozen sleek greyhounds were being led onto the track by their handlers. From time to time, a dog would resist the tug of the leash, lower its haunches, and try to pee; the handlers refused to interrupt the post parade, yanking the greyhounds along behind them. The dogs' eyes were mournful and filled with dumb canine embarrassment, reduced to a froglike hopping as they tried to relieve themselves.

Another race, another Bloody Mary. I chewed on a swizzle stick, having second and third thoughts about what we had in mind. The longer we waited, the more I began to hope that Gerald had taken the day off, stayed home with his sister. I pictured them sitting by the fire, Gerald polishing his brass knuckles, telling her about all the faces he'd smashed with them. I fidgeted and watched the lounge entrance uneasily.

Beth said, "Is something bothering you?"

"Gerald used to beat people up for a living. That was his job."

"But didn't you say he likes you?"

It was a little difficult to explain. I told her about a news clip I'd seen on TV a couple of years back, about a female gorilla in the National Zoo. The gorilla had been raised in captivity, and in order to prepare her for motherhood, the zookeepers provided her with a surrogate, a small kitten upon which to practice her maternal technique. The news footage was touching; the gorilla eagerly mothered the kitten, jealously protecting it and lavishing it with affection. Of course, the gorilla was still a gorilla, and in the midst of all the affection, it managed to drop the kitten on its head a couple of times. It was touching, but it made you cringe, too.

Beth was looking at me strangely. "Did I miss something? What's the point?"

"The point," I said, "is Gerald. Just because he likes you doesn't mean you won't get hurt."

I watched the fourth race—the antic dash from the gates, the inevitable pileup at the first turn, then *poof!* the finish line seconds later—increasingly convinced that dog racing was as inane and comical as horse racing was majestic and freighted with meaning. At best, I supposed, a dog race offered a perverse metaphor for life: all the contestants looked the same, it was over before you knew it, and you couldn't make much sense of what had happened. Or was that a metaphor for sex? I finished another Bloody Mary, tried to get the attention of the waitress, and . . .

There he was.

Gerald Valentin was walking toward the bar, wearing a white shirt, beige windbreaker, and trousers with a small black-and-white check. Big and Tall Shop, I guessed, all fit and no style. Everyone in the bar was making room for him, sneaking glances at him after he passed by. He looked even larger and more menacing than I remembered. Some of that was simple contrast, of course; the dog players around him seemed uniformly stunted and skulking, smaller than life.

"Wait," Beth said, "that's Gerald?"

I nodded.

"I was expecting someone younger, I don't know, someone like a . . . "

"A pro-football lineman? Unh-uh," I said, "football has rules."

We watched as he stood against the bar and gripped the railings with enormous hands. He exuded power, but it wasn't athletic power and it had nothing to do with coordination or weight-room muscles. Gerald's was an old-fashioned kind of power that came from the center. He fell into a category of creatures who derived their strength from the massiveness of their torsos: Russian weight lifters, giant African beetles, Italian opera singers.

I pushed away from the table and took a deep breath. "Well, here goes."

"Thomas, if you don't want to do this, just say so."

I said, "I don't want to do this."

But I eased up to the bar—no sudden movements—and hovered a couple of yards away from him. Gerald wasn't the sort of man you approached from behind and slapped on the back, saying, "Hey, big guy, how ya doin'?" I stood there, waiting for him to become aware of my presence; it was a self-effacing technique said to be favored by servants who attend kings.

His massive head swiveled toward me. Other than raising his eyelids another quarter inch, his features remained unanimated, as if we'd talked just the other day, not two years ago.

I got right to the point. No small talk, no handshake, no awkward expression of sympathy at Cuillo's death. I told him that we needed his help, and then I told him about

Byron Choate and Sheena Sands, what we knew, what we suspected, and what we planned to do. Getting Sheena away from Byron Choate, I said, might be dangerous or it might be relatively simple. Choate himself didn't pose much of a problem, but there were a few unpredictables. One was a guy with a skin problem named Teddy. Another was that we didn't exactly know where she was. The loft where I'd seen her was probably Byron Choate's home, but he wasn't listed in the phone book, and we hadn't yet come up with an address. The only time I'd been there, I'd arrived with a bag over my head.

At least Gerald didn't say I was crazy. He just listened impassively, and I saw in his face an inscrutability that comes with the knowledge of another, more violent world. It occurred to me that plots of kidnapping and rescue sounded a lot crazier to me than to him.

Then I described our options, keeping everything brief and businesslike, trying not to babble. I said there were a couple of ways we could proceed. We already knew the location of Venture Productions, and we knew about his club, Manray's. If Sheena was being held at Choate's home, it shouldn't be too difficult to come up with an address. But the smart thing—here a quick nod of deference—the smart thing might be to get as much information as we could before we walk right in and confront people. Maybe we should go to Manray's first, I said, and talk to the male stripper. Find out what Sheena's costar knows about her. Get the lay of the land, I said. Find out what's what.

I finally shut up, relieved that I'd gotten it all out. Telling him hadn't been so bad, after all.

I looked at him and waited. Gerald slowly lifted his eyelids another good quarter inch.

He said, ''Who are you?''

17

Marie Tenebrusco of Watertown: "Nobody forces you. I mean, if you don't want to watch a porn movie, just don't rent one. What's the big deal?"

Roger Neville of Newton: "All points of view, however reprehensible, must have access to the marketplace of ideas." His wife, Tanya: "Yeah, and we like those movies, anyway. We rent them all the time. We think sex is beautiful."

Howard Vincent, owner of a newsstand at the corner of Beacon and Tremont: "Proposition Six? You know how a lawyer explained it to me? He said if a woman walks by my newsstand, sees some girly pictures, and gets depressed, she can sue me for a couple of million bucks. You call that fair?"

Mimi Drabeki of Charlestown: "Sure, I feel bad for that lady who died, but it's some nut on her side who did all that bombing, right?"

For the last week, the Coalition of Women Against Pornography had employed a simple strategy: expose the production of porn videos in Boston, then tap into the resulting outrage for votes. The problem was, the referendum vote was only two weeks away, and no one seemed particularly outraged.

The revelations about Venture Productions stirred up the city for a couple of days, offering a new angle on an increasingly stale news story. But Samuel Dodds's acquisition of Channel Eight, strictly a business read, was earning almost as much coverage, which suggested how quickly interest in Proposition Six was fading. Of course, the Dodds TV deal was hard for TV to resist; given the choice, the media is always more comfortable covering itself.

The demonstrations at 29 Duffy Street were dutifully aired each night, but the office of Venture Productions refused to provide a compelling visual image. No memorable photos appeared, no pornographers creeping out of the smut factory while small children played nearby, no greasy men chomping cigars and ducking the taunts of the demonstrators. The images not only lacked drama, they were contradictory: the Coalition carried placards attacking Venture Productions, so when the cameras zoomed up to the office itself, why did the sign on the door say Tele-Techniques?

Byron Choate's lawyers earned their money, blasting the allegations that swirled around him—outlandish, slanderous, unworthy of a response—denials couched in precisely the sort of language that has come to signify guilt. His lawyers charged malicious harassment; they threatened lawsuits.

I ordered another cup of coffee and thumbed through the rest of the newspaper, convinced that the world it described, however improbable, was a lot simpler and more comprehensible than the one I inhabited. Nine-thirty, Tuesday evening, and I was sitting in a booth at Dunkin' Donuts on Route 1, about half a mile down the highway from Manray's. Tonight was ladies' night at the club, and Beth was already there, making sure this evening's roster of male strippers included Sheena's costar in *The Right Stiff*. Beth would be returning here to join me in a couple of minutes.

We were up to no good.

Gerald Valentin sat across from me in the booth. I still had no idea whether he was serious when he'd asked who I was. I'd told him anyway, in the process succumbing to my compulsion to babble. Whatever I said must have satisfied him, because he was here, and that basic alliance having been established, he apparently felt relieved of any further obligation to communicate. Now he just sat there, a lot more comfortable with silence than I was; somehow that only deepened my belief in his abilities.

At a little before ten o'clock Beth walked in, slid onto the seat beside me, and greeted Gerald as if she'd known him all her life. Elegant and composed. Nothing in her face hinted that for the past hour or so she'd been watching nude men cavort wildly on stage.

"Well?"

"Tacky," she said, "very tacky."

"And our man's there?"

She nodded. "I sat through Johnny Tigre and the Amazing Something-or-other before he came on. He does a bumbling accountant routine, just like his character in the movie. He comes out wearing a nerdy suit and horn-rimmed glasses, carrying a slide rule. Stiff, no rhythm—"

I arched an eyebrow. "Stiff?"

"Stiff as in awkward, Thomas, uncoordinated. But the more clothes he takes off, the less and less nerdy he acts. He does a couple of things with the slide rule that really get your attention. By the end of his routine, the sound system's blaring 'Taking Care of Business,' and he's pumping his pelvis to beat the band."

"Having fun, are we?"

Elizabeth smiled. "If these guys would submit to head transplants, the results might be interesting. I've never seen so many gnarled stomachs in my life."

While we finished our coffee, we tried to anticipate things that might go wrong. All we had in mind was asking a few pointed questions—a snap, right?—but recent experience had taught me that nothing in my life was likely to unfold according to plan.

"Maybe we should sit tight until closing time," I suggested, "wait for him to leave. If he's feeling skittish, at least we'd have some privacy."

Beth shook her head. "I know it's hard to believe, but someone told me that after hours women wait around for these jerks. Apparently, about three o'clock in the morning, you'll find about a half dozen Cadillacs in back, windows fogged, rocking on their wheels. I don't have to tell you what everybody's up to."

I said, "Bobbing for apples?"

We thought of a few more possibilities, until I noticed a frown at Gerald's lips, a shadow of impatience in his eyes. He was accustomed to listening and following orders; he was also accustomed to associating with people who knew what they were doing.

I looked at him. "Any ideas?"

He spoke slowly, his voice a raspy growl. "All you want to do is talk to this guy, right?"

I nodded.

"So why don't we just walk in and talk to him?"

"That would be fine, except the club doesn't allow men inside on Tuesday night. It's a rule."

Gerald eased himself out of the booth and stood up, looking down at me as if I were some exotic species of bird at the zoo. He said, "We ask nice, maybe they'll make an exception."

We drove over in Gerald's Riviera, primarily because that was the car we were certain he would fit in. We merged into the traffic on Route 1, barely reached minimum speed before turning off beneath the sign for Manray's. We decided that Beth should wait for us inside, so we dropped her off in front of the club. The same hulking young man in a tuxedo who'd turned me away the week before was guarding the door. We watched as he stepped aside and greeted Beth familiarly—heh, heh, back so soon?

Gerald and I parked and got out. When the doorman saw us approaching, he spread his feet slightly, improving his stance, suggesting a mental adjustment of roles from courteous doorman to bouncer.

Before he had a chance to say anything, I smiled agreeably and raised my palm. "I know, it's Tuesday. All-male revue. No men allowed."

"That's right, sir."

I don't think he recognized me. Gerald stood a couple of yards behind me, deferentially.

"The thing is, my friend and I"—I nodded behind me—"were hoping that you would make an exception. We need to speak with one of your employees, a dancer. I assure you that we don't want to cause any trouble for you or your customers, and we will take all possible pains not to inconvenience anyone. But we do need to step inside for just a few minutes. I realize that you have a job to do, but this is important."

I might as well have been reciting the multiplication tables. I hadn't expected to talk my way in, but if Gerald said to ask nice, I was going to ask nice.

"Sorry, gentlemen, I'm afraid I can't permit that. Tuesday is ladies' night. No men allowed." He added dismissively, "Now if you'll excuse me . . ."

"Okay, here's the deal," I said. "My friend and I are going in and there's not a damn thing you can do about it. I was hoping we could do this the easy way, but it's up to you."

He tilted his head and squinted at me with fresh interest. I'd finally said something that didn't bore him.

"I'm not a problem," I said, again nodding toward Gerald, "but if you fuck with him, you'll require immediate medical attention."

"That guy? He must be pushing sixty."

"You're just going to have to trust me on this one. He can do it. On your best day, he could rip off your head and shit down your neck."

By now a few women were hovering nearby, waiting to enter the club. It was obvious that the bouncer was aware of them, and his ego was coming into play.

He grinned and said, "Why don't we ask Granddad there what he thinks? All I'm getting from you is bullshit threats."

He brushed past me and took a step toward Gerald, up on his toes, his legs springier. You could almost sense his glands kicking in, giving his blood a little hit of adrenaline and testosterone. He put his face up close to Gerald's. Actually, he was a lot bigger than I thought.

"So Granddad, somebody put something in your Geritol this morning? Your friend's running up a big tab with his mouth. He says you're gonna pay it."

Gerald didn't move. He was looking past the younger man toward me. I was aware of a flicker of meaning in his eyes, as if he were trying to tell me something. For a split second I thought, Shit, no, don't tell me he's scared, but I kept looking at him, wondering what . . . oh, I thought, right. Of course. Now there was no one between me and the door, nothing to keep me from going inside. I started in.

"Hey, wait—"

The bouncer turned to stop me and that's when it happened. Gerald dipped and swung his right arm like a scythe, raking the young man's ankles. His legs flew out from under him, and he hit the pavement chest first, hard. He literally bounced. And then Gerald was standing over him. He placed his shoe on the back of the young man's neck, pinning his head down against the pavement. When he started to flail his arms, Gerald simply weighted his shoe until the flailing stopped.

". . . offa me . . . get him offa . . ."

The bouncer managed to turn his head a few degrees and now his mouth protruded from the edge of Gerald's shoe, squished sideways, as if he were attempting an impression of a fish. The women who'd been watching were standing a lot farther back now. I'd taken a few steps back myself. We were all impressed.

". . . offa . . ."

I leaned down and said, "I told you. Everything else I told you was true, too. We don't want trouble. Just give us an hour inside and we'll just forget this ever happened. Fair enough?"

Even though Gerald was standing on his head, he managed to nod. His eyes were frightened and he was straining to look up at us. We helped him to his feet. I smoothed the lapels of his tux and reassured him, "There, no harm done.

Easy does it. We're going inside now. We'll be back in a jiffy.''

He looked less like a bouncer than a scared twenty-year-old who hadn't lost his baby fat. A crease appeared on the side of his cheek, slowly reddening. Curved, like the imprint of a shoe. About a 13EE, I'd say.

18

A cavernous space with mirrored walls. A gleaming hard-wood stage, gymnasium finish, and a long runway extending into a sea of women. A sound system of apparently unlimited wattage blasted the room, until the air itself seemed to vibrate. A stripper with a swimmer's physique posed at the lip of the runway, his back toward the audience. A spotlight had targeted his rear end, and he expertly flexed his butt muscles to the intricate rhythms of a drum solo. The women shrieked with delight, pelting the stage with wadded dollar bills, urging him to even lewder movements. Some women abandoned their tables and surged toward the runway, egged on by their friends as they grabbed wildly for the stripper's ass. Rowdier, I decided, more demonstrative than a men's bar, but the general principles were the same; it all seemed a little asinine when you were sober.

Elizabeth, Gerald, and I squeezed single file through a crush of women, moving purposefully, trying not to appear furtive. We spotted a small table in a dark corner of the club, far away from the action onstage. I could sense the waiters and bartenders eyeing us as we passed by, wondering what we were doing there. That we were already inside bestowed upon us a certain credibility, but I doubted that would be enough. As soon as we were seated, I matter-of-factly beckoned a waiter.

"Yessir?"

He wore the basic uniform: sleek, black tuxedo pants, suspenders, and bowtie, being otherwise bare chested. Midtwenties, I thought, maybe six three, and as it happened, gullible as hell.

"Don't mind us," I explained amiably, ordering three club sodas, "we're business associates of Mr. Choate's, just having a look around. We cleared it with the gentleman at the door, but if you'd like to check—"

The waiter hesitated a moment, then said, "No, that's okay, sure, yessir."

In a moment he returned with the drinks, insisting they were on the house. I thanked him, dropped a ten-dollar bill onto his tray, and began to feel slightly more relaxed. Gerald endured the proceedings with stony patience, and Beth busily scanned the crowd for Sheena's costar. After a moment she touched my arm.

"There he is."

I followed her eyes to a table on the other side of the runway, where our man was preening among a group of maybe six women who vied for his attention. Holding court, it seemed, acting less like George Dufus than George III. Unless we were looking for an autograph, getting near him wasn't going to be easy.

Beth said, "So much for the element of surprise. Looks like we're going to have to stand in line."

I smiled. "You were expecting to catch him with his pants down?"

"Any bright ideas?"

"A few," I said, "but none that would work."

We both turned toward Gerald, who was shaking his head wearily. "When's the guy go on?"

"One more set," Beth said, "then he's on deck."

Gerald, whose work for Cuillo had brought him into strip clubs almost daily for the last two decades, had obviously inferred some basic principles. He pointed toward the rear of the club, to a small vestibule tucked in the shadows at the right of the stage. There was a pay phone, two cigarette machines, and a men's room.

He said, "Dressing room's back there. When he goes back to change, we do it then."

There was something scary in the way he said "we do it then," something that hinted at an earlier time, when "doing it" probably didn't mean conducting an interview.

And so we waited. Onstage, still another dancer with the obligatory physique—tan, wasp waisted, with a hairless, well-muscled chest—concluded a routine with a jungle theme. For the grand finale, he wore only a mask strapped to his loins, a replica of an elephant's head, the gray ears spreading out on either side of his groin; the trunk, of course, swung prodigiously down between his legs. By manipulating his pelvis, he achieved a variety of effects; the elephant's trunk twirled clockwise, then counterclockwise, and finally back and forth in a bullwhip motion. These maneuvers proved enormously popular. The dancer grinned wickedly, then pursed his lips in a model's pout.

I leaned toward Beth. "That's fine," I said, "but can he eat peanuts with it?"

"Feeling a little insecure, are we?" she said, sipping her club soda meditatively. "You know, I'm curious why all these guys are so pleased with themselves."

"Excuse me?"

"Those G-strings and bikinis they all wear, with the little baskets they carry their gonads in. That pulls the scrotum up close to their bodies, which overheats the testes, which in turn kills sperm. Chances are they're as barren as mules."

"Ah," I said, "that must be nature's way of controlling the population of insufferable assholes."

Again, what struck me more than anything else was the blandness of it all. I found myself puzzled, trying to reconcile the freakishness of Byron Choate's vision with the reality of Manray's on ladies' night out, watching some bubblehead twirl his pego. Maybe I'd misread Choate, but would he have really committed murder and arson for this, a sanitized, innocuous exercise in suburban titillation?

Soon, the loudspeakers crackled as a microphone engaged; an announcer's voice boomed with bawdy patter as he introduced the next act. And sure enough, now on deck, Gorgeous George excused himself from his group of admirers, weaved unhurriedly through the crowd, circled the runway, and walked right past our table, heading toward the rear of the club. His blond hair glistened with mousse, gathered into spikes that sprung rakishly from the top of his head. He was handsome enough, although his face was the sort women have always described to me as "too pretty"; judging by the untroubled confidence of his demeanor, I gathered that criticisms of this sort had been successfully concealed from him.

Our table was one of the few that offered a better view of the rest rooms than of the stage. We watched as George paused to place a telephone call, then a minute later turned a corner and disappeared. I got up and followed, trying to appear as inconspicuous as possible considering I was male, fully dressed, and hadn't been near a weight room for maybe ten years. I stopped in front of the cigarette machine next to the telephones, reached in my pocket for change, taking the opportunity to sneak a look around. I saw a small hallway leading behind the stage with a door at the end of it. EMPLOYEES ONLY. ABSOLUTELY NO ADMITTANCE. I thought: Ta-da. I looked back at Beth and Gerald, who were still sitting at our table, watching me. I nodded once, resisting an impulse to signal them by touching my forefinger to the tip of my nose and flicking it.

They joined me, Beth appearing completely composed and Gerald—well, his facial muscles were probably incapable of expressing anxiety. We turned down the hallway—quieter here, the music muffled—and a moment later we stood in front of the dressing-room door. We waited a few seconds; no one followed.

Without a word Gerald and I positioned ourselves on either side of the door, out of sight. Elizabeth took a deep breath, giving me a look of "Here goes" before she turned the knob and opened the door.

I heard George say, "Ladies' rest room is the first door you come to. If you go back—"

Beth didn't budge, except to cock her hip. She said, "I know."

"No ladies allowed back here."

"I watched you dance earlier," she said, her voice dropping a register, throaty, hitting a note of seductiveness that impressed me. I was impressed, too, when she told him with a straight face, "I was hoping you'd show me how your slide rule works."

"Sorry, but we—"

He paused, and I could sense that he was thinking fast, reevaluating the situation, maybe even checking his watch to see how much time he had. And then I heard a chuckle, a small self-confident chuckle, full of superiority.

He said, "Ooo, baby, you just couldn't wait, huh? You want it bad, don't you?"

"Yessss," Beth cooed breathlessly, "I want it bad. And it looks like we have the dressing room all to ourselves."

That was our cue. Beth stepped inside the dressing room, and Gerald and I followed her through, closing the door behind us. Gorgeous George had been sitting there, only a towel draped across his lap, striking a cavalier pose, balancing on the rear legs of a wooden chair. When he saw us, he froze. Gerald took a step forward, raked the front left leg of the chair with his shoe, sending George over backward, shouting "Hey!" until he hit the dressing-room floor. When he tried to get up, Gerald shook his head no.

"Wha . . . who the hell is he?"

"This is Gerald," I said. "He wants it bad, too."

He stared up at us, beginning to panic. Strange men in the room changed the social equation, and his nakedness bothered him a lot more. He stayed down, one hand pulling his towel close about him, the other rubbing his head. He was looking up at Beth as if for assurance that some practical joke was being played on him.

"Sorry," she said, "I prefer my men in a nice pair of boxer shorts. No fast-food slogans." Then she calmly looked at me. "You know, it's true."

"What?"

"Film makes everything appear larger."

I said, "Yes?"

"Looks like a Whopper Junior to me."

I helped George back into the chair, thinking I'd found my niche: helping people up after Gerald got through with them. I said, "As much as we're enjoying this, we really don't have time for chitchat. So if you'll cooperate, we can make this quick. You feel like answering a few questions?"

He didn't take his eyes off Gerald. "Sure . . . I mean, Christ, why didn't you just say so? What kind of questions?"

"We want to know about Sheena Sands. Just tell us about Sheena."

"Sheena Sands?"

"Come on, George, put your brain in gear."

"Jesus, Sheena . . . what about her?"

"For starters, where is she?"

"How the fuck would I know?" he said, reaching amid the clutter on the dressing table for a pack of cigarettes. He shook one out, lit it, and drew on it nervously. "I saw her, I don't know, maybe three, four weeks ago. There was a party for some of us who'd worked together on this, uh, project. . . ."

I said, "No secrets among friends, George. We already know about your secret life as a minor film star. So there was a party?"

"Yeah, sort of like a cast party for Venture Productions. I don't remember too much about it, but I'm pretty sure she was there." He paused, eyeing me. "Sheena? What, you got a thing for her?"

"We're just trying to find her. We think she may be in trouble."

"Trouble? A nineteen-year-old girl doing fuck films? What makes you think she's in trouble?" He grinned and once again balanced on the rear legs of the chair, beginning to relax. "Look, if I knew anything, I'd tell you. Sheena seems like an okay person, but I don't really know her. Sometimes it's easier to work in this business if you keep everything nice and professional. Just have a nice, working relationship. Now, if you say she's in trouble, I wouldn't know anything about that. If she's not around, maybe she just quit, you know, got fed up and split. It happens all the time. Or maybe the prissy little preppie canned her."

I said, "The prissy little preppie to whom you refer is Byron Choate?"

He nodded. "Or maybe it was Theodore. Maybe she just got sick of the creep hanging around, being on her ass all the time."

"Theodore," I said. "You mean Teddy?"

"Yeah, Teddy. Theodore Spanelli, Teddy Span, Teddy the Techie. He works for Byron, but you ask me, he's out of control. Always hanging around the set, harassing the girls, giving everybody the willies." George started laughing. "You know why he got his face scraped? He had this idea if he improved his appearance, Byron might put him in a movie. The crazy fuck. Yeah, they might put him in *Nightmare on Elm Street, Part Ten*. Save a bundle on make-up."

"You said maybe Byron fired Sheena. Why would he do that?"

"Let's just say she didn't take direction all that well. Sheena could be wild, really into sex, but she was a little weird, too. She had all these ideas, college-girl ideas. Politics. Can you believe it? She brought books to the set, read whenever she got a chance. All this heavy-duty feminist shit. She wanted all the sex scenes to have this equal power, you know, showing women in control. I used to tease her sometimes, ask her what about equal work, equal pay. This is one business where women get paid four or five times what guys make. Anyway, her and Byron were always arguing about the scripts, always climbing up each other's ass. Sheena was good at what she did, but she had some rules, a few things she wouldn't do for the camera."

Beth said, "Why do you think she did any of it?"

"Who knows? Girls have all kinds of reasons. Some of them just like sex, simple as that. Some of them want to hurt their parents, or maybe hurt themselves. Some have asshole boyfriends who talk them into it, telling them how gorgeous they are in one breath and telling them to spread it for some stranger in the next. If you're eighteen or nineteen, maybe you think that's true love. Others just like the money, or they like the drugs. What was going on in Sheena's mind, I don't know. She acted like maybe she wanted to change the world. I don't think she was having much luck."

I remembered the stupefied girl I'd seen at Choate's. "Did she have a problem with drugs?"

He laughed and blew a lungful of smoke into the room. "A problem? None of us really had a drug problem. That's one good thing I can say about Byron, he always keeps plenty of drugs on the set. So I can't really say there was a drug *problem*. How do you think these movies get made, my friend? It's a speed show."

"So you saw her at a party about a month ago?"

"Yeah, at Byron's. That party was about the only time he ever did anything for us he didn't have to. Not a bad party, what I remember of it. No drug problem there, either. Byron's got those photographs all over his walls. You eat a little cake and stare at those, man, you can get seriously weirded out."

"Did you talk to her?"

"Unh-uh. Now that you mention it, I think her and Byron were going at each other then, too." He narrowed his eyes and eased some smoke from his lips. He was remembering something. "A couple of business suits show up . . . yeah, friends of Byron's, VIPs, and I think what Byron had in mind was to show 'em a good time, get their ashes hauled. The reason I remember is that I figured they were the reason Byron decided all of a sudden to get generous and throw a party. Anyway, Sheena freaked when it dawned on her what Byron was up to.''

"Which was?''

"He wanted her and the other girls to service these business suits. Byron was treating her like a hooker, and it pissed her off. Like I told you, she had these ideas; she made some interesting distinctions. I think that's what was going on. Maybe not. I was a little out of it.''

I asked him where Choate lived, and he snorted and said he couldn't find it again if Byron was inside handing out free money. And then he said something I hadn't counted on.

"You got all these questions, why don't you just ask him? He's got a flick in production right now. I'm sitting this one out, but I hear it's kind of a health spa, bodybuilding thing. I think they're calling it *Love Muscles*.''

We just stared at him.

"You didn't know? Yeah, Byron thinks it's a hoot, gets a real kick outta doing it while all those feminists are picketing the building, thinking they got him shut down. It's easy. He just shoots the exterior scenes wherever he pleases, then shoots the money scenes, the hard-core scenes, on the soundstage at night. Most of that building is a warehouse, anyway, so the crew just parks around back near one of the truck bays, and goes in through there. Nobody sees 'em coming or going. No sweat. I heard Byron owns the whole damn building.'' Gorgeous George shrugged. "Things start hopping around midnight. Check it out. Shooting porn is night shift work, anyway.''

19

His jaws aching, his tongue weary, he feared that she would never come. But he set about his labors with renewed vigor, flicking his tongue as rapidly as fatigue would permit, teasing the upper edge of her soft, warm notch. . . .

Beth looked up from the manuscript and suppressed a smile. "Notch?"

I said, "You should try it sometime. It's not easy."

"Yes?"

"I mean describing it."

If I had to endure criticism, I thought dreamily, this was the only way to go. For the second time that week Elizabeth and I were in bed together, sated amid a tangle of sheets. She was straddling my hips as I lay there, her blond hair appealingly disheveled, our torsos still warmly and wetly joined, both of us ridiculously content. She'd spotted the latest pages from *Naked Laughter* on the bedside table, and spread them before her on my chest. She'd been reading aloud, feigning an expression of severity as she peered down at the typescript, occasionally erupting into laughter.

"Ooo," I said. "Do that again."

"Do what?"

"Laugh. I feel it when you laugh. It gives me a little nip."

. . . and still he could not fetch her. His tongue burned with weariness now, moving unrhythmically, feeling

strangely unconnected to him, alien, as if it were someone else's tongue. All the while he watched her above the soft swell of her pudenda, her eyes tightly shut in concentration, her body foreshortened before him, the plains and hillocks and valleys of an unconquered land. Just when he was sure he couldn't continue a moment longer, she began to tremble and quake beneath him. He became aware that a threshold had been crossed. Suddenly every caress of his tongue, however awkward, seemed only to incite her. Her thighs opened wider and quivered, and she began to buck, clutching his hair spasmodically—ow!—wriggling and heaving, until with a low yawling, half moan, half sigh, she came. . . .

Beth said, "So where's the part with the redeeming social value?"

"I put it in an appendix. I didn't want to break up the rhythm."

It was eight-thirty Saturday evening, and what we were supposed to be doing was conserving our energy. Later we'd planned a midnight excursion to Venture Productions to see if Gorgeous George had been telling the truth about a night shift at the smut factory. Nothing complicated, just meet Gerald, drive to the building at 29 Duffy Street, park out of sight, and see who showed up. And if that happened to be Byron Choate and his merry band of pornsters? Well, we'd improvise, I thought, assess the situation, identify and analyze our options. And when that didn't work, let Gerald tell us what to do.

Beth and I had met for an early dinner at Grendel's, then returned to my apartment at seven, which left us with three hours to rest up. Given the chance we'd be up all night, we decided the best thing to do was take a nap.

A nap. We should have known what *that* meant. We fell into each other's arms, wordlessly, of course, neither of us eager to contemplate what our recent romantic unions might signify. A step toward reconciliation? An unthinking aberration? The inevitable consequence of spending so much time together? I knew this much: The last hour had been memorable, our lovemaking the beneficiary of our months apart, an ideal mingling of the familiar and the novel, which left me wondering: Was this, finally, the prescription for a happy marital bed, lovemaking on successive weekends every other year?

Afterward Beth had spotted the pages, another prop to distract us, a focus for our evasive joking.

. . . *and then she came again, and yet again, ever more quickly, as if the voluptuous moment he had sought for her, having arrived, would not pass. "Enough," she breathed. "I can't take any more," but so inflamed of mind and groin was she that when he withdrew his tongue, she came again, not from his touch but from the very idea of his touch.* . . .

"How original," she said, "multiple orgasm."

"Exaggeration is the essence of the literary imagination."

She goosed me. "When we were married, I had the impression you thought multiple orgasm meant having two in the same week."

. . . *His brain seemed on fire as he pulled himself on top of her, ironbound, priapic, push, push, pushing as he, too, succumbed to that sensual ache at the very root of his being. Behind closed eyes his mind teemed with images. He perused that secret gallery, the residue of his remembered sex life, the obscene stash of the mind's eye. Anonymous genitalia, disembodied and glistening, cavorted in his brain, the pornography not of the page or screen, but of the retina. And then his mind went blank, riding the crest of an exquisite spasm, which carried them together past all thought.*

"Ah," she said as she dropped the pages fluttering to the floor, "Dostoyevski meets *Penthouse Forum*."

I was about to roll out of bed, but she pushed me back into the pillows. She hovered over me, nuzzling my neck, playfully kissing my throat and chest.

"You know what they say," she whispered. "Those who can, do. Those who can't, write."

"Teach. Those who can't, teach."

Her hand moved down between our bellies, manipulating my flesh. There was a challenge in her eye.

She said, "You want to split hairs or you want to make hay?"

"We've already made hay. My haymaker is taking a break—"

"Oh, I know just the thing," she assured me, planting light kisses all over my chest. "I wouldn't worry about that. Just give me a minute, I can bring him right to attention, remember?"

I regarded her with mock fear and spoke in a high, squeaky voice. "Oh no," I said, "not the splints."

An hour and a half later we were in Gerald's car on our way to 29 Duffy Street, preparing for amateur surveillance night. Beth sat up front, asking Gerald about the old days in Boston, before the city had evolved from tough waterfront town to four-year camp for college students. I was in the back, yawning and blinking, trying to recover from the effects of our rest period. A pair of binoculars and a Thermos of coffee rested on the seat beside me. We were dressed in dark clothes.

Beth and Gerald, I'd noticed, seemed to be developing a curious rapport. He still had trouble taking me seriously—who blamed him?—but his manner toward Beth was charmingly, if awkwardly, genteel; as he described the rough dives and fearsome inhabitants of Sculley Square, the red-light district that preceded the Combat Zone, I heard him strive for delicate phrasings. For her part, Beth listened with genuine interest, settling into the relaxed, accepting demeanor of a psychologist, her own ease putting him at ease.

At one point Gerald mentioned his stint as a pro wrestler in the fifties, which somehow inspired the following exchange:

"Real blood?" Beth asked.

"Uh-huh. Real blood."

"I know it looks real, but it can't be. Don't they fake that just like they fake everything else?"

"When I was wrestling, the blood was real," he insisted. "I don't know what they do now."

"Wait a minute. When a wrestler got bashed over the head with a chair, or whatever they do to each other when they get carried away, and the blood gushes, you're saying that was on the level?"

"Only the blood," he said. "We faked the other stuff. Real blood was the key. That made believers outta everybody."

"How? I don't get it."

"It was easy," he explained, and for the first time I saw him grow animated, his face lit with enthusiasm. "Say a guy bangs you with a chair, or bounces your skull on the cement outside the ring, something. That's fake, but you go down, grabbing your head like you're dying. The thing nobody sees is that you're palming a razor. Just an old Gillette razor blade all covered with adhesive tape except for one tiny little corner. So there you are on the floor, wriggling in pain, but what you're really doing is pulling this razor across your forehead, just enough to break the skin. You finally stagger to your feet and your hands come away from your head"— he paused triumphantly—"and the blood starts to flow. Real blood. Gets mixed in with your sweat and pretty soon it's everywhere. Drives 'em crazy. Even the cocky ones, the fans who think they know everything's fake, are scratching their heads. The thing about real blood, you know it when you see it."

I sensed that Beth was having trouble maintaining her neutral, all-accepting demeanor.

She said, "You cut yourself with a *razor*?"

Gerald reached back and flipped the overhead light. Eyes on the road, he leaned slightly toward her to display his forehead. I sat forward for a peek, too. Sure enough, just beneath his hairline was a series of scars, long and perfectly straight, whitish and faint with age.

Beth said it again. "You actually cut yourself?"

Her innocence pleased him. "Sure. You had to. You didn't trust no one else to cut you. That would be stupid."

Yes, I thought, that would be stupid. But I didn't permit myself as much as a smile. I was too conscious of the irony of my own situation to relish the irony of someone else's. I stared out the rear window as the dark streets of Boston flew by, and pondered the strangeness, the almost surreal aspect of the moment. Was I really here, on this midnight errand, listening to my ex-wife and a former Mafia enforcer explore the mysteries of professional wrestling?

"Wait," I said. "Slow down. I think we're here."

We stopped. Beth said, "Are you sure?"

It didn't really look like the place where barely a week ago she'd dropped me off for my audition. At night everything appeared more desolate, more sinister than I remembered. From the street the building presented only a stark, utilitarian profile against the black sky. The gestures of renewal—the freshly sandblasted brick, the passageway of scalloped arches along the first floor—were hidden in the darkness, as if after hours the structure resumed its former architectural status, a warehouse. But the small park was there, just across the street, so I knew we'd come to the right place. The park, too, appeared bleak and foreboding. Good place for a midnight stroll, I thought, if you owned a pit bull.

We made a slow pass in front of the building, and I carefully studied the dark windows. No nude silhouettes appeared on the drawn shades. No muted cries of "Action! Roll 'em!" drifted from within.

Gerald took a left, turned off his headlights, and eased along the side street on the north side of building. A rear parking lot was enclosed by a high chain link fence; the entrance gate was chained and padlocked. Beneath a few dim security lights, we saw a concrete loading platform, several truck bays with lowered doors of corrugated metal. About fifty yards down the deserted street, Gerald made a U-turn and pulled over to the curb. We parked in near darkness with a clear view of the rear of the building.

If there was anything to see, we would see it.

For the next half hour we had the place to ourselves. Beth

and I made short work of the Thermos of coffee, and Gerald, encouraged by the awed response to his forehead, had grown loquacious, giving an account of various scars on his forearms and neck. We were saved from a history of more private wounds when a white van turned off Duffy, moving slowly, its headlights aimed our way.

I whispered, "Company."

The van turned at the entrance to the parking lot and stopped with its front bumper a yard away from the gate. I raised the binoculars to my eyes. The driver got out, walked around to the front of the van, and tested the gate. I'd never seen him before. Slim and bearded, thirtyish, wearing a black baseball cap and a down vest. He was alone, and he leaned against the front of the van, smoking a cigarette, waiting.

"Recognize him?" Beth said.

"With a beard and baseball cap, I don't know, he looks a little like Steven Spielberg . . . naah."

A couple of times he glanced in our direction; I don't think he could see us, but if he did, it didn't seem to bother him. Mostly he was looking the other way, toward Duffy Street, and about five minutes later, we were all rewarded by the sight of a second pair of headlights entering the side street and heading toward us. A taxi. When it reached the van it pulled over and stopped.

Byron Choate emerged, a felt hat pulled low over his patrician brow, a leather valise in hand, long dark overcoat and flowing scarf worn over jeans and sneakers. The *auteur* himself. With his free hand he reached into his overcoat pocket, tossed a ring of keys to the man in the baseball cap, and climbed into the van on the passenger's side. The bearded man unlocked the gate and swung it open, then hopped back behind the wheel. The van eased across the asphalt lot and parked at the far end of the loading platform, near some concrete steps. The two men got out, mounted the steps, and crossed the platform to a steel door. Beneath a dim security light, Choate flipped through his keys— holding them out from the shadows of his body—until he found the one he wanted. He opened the door, and they disappeared behind it.

"If that door's green," I said, "we're onto something."

Surveillance, I discovered, wasn't such a mind-numbing, soporific chore, after all. Over the next half hour, a steady stream of people showed up—not a cast of thousands, but more than I'd expected—in cabs, dropped off by friends, driving their own cars, mostly subcompacts so uniformly battered that I was convinced that porn didn't pay.

So far we'd counted fourteen people, six women and eight men. No Sheena Sands, sedated or otherwise. No Ugly Teddy, either. Beth remembered two of the men as dancers from Manray's; I recognized Sandy Lofton, the woman who'd set me straight about job qualifications for fluffer. All the other faces were unfamiliar, although it was fairly easy to guess which side of the camera most of them worked on. Some entered the building with a dutiful air, workmen about to punch the clock. Others literally bounced inside, their spirits spectacularly, unnaturally high.

During the next half hour, the pace of arrivals eased. During one lull, the bearded man in the baseball cap reappeared, hopped in the van, and drove away. A few minutes later, a Toyota station wagon turned into the lot and dropped off a latecomer, an attractive young woman with a huge mane of blond hair, wearing tight jeans and a sweatshirt, a canvas bag slung over her shoulder. There was something endearing in the way she circled the station wagon and leaned through the driver's window, lingering for a few sentimental good-bye kisses. A golden retriever in the backseat followed her movements alertly. Ah, I thought, the clichés of domesticity applied here no less than in the suburbs of Acton or Braintree. A job is a job, I thought, watching the couple engage in another, more passionate kiss. Spouses and girlfriends must be dropped off, and kissed and hugged.

As the station wagon pulled away, I got a better look at the driver, and I thought: Whoops. I'd just witnessed domestic bliss, certainly, though not the particular bliss of clichés. Behind the wheel of the station wagon was another young woman.

We waited another half hour for good measure. About one in the morning, the man with the baseball cap returned. He idled the white van just inside the gate, got out, swung it closed, and locked it. Then he parked and went inside, and the purpose of his errand was clear. He was carrying a large stack of white cartons. Pizzas.

"No," Beth whispered solemnly, "that's definitely not Spielberg. They wouldn't send Spielberg out for pizza."

No one else arrived. Except for the battered subcompacts parked along the rear of the building, the scene appeared exactly as it had when we'd first parked here two hours ago. An obvious, unspoken question hung in the air, until Beth finally asked it.

"Now what?"

To me, at least, the answer was clear. All we had to do was wait. Quitting time would roll around, eventually everyone would leave, and then we could follow Choate. We might be here until dawn, yes, but there was a very good chance Choate would lead us right to Sheena.

My advocacy of this approach was interrupted when Gerald turned the key in the ignition, flipped on the headlights, and drove away. I wasn't sure what to think. Had the sight of the pizza made him hungry? But we didn't go far. We turned onto Duffy, drove another twenty yards, and parked right in front of the building.

Gerald said, "You said one of those doors is theirs?"

I nodded.

"Which one?"

I pointed in the general direction of Tele-Techniques.

"Does it connect?"

What did he have in mind? I began urging the virtues of patience. After all, I reminded him, tonight was surveillance night. Breaking and entering was another skill entirely, one to be mastered on another night, a night when we were fresh and there would be less chance of confrontation, not to mention a lot fewer people to confront. Waiting might not be glamorous, I told him, but it would be effective, and it would be safe. Hah, I said, both safe and effective. Free of worry.

"You still don't have the hang of this, do you?"

I said no. He eased himself out of the car, unfolded his huge, hulking frame, and peered back at me through the open door.

"We don't worry about them. We make them worry about us."

He opened, then closed the trunk, and a moment later we watched as he headed up the concrete walk toward the building. Jesus. He was carrying a crowbar and making no effort to conceal it. Not the modest, nail-prying bar of backyard workshops, but much larger, the kind of tool you might see on a construction site. Beth and I exchanged a panicky glance, but we got out and followed him anyway, vaguely humiliated, like children who don't want to go, but who don't want to be left behind, either.

Things happened quickly. Up ahead, Gerald was already at work, wedging the flat tongue of the crowbar into the doorjamb just below the knob; he wielded the tool deftly, as if it were as light as a magician's wand. He caught the opposite end of the bar against his stomach and levered it with his weight. I cringed at the loud metallic pop, the sound of wood splintering. By the time we reached him, he'd repeated the procedure, dropping the bar to a lower point, finishing the job. Someone with a key couldn't have opened it any faster.

"Shit," I whispered tensely, "shit."

I couldn't believe it. Splintered, dangling limply within the jamb was the door to Sun God Tanning Salon. Shit, shit, shit, I cursed. Gerald had popped the wrong fucking door off its hinges. I resisted an impulse to ask for a second look at the scars on his forehead, to see just how deeply he'd gouged himself. To his credit, he didn't seem especially troubled when I pointed out his error. He simply moved down one door, to Tele-Techniques, leaving me to restore the entry to the tanning salon to some semblance of its former state. I propped the door cosmetically within its frame.

Beth was watching the dark street uneasily. "I'll let you know as soon as I hear the sirens."

"Another wrong door and we'll have the makings of a pretty good insanity plea."

Gerald now worked on the entrance to Tele-Techniques, and I stood behind him, again cringing at the sound, feeling more vulnerable and exposed with every passing second. For someone who'd resisted the notion of illegal entry moments ago, I was surprised how badly I wanted to be inside now.

I got my wish.

20

The small office was quiet and full of shadows. I replaced the outer door as best I could—my new specialty—and then we waited and listened. I tiptoed across the room and tested the inner door, not giving Gerald an opportunity to bring his crowbar into play. It was unlocked. I opened it a few inches and stood perfectly still. A moment later a woman's voice echoed from inside, eerily distant and hollow.

"Oh baby yeah. Ooo, yeah. That's so good. Hmm."

Thank God, I thought, still at work; at least they hadn't heard us break in. I tried to relax and put myself in a better frame of mind. In a sense, Gerald was right about who should and shouldn't be nervous. After all, I told myself, wasn't Byron Choate the skulking pornographer, and weren't we on a mission of mercy? He was the one who'd switched his shooting schedule to the middle of the night; he'd likely be as skittish, or even more skittish than we were. And Ugly Teddy, as far as we could tell, wasn't around to help him.

We stepped through the inner door into a small vestibule that led into the enormous open shell of the building itself. Concrete floors, unfinished brick walls with ragged mortar. All that kept us from seeing or being seen were shipping cartons, hundreds of them, stacked high upon row after row of industrial shelves, which rose toward the ceiling on steel frames. We crept along a narrow aisle, down among the close stacks of cartons, until we reached a wide center corridor that bisected the rows of shelves. We turned left, heading toward the far side of the building, moving carefully, making certain our sneakers didn't squeak on the concrete floor. Gerald, I noticed, wore Hush Puppies.

"Oh yeah, baby. That's right. That's so good. Soooo goooood."

There, at the end of the corridor, beyond the last row of cartons, a halo of bright light reflected against the ceiling. And from there, too, the woman's voice drifted toward us, clearer now.

"Hmmm, hmmm, yeah. That's good."

A male voice offered encouragement. "Come on, Tina, come on. Give it to me."

Each step took us closer to the sound of the voices, closer to the bright halo of lights beyond the last wall of boxes. Two forklift trucks were parked at the end of the corridor, and just before we reached them we turned off, slipping back among the narrow aisles between the shelves. We crouched in the shadows, no more than a few feet away now, only a single shelf separating us from the moviemakers on the other side. Here and there, I noticed, enough boxes had been removed so that shafts of light broke through to our hiding place.

I found an opening near eye level and peered through it.

Two large backdrops formed a V and the space within it created the illusion of a health spa. Various pieces of exercise equipment were positioned on a low stage, in front of large mirrors and a dance bar. Out from the stage, set down amid a tangle of cables, were lighting stanchions and reflectors and tripods, and some other equipment I didn't recognize. There were space heaters, too, around the periphery.

"Hmm, yes, yessss . . ."

She lay on an exercise bench at the center of the set, fully clothed. Blue bodysuit, hair pulled back in a ponytail, braided terry-cloth headband. The bearded man with the baseball cap was leaning over her as she lay there. He, too, was fully clothed, and he held a camera, taking an extreme close-up of her face.

Byron Choate stood nearby, studying a clipboard, sleeves of his white shirt rolled up to the elbows, looking very much the preppie pornster.

The bearded man with the camera said, "Come on, Tina, give it to me. Come on, sell it. Really sell it."

Tina resumed her expressive moans and ruttish squeals, peering directly into the camera. She rocked her head from side to side, in the throes of imaginary ecstasy.

"That feels sooooo gooooood. Soooo gooooo—" and then she broke out laughing.

Byron Choate glanced up from his clipboard, annoyed. Tina brushed the cameraman aside and sat up. Craning her neck, she looked beyond Choate, offstage, where the other actors and crew had crowded around a table.

"You shitheads," she called out, "you better save me some pizza."

It was much easier now to distinguish the talent from the technicians. Most of the women around the table had changed into flashy workout gear, the colorful swatches of spandex now de rigueur at health clubs for singles. Everyone was wearing considerably more jewelry than I associated with authentic exercise, and the outfits were so revealingly cut that even modest movements would be rendered obscene. Which, of course, was the point. One girl— the blonde who'd been dropped off by her girlfriend—was leaning backward, giggling as she positioned a slice of pizza above her open mouth. She was wearing a billowy red jacket clasped at her waist and thick leg warmers that rose almost to the tops of her thighs; she remained bareassed in between.

At the edge of the stage Byron Choate massaged his temples and frowned at his clipboard; he was conferring with Sandy Lofton, who carried a clipboard of her own. She, too, was displeased.

"We may get caught a little short at the end of twenty-six," I heard her say. "We could really use another hard-core shot. Randy didn't really have his pump primed."

"Tell me about it."

They seemed to rely on a lot of movie talk, interspersed with various euphemisms, which I suppose elevated their exchange and buffered them from the indignity of saying something like, "Let's point the camera at Bubba while Betty doodles his pud."

"What about twelve?" Choate asked. "How was Randy in twelve?"

"Better. Not exactly Old Faithful, but better."

"Tell you what. If we get in a bind, we just take the wet shot from twelve and splice it in at the end of twenty-six. Repeat it slo-mo if we have to."

"Can we get by with that?"

Choate's reply was a dismissive roll of his eyes. "Tapioca is tapioca."

In unison they flipped the top pages on their clipboards and folded them under, another cinematic crisis having been resolved.

"So we can get started with the orgy scene?"

"Round 'em up," Choate said, "move 'em out."

I stepped back from my peephole and glanced over at Beth and Gerald. Narrow beams of light angled near their faces as they quietly spied through peepholes of their own. Gerald appeared especially calm, considering he'd passed a good ten minutes without making anyone nervous. Maybe he was a little starstruck.

"Scene twenty-seven, *Love Muscles*," Sandy Lofton called out, summoning the performers to the set. Muttering and groaning they pulled themselves away from the pizza and gathered on the low stage, where Choate arranged them in twos and threes among the sleek exercise machines and on the low padded benches of a Nautilus. He continually referred to his clipboard, explaining the orgy scene as he went. The gleaming apparatus, I now saw, had been selected less with an eye to fitness than to erotic possibility.

"Nicole, hon, toward the end of the scene, after you and Brandy finish your thing with the dildo, I want you to go over to the Stairmaster and help Kelley fellate Roddy. Be sure to keep your bottom toward the camera," he added, "give us a nice peek, okeydoke? Now Cody, sweetie, you go"—he looked around, momentarily puzzled—"No, no, wait, Cody, I want you over here on the Nautilus with Randy. We'll have him lying right here on the bench, and you're going to hang from this bar and sort of lower yourself onto his face, okay?"

How sweet, I thought. Young people in love.

Choate began demonstrating this bit of stagecraft to Cody, coaching her as she hung from an aluminum bar above her partner's head, Choate saying, "Lower, lower, that's it," until the actor whose face lay beneath her descending buttocks sounded a muffled alarm and struggled free.

"You want her like that," he said to Choate, "you gotta get me a snorkel. I can't breathe."

Choate sorted out this and other snags and continued around the stage, until another small commotion erupted behind him. The young women he'd called Nicole and Brandy had begun to argue, each of them tugging at the flesh-colored straps attached to the base of a rubber phallus. Apparently there was a difference of opinion about who wore the dildo in the dildo scene.

"Read the script," Nicole said. "I pitch, you catch."

"Unh-uh," Brandy said, turning to Choate, "no way. It's my turn. She puts this on, she goes crazy. She thinks it's her big chance to rule the world or something. You don't pay me enough."

Choate looked back and forth between the two young women, as each advanced a claim on the knobby appendage. It wasn't the sort of dilemma, I was thinking, that required a Solomonic display of wisdom. Choate finally awarded the prosthesis to Nicole.

"Nicole, sweetheart, do me a favor. Nice and easy with the dildo, okay? Remember, you're supposed to be making love to her. You're not trying to punish her for her sins."

Nicole scowled. "Yeah? Tell that to a guy sometime."

When the nuances of the orgy scene had been explained more or less to everyone's satisfaction, Sandy Lofton assembled the players at the center of the stage. Choate hopped onto a bench and raised his hands to quiet them.

"Okay, people, even if you're not in the primary shot, stay alert. Always know where the camera is. I don't want to pick up anyone in the background yawning and checking their nail polish, got it? Once we commit, there's no turning back. Camera, sound, same goes for you. We have a lot of mirrors in the background, so please don't get caught in the frame."

As I watched him, he suddenly appeared to me in a different and lesser light. I struggled to imagine him the shrewd schemer, the real-estate speculator, the powerful, unseen manipulator of Boston's underworld, the overseer of some new realm of porn. He now seemed strangely reduced, innocuous, even clownish. The image that kept popping into my mind was Mickey Rooney standing on a chair among the neighborhood kids. Was this the show they finally put together in Mr. Anderson's barn?

He glanced at his wristwatch. "Let's be ready to roll in fifteen minutes. Sandy will be passing around a few treats, laying out a few lines that should assist you in focusing your energies." He smiled at them. "Please, just enough to give you an edge. Don't lose your blink reflex."

At the precise moment Choate finished this speech, things began to happen quickly. I became aware of a rustling, a stirring of air as Gerald squeezed past me in the narrow aisle. I turned to see him step out into the corridor, clutching the crowbar menacingly, eager to test the nerves of the pornographers.

I whispered after him, "Wait, let's think of a—" but he didn't stop.

Beth was at my elbow now, and we heard a noise that further confused and unnerved us: the sound of a motor starting, an engine being revved. Grimacing, we eased out of our hiding place. I stuck my head into the corridor, and there was Gerald, atop the driver's seat of one of the fork-lifts parked in the corridor. Once again he'd managed to transform a period of quiet surveillance into utter panic. He revved the engine some more—surely they'd heard it by now—and popped it into gear. He was still gaining speed as he passed me; if I hadn't jumped back among the cartons, one of the steel prongs would've nailed me.

He took the corner at the end of the corridor too quickly; the rear end of the forklift slid out, clipping a protruding shelf. His entry onto the movie set was accompanied by a deafening crash of cartons, tumbling down from the high shelf, thudding in his wake.

I followed just far enough to peek around the corner. What I saw immediately confirmed Gerald's knowledge of confrontation, his instincts about who would run and who would stand and fight. The crew of thespians were squeal-ing and scurrying like mice. Of course, why shouldn't they? He'd caught them midsnort, inhaling drugs between takes of a skin flick. And if that wasn't enough, they no doubt possessed other guilty fears of which we were unaware.

Gerald surged forward into the rapidly emptying set. A few of the actors lingered recklessly over the white powder, risking final snorts, noses down, eyes up and wide, riveted on Gerald, making desperate calculations of distance and time as the prongs of the forklift bore down on them. At the last possible moment they, too, fled, and Gerald plowed through the table—drugs and pizza boxes flying—catching the table and carrying it forward, impaled on the lift. An instant later the table sailed into the air when Gerald plowed into the stage.

Choate? I thought. Where was Choate?

I frantically scanned the fleeing swatches of spandex, looking for a plain button-down white cotton shirt. God-damn it, where was he? If he escaped, everything was wasted, the entire night's work was pointless. Why hadn't we just stayed in the car? Why hadn't we just sat there watching, like I'd wanted?

Gerald leaped down from the truck, gripping the huge crowbar like a sword. He circled the stage, swinging it before him as if bushwhacking through the jungle, mauling the cameras and tripods, pulverizing the lighting stanchions, sending it all flying. Sparks flew. Mirrors shattered. Of all the things that might have come to my mind, I thought of Jesus. Jesus expelling the money changers from the temple. A very big Jesus. A very ugly Jesus.

There he was. Slinking along the far wall, I got a glimpse of Choate. He paused in a crouch, casting an uneasy eye toward Gerald. He seemed to be biding his time, circling back, planning an alternative retreat, hoping to avoid the traffic jam that had developed at the rear exit. I watched him watching Gerald. Soon he picked his moment. With a crouching, loping gait, he crossed the open space behind Gerald, apparently in the hope of sneaking down the corridor and out the front office.

He was heading directly toward me.

I eased back into the shadows. When he was about ten yards away, I stepped out into the corridor and blocked his path. I thought mean thoughts. I made my voice harsh.

"Right there, asshole," I barked. "Hold it right there."

He skidded in his tracks until he came to a complete stop; surprised and frightened, he squinted at me in the shadows. I didn't think he could see more than my dark outline, much less enough to recognize me. I made my hand into a gun and pointed my forefinger at him. It was the same forefinger with which I'd shot the pigeon, but somehow this time I didn't think it was going to fire.

I said, "Don't fucking move."

Very slowly he started backing up, raising his palms toward me, saying, "Easy, take it easy," as if he expected me to pull the trigger at any moment. His patrician face was full of fear and profound puzzlement, as if he were sifting mentally through any number of bad things that might be happening to him.

"Why now?" he began to plead. "Just when we get everything under control. Didn't I just talk to him last week?

Everything was okay then, and everything's okay now. Just tell him everything is okay.''

I continued to hold him at fingerpoint while he babbled more nonsense. Behind him, Gerald completed his demolition of the set.

I said, ''Everything is not okay.''

21

The South End of Boston is a neighborhood at some uneasy stage of urban evolution. At this time of night, the young gentry lay sleeping in renovated row houses, snug beneath goose-down comforters, on sleek platform beds pushed against exposed brick walls. Outside, the sidewalks yield to a furtive commerce, a merchant class and a nomad clientele, brought together on these dark streets by the usual addictions of body and mind. And there were other hunters, too, and other prey.

It was three o'clock in the morning, and we were driving along Washington Street. I was behind the wheel of the Riviera and Elizabeth was beside me. Gerald had wedged himself into the backseat, the better to keep an eye on Byron Choate, our hostage.

Only he wasn't acting very much like a hostage. From the moment I stepped out of the shadows at the movie set, and he finally saw who I was, he regained his composure. "Oh," he said, "it's you," more relieved than frightened, apparently deciding that the predicament in which he found himself was of a lesser order than the one he'd feared. "You had me going there for a minute, Professor."

We stood without speaking, until he looked down at my forefinger, which was still pointed at him. A hint of a smile crossed his lips.

"I'd put that away," he said, "unless you plan to use it."

I told him why we'd come, and he listened with suppressed amusement, trying to maintain an air of earnestness, as if he were hearing a small child confess some outlandish ambition—say, to become president of the United States. He offered no resistance when we led him back among the aisles of cartons, through the front office, and outside to the car. Gerald followed behind him, the crowbar resting on his shoulder like a baseball bat.

"I see, I see, a fairy-tale rescue, and you've brought Beauty and the Beast to assist you. I suppose I can visualize you as Prince Charming, though you're going against type. But Sheena Sands as Snow White? Our young porn starlet? Well, perhaps. There have been unfortunate rumors of bawdy goings-on with the seven dwarfs." Gerald opened the rear door of the Buick, and Choate hesitated at the entrance, as if it were a dark hole into which he might fall. "I don't know about you, but I find fairy tales a very bleak, very depressing business. Beneath the sunny sentiments and happy conclusions, there are all manner of dark meanings and violent twists of plot."

As we drove away, I glanced in the rearview mirror, and for a moment his eyes caught mine. "Tell me, Professor," he said, "do you have any idea what you're getting into?"

"We're just trying to help Sheena."

"You still don't have a clue, do you?" he said, laughing. "Well, so am I. In my own modest way I'm trying to help Sheena, too. She'd be dead now if it weren't for me."

Gerald didn't have to pound anything out of him. Choate volunteered directions to his loft, and he told us about the small studio apartment on the floor above, where we would find Sheena. If anything, he grew more talkative as we drove, more annoyingly sociable.

"Can you believe it! Who do I hire as the future queen of porn? Not just a college girl," he said, "but some fire-eating Barnard dropout, an admirer of Emma Pierce. Half bookworm, half sexual anarchist! It would be funny if it weren't so pathetic.''

The sound of his own voice, I realized, buoyed him; his bravado offered a final vestige of control.

''The girl's full of raw animal spirit, I'll say that. She exudes sex. With some people—I don't know why—it just seeps out of their pores. But God is she naïve! Always complaining about the scripts, always asking for changes, as if we were all dying to strike a blow for sexual equality. You know what she wanted, of course. Positive images of women, happy women having happy sex. Positive images? Jesus Christ, in porn! Well, everybody has to suck it up sometime; the damn movies aren't exactly what I had in mind, either. I said, sure, we can cut out some of the extreme stuff, but don't throw out the baby with the bathwater. I had to tell her: If you get rid of everything that debases women, you get rid of the porn, too.''

There was something else in his voice, too, something of release, as one who has clutched the lip of a ledge too long and has finally let go. His speech had something in common with the long, luxurious scream of one who is falling.

''You know what the problem is? Sex itself. The very act of penetration. Every feminist knows in her heart that copulation isn't equal or progressive; that's why it's so bothersome. Men mount women and penetrate them, and there's no getting around it. That's the one thing you can't finesse in a porn film. In a novel you can finesse it with romance, in a painting you can finesse it with moonlight, but in a porn film, there's no finessing the old piston shot. No matter how sentimental the preliminaries, the world is eventually reduced to an image of a woman getting jabbed. The image can't be salvaged, and it can't be explained away. No amount of social engineering can redeem it. An image of a piston shot has been seared onto our brains; it informs our lives, our very language. How do we scorn our enemies? We say, Fuck you. How do we humiliate them? We fuck them over. And when the latest young accountant from Wall Street is sent to prison, what is his greatest fear? Not confinement. Not the cuisine. What terrifies him is the likelihood that someone will ask him to be a woman, that some hulking man will get into his pants. He fears that he will wind up on the wrong side—the female side—of a piston shot.''

Held captive to Choate's dark monologue, I was thinking that someone ought to revise all the old insurance-salesman jokes and substitute pornographers. We were heading down River Street, along the nameless side streets of the South End. The going was easy on the deserted avenues, and we were getting near the address he had given us.

Beth, who'd been listening without visible reaction, turned and looked at him across the seat.

''Is Sheena okay?'' she asked quietly.

''She speaks,'' he said, staring straight at Beth. ''She speaks at last. I haven't quite figured you. You don't fit in with all those sour harpies with their butch haircuts, always displeased. Hah-hah. I'll let you in on a little secret. Your lesbian friends are right. This country doesn't simply tolerate pornography, this country loves pornography. The reason is simple. This country hates women. I've thought about it for a long time, and I don't know of another name for it except hate. Everything else is subterfuge and rationalization, flowers and candy. Do you ever listen to those ACLU lawyers on the local talk shows, deploring Proposition Six? Oh, your enemies are clever. Oh, it hurts them so. They frown with pain while they tell you that porn is the high price we pay for free speech. Take a peek under their pillows sometime. You'll find the latest issue of *Shaved Pink*.''

A soft, nightmare laugh sounded from the backseat, and when it subsided, Beth asked him again, ''Is Sheena okay?''

''Three weeks of phenobarbital is no picnic, of course, but I'd say she's fine. A few cobwebs in the noggin, no doubt extremely depressed, but fine. She's a healthy girl.'' He sighed wistfully. ''A lot healthier, I promise you, than if she'd been free to go around spreading a lot of wild rumors.''

''What sort of rumors?'' Beth said. ''What are you talking about? What threat could she possibly pose to you?"

"To me?" he replied with an odd lilt. "None. None at all."

Arriving at Byron Choate's residence was a far less intimidating experience, I decided, with Gerald in the backseat and without a hood pulled tight over my head. Six Hundred Eighty-two Reynolds Street was a carriage house with a curb break and private garage, a rarity in the city. The short drive sloped abruptly to a crescent-shaped garage door below street level. Posted on the door was a sign: PRIVATE DRIVE. DO NOT BLOCK. There were two more No Parking signs at the curb, and still another stenciled in yellow paint on the sidewalk itself. The sheer number of warnings suggested that here was another of those luxuries more appealing in theory than in practice. But the No Parking signs had worked tonight, so I pulled over and blocked the drive.

We got out of the Riviera and from the sidewalk stared up at the dark facade. Shades were drawn behind the top windows, and a dim light illuminated them. Choate whispered, "I should warn you, Prince Charming. She probably won't waken with a kiss. You'll need a bucket of cold water, at least. Maybe even a few hard slaps to her cheeks."

By now, we'd pretty much had our fill of Byron Choate. I turned and put my finger on his breastbone, and explained a couple of things. He was going to take us up to Sheena, and we were going to ask her to come with us. And we all hoped for his sake that she would be in a condition to leave.

"Now, the thing we have to know," I said, "is where's Teddy Span? Is the mad bomber upstairs?" Choate shook his head, and I said, "Let's be clear. If he's here, have him stay out of our way. If he interferes, Gerald will have to hurt you."

Inexplicably, Choate started to laugh.

"You're just not up to speed on this one, are you, Professor? Even if Teddy were here, I doubt very much he'd listen to me. At the movie set, when you confronted me from the shadows, why do you think I was so afraid?"

"You thought I had a gun."

"Yes, of course, I thought you had a gun. I also thought you were Teddy . . . but that's another story. He isn't here. Oh, there was a time when he was quite infatuated, visiting his young captive almost every night, keeping a very close eye on her. He's held her here for nearly a month now. I think he was exploiting the situation, taking advantage of her plight. With the sedatives, she's been quite vulnerable. A bitter irony for her, I imagine, given her advocacy of equality in sexual relations. The two of them together doesn't conjure up such an appetizing image, does it? Even under more favorable conditions—even with consent—Mr. Span isn't someone I'd call an appealing lover."

I put my hands on Beth's shoulders and stepped between them to keep her from hitting him. "It's not worth—"

I didn't see the blow. All I saw was Gerald retrieving the huge slab of his hand from the vicinity of Byron Choate's face. Beneath Choate's nose there appeared a mustache of blood, black in the darkness. He didn't cry out. He touched his lip gingerly and then examined his fingertips. He studied the blood as if it had nothing to do with him.

Gerald looked at me without expression. "Guy talks more than you do."

Thus subdued, Choate opened the wrought-iron security door of his carriage house, and we followed him into a small foyer, and then into a hallway. We climbed a flight of stairs—on the second landing passing the door to Choate's apartment—and then up two more flights until we reached the top floor. At the head of the stairs, Choate stopped in front of a gray door and fumbled at his key ring. The mustache of blood had drooped down his chin, and he smeared it with his shirtsleeve. He handed me the door key and stepped out of the way.

"She's your problem now. I give her to your care."

The hallway light fell on a closet door and a small galley kitchen. The air inside the studio apartment carried the odors of confinement, unfresh and used. We found the light switch and flipped it on. At the opposite end of the room, beneath two windows, a girl lay on a mattress on the floor.

Her back was toward us; she was on her side with her knees pulled up toward her chest. She was naked except for the flimsy slip she'd worn weeks ago, which was twisted up around her waist. As we moved nearer, we saw bruises on her thighs, beginning to yellow. She didn't move.

Beth reached her first and covered her with the snarled sheet that lay at the foot of the mattress. She leaned down and spoke to her, saying, "Grace, Grace," with no response. She turned her and gently lifted her shoulders, and the girl's head lolled, like a child being wakened in the night. When Beth shook her—gently at first, then more firmly—the girl began to come around. She slowly lifted her head, eyes puffy and heavy lidded but trying to squint at the strangers who surrounded her. Blond hair matted, rough as straw, and heaped to one side; forehead lined with the impressions of wrinkled bedclothes. It was impossible to match this frail being to the young woman I'd seen in the movie.

Sheena Sands looked past Beth to me and then to Gerald. As her focus improved, her fear increased. She cringed and whimpered and scuttled back against the wall. Beth didn't have to tell us to wait outside.

Choate was gone. He wasn't behind us, and he wasn't in the hallway, so I left Gerald there and hurried downstairs after him. I didn't have to go far. The door to his apartment was wide open and the lights were on. I stepped inside and crept through his gallery of grotesques—the eyes of the freaks eerily on me—before passing into the open living room.

I found him atop a small ladder which leaned against a wall of shelves, a vast library of videocassettes. He was searching for something, and when he looked back at me over his shoulder, I saw that he'd washed his face. A clump of white tissue protruded from one of his nostrils.

He said, "I thought you'd want back the tape of you and Sheena."

I'd almost forgotten it.

"Yes," he said, "yes, here we are," stepping down

from the ladder and popping a cassette into the VCR. The TV was recessed into the wall of shelves, and he stood before it with a remote control in his hand, rocking back on his heels, waiting. The blank screen soon filled with bright snow, which seconds later gave way to a humiliating image of the girl and me, naked on Choate's bed, one of us debilitated by drugs, the other debilitated by fear.

"Ah," he said, "yes. Here we are."

I looked away. It really wasn't an image I wanted to carry around in my mind.

"If you don't mind my saying, it's a very listless performance by all concerned. Completely unconvincing. I don't blame you for not wanting it shown."

As I listened to him, it was finally dawning on me. Why it hadn't sunk in before now, I'll never know. There'd been signs all along, only I'd refused to see. But it was becoming painfully obvious. No wonder Byron Choate didn't worry about Proposition Six or arson or murder, didn't give a thought to the consequences. Why should he? Byron Choate was just a functionary, a lackey. He was a hired hand.

I tried to remember what he'd said at the movie set, before he saw it was only me pointing my finger at him. I visualized the situation from his point of view. He thought I was Teddy? So what had he said?

Why now? Just when everything is okay. Something like that. Telling Teddy to tell someone else everything is okay. Tell him everything is okay.

Tell who everything is okay?

From the hallway Elizabeth called me, and I went out to find them heading down the stairs. She must have struck some bond with Sheena, because the girl had permitted herself to be carried outside by Gerald. She was bundled in Beth's coat, and she looked very small in his arms.

"How is she?"

"Out of it," Beth said. "Scared to death. We'll take her right over to the ER at Brighams and get her checked out. I have some friends there. If she's up to it, I'll bring her home with me until we figure out what to do."

Outside, we settled Sheena in the backseat of the Riviera, and Beth followed her in. Gerald got behind the wheel. I remained at the curb.

"You're not coming with us?"

"I'll stop by your place first thing in the morning. I have some unfinished business."

"You're not going to do anything rash?"

"For once I'd like to," I told her before they pulled away. "I think I really would like to do something rash. I just don't know what that would be."

Choate seemed to take no notice of me when I reappeared. He'd changed into a fresh shirt; he'd fixed himself a drink. There he was, having a cocktail, contemplating his gallery of grotesques.

I said, "Tell who everything is okay?"

"Come look, Professor. This is my prize."

He stood before a stark black-and-white photograph. It was an outdoor scene, and the light suggested dusk. In the foreground a group of young girls—nine, ten years of age—are celebrating Halloween. There is a glimpse of a chain link fence and dingy grounds which hint at a hospital or, more likely, an asylum. The young girls are smiling and happy, full of innocent joy, their heads poking through white sheets as they hold dime-store Halloween masks near their faces. But the photograph carries a terrible irony. The young girls are afflicted with unspeakable retardations, and their smiling faces, stubbed and blunt, are more frightening than the plastic masks they hold.

"I thought we could contain it," Choate was saying. "What do the politicians say? Stonewall it. First it was only Sheena, and I told him I could keep her out of the way. But she involved Emma and Emma involved you. Well, we thought Teddy took care of that—that was a bit of luck, we thought, two birds with one stone, and the videotape burned to a crisp. All we had to do was wait it out, that was what I kept telling him. Wait it out. We had Sheena safely out of the way, and when Emma Pierce died, that was that. The media got all stirred up, but what did they know?

"And then you came nosing around. I thought the dirty pictures of you with Sheena would take the wind out of your sails, but here you are. The funny thing is, you still don't know. You still haven't figured it out. Even Sheena herself doesn't know what she knows, really. She had the video-tape, yes, but she thought it all boiled down to Proposition Six, too. That's why she went to Emma Pierce. She should've gone to the *Wall Street Journal*."

"Tell who everything is okay?" I repeated.

"Unless you have more plans for me, I wish you'd leave. Your fairy tale is winding its way to a bleak conclusion. Don't forget your tape. I didn't bother making copies."

He indicated a coffee table of tinted glass. The cassette was there, and next to it, a cardboard box. I recognized the box immediately. It was a shipping carton, and I knew where I could find hundreds more just like it. An entire warehouse full of them. Not more than two hours ago, I'd had my nose pressed up to one just like it.

I was aware that Choate was observing me as I looked at the carton. It hadn't been there before. He'd put it there for me to see.

My first thought was porn videos. A warehouse of ship-ping cartons, each brimming with cassettes. But no, the gesture of putting the carton there was too studied, too significant for something so obvious. My second thought—after all, I lived in America at the end of the twentieth century—was drugs. Boxes laden with those plump little pillows of cocaine that pop up to resolve every detective hour on TV.

I squatted by the carton and pulled at a cardboard flap. When the staples finally gave way, some packing spilled out, Styrofoam popcorn. I swept the rest of the packing aside and saw what there was to see. I wished it was co-caine; at least that would've made sense. That would have made things simpler. But there were no drugs in the carton. Food for the mind, perhaps, but not drugs.

When I looked back at Choate, he'd returned to his gal-lery of freaks, once again contemplating the photograph of the young children with their Halloween masks and Halloween faces. Both of his hands were at his face, and he was delicately running his fingertips over his own features.

"Unnerving, isn't it," he asked quietly, "to discover that the face behind the mask is even more horrible than the mask itself?"

22

I walked. My head buzzed from lack of sleep, but the pre-dawn breeze freshened me. After about a mile, fatigue re-turned and my gait began to feel awkward, as if I were walking for the first time. I was thinking about sex scenes. Not sex, but sex scenes. I'd witnessed a lot of them lately—on-screen, onstage, in print—and when I reviewed them in my mind they all left me depressed, even the ones I'd man-ufactured myself. It was curious, I thought, very curious. The ostensible goal was to give pleasure, but somehow they achieved only an impression of unbearable grimness.

The streets I was following weren't especially safe, but no one bothered me. My expression must have been slightly crazed, which kept people at a distance. Drug dealers re-fused to approach me; hookers eyed me and let me pass; even a couple of drunks stepped out of my way. I felt curiously protected, as if my vaguely manic demeanor be-stowed on me a privileged status not unlike that afforded insane persons by certain tribes of Indians.

An hour later I'd made it all the way back to the ware-house at 29 Duffy Street. I sat on a bench in the little park and smoked a cigarette. No one was around, and the park was peaceful, almost serene. Dawn was just beginning to break, and a band of pale lavender hung low at the horizon. The warehouse itself appeared undisturbed, with no sign that the police had ever arrived, but then again, who would have called them? You see, Officer, we were minding our own business, just getting ready to shoot the orgy scene and doing a few lines, when all of a sudden this maniac . . .

The door to Tele-Techniques was just as I'd left it, propped within its frame. When I entered the office this time, I didn't tiptoe, and my heart didn't pound. Soon I stepped out into the open shell of the building, out among the high shelves of cartons. I turned down the center corridor and stopped near the end of it. I looked at the movie set. Gerald had trashed everything except the Nautilus equipment, so it now looked as if someone had tried to set up a gym in a war zone.

Maybe a dozen boxes lay scattered at my feet, ones that had crashed down when Gerald took the corner too sharply with the forklift. These would be as good as any. I kneeled among them, and ten minutes later they were all open.

The shipping cartons were filled with books. Each held about thirty volumes of a single title. Pristine condition; shiny new dust jackets. One contained an early novel by D. H. Lawrence. Another, a history of colonial America. A critical edition of Whitman's *Leaves of Grass*. *Emerson's Essays*, vol. II. An anthology of Puritan sermons. Formidable, prestigious titles, but what else would I expect to find in the warehouse of such a formidable, prestigious publishing house?

I pulled one book from each carton, stacked them, and turned them on edge. The same two words were printed over and over near the base of the spines: ADAGE PRESS. ADAGE PRESS, ADAGE PRESS, ADAGE PRESS.

At a little past eight, I'd walked another mile and a half, which brought me to the periphery of the Combat Zone. I was standing across the street from Lounge Fifteen, the bar where Monkey Poussin handicapped the races each morning. It was one bar that I knew opened early, and I was desperately craving a beer. I also wanted to talk to Monkey Poussin, but mostly I was craving a beer.

Even at this time of morning, the sidewalks were alive. A

few businessmen ducked inside the bar with collars up-turned, scurrying out seconds later, three fingers of vodka in the belly and no one the wiser. Even here, the world refused to be simple; it insisted on presenting a mysterious and theatrical face. I watched as more businessmen slinked in and out of the bar; countless miniature dramas were being played out before me, all ripe with the fear of exposure and the effort to conceal. Even here, men were taking risks, making decisions, succumbing to weaknesses, learning un-pleasant truths about themselves.

I, too, was in the process of learning an unpleasant truth, one that I wasn't sure I was prepared for. I tried to postpone it by not thinking. I might have been a member of some flat-earth society, and someone had come knocking on my door, shouting news of Columbus's voyage. I covered my ears. Go away, I said. I don't want to know. I like my world flat and small and manageable. I prefer it that way.

"Come on, Arnie, stick with me. I feel it. I'm coming back. Bam! bam! bam! I just can't miss with these."

Monkey was just inside the door, talking on the pay phone. When he saw me, he raised his hand and began tapping two fingers against his pursed lips. I shook a ciga-rette out of my pack, and Monkey gave it a brief look of disapproval, hung it on his lip, and kept talking.

"I can handle it, Arnie," he said, "I can handle it. I just want to know if you can handle it. Now gimme St. Mary's, giving three, and South Alabama, even. A yard each. You think you can remember that?"

I waited at the bar, flipping through his *Racing Form* until he joined me. The bottle of Rolling Rock tasted even better than I thought possible, so I had another. The fifth race intrigued me. All of the old urges were rising up in me like sap.

"So, Monkey, what looks good?"

"Everything," he said, "and nothing." His eyes were bright and his spirits jaunty, despite the argument with his bookie. Like a lot of gamblers, he whined from force of habit. Monkey looked at his wristwatch and then at me.

"You just getting started, Tommy, or you just turning in? You look a little green around the gills."

By the time I finished the third beer, I felt better prepared to explore a larger world. I said, "You remember the parable about real estate? The one that takes place in the arson capital of the world?"

His eyes turned glassy and distant, the eyes of a salesman who senses a customer is about to ask for a refund.

"What's up, Tommy?"

"I met Byron Choate."

"Yeah?"

"The thing is, Monkey, he's a little weird, and he has some funny ideas, but he's not a big leaguer. He's not a powerful person. He's just not scary enough."

"Okay," he said, "Byron Choate's a wuss. So?"

"So, in this parable of dark deeds, we weren't talking about Byron Choate, were we?"

"You're the one kept saying his name."

"I know that. I jumped to the wrong conclusion. But the stakes are a little higher now, so I need to know what's what. What it comes down to is this: I think I may be standing in shit, and I just want to know how deep it is."

My crazed expression must have reappeared, because just then, Monkey stopped himself short. For a brief moment, he appeared almost sincere.

"I don't know for sure. I hear things, Tommy. They don't sound too promising. Just to be on the safe side, I'd get some flippers and a mask."

I took a cab to Cambridge, showered, shaved, and put on fresh clothes, and by late morning I'd taken another cab to Beth's. Sheena Sands was asleep in the bedroom. Her name was Grace Alice Perry, and all things considered, she was in pretty fair shape. She was still suspicious and confused, and she'd had a rough night, filled with nightmares and delirium. But Beth was slowly gaining her trust, and the girl had begun to confide in her.

Now, as Beth began to piece things together, her voice became an excited whisper. "It was right there all along," she said. "When Grace sent Emma the videotape, the point wasn't just to show her *The Right Stiff*. The point wasn't just that porn videos were being made in Boston. That was part of it, but only a part. What Grace told me was to keep running the tape for maybe ten minutes after the movie ends. You'd never know anything was there unless you knew to look. She never had a chance to tell Emma, but it was right there on the cassette all along."

I said, "What was there?"

"Another video clip," she said. "Grace copied it onto the blank part of the tape near the end of the reel. You remember the party Gorgeous George told us about? The one at Choate's where he last saw Sheena? Well, Choate's cameras were going and it's on film. When the business suits showed up looking to be entertained, Choate told her that one of them was special. One of them wasn't just any old VIP. Choate told her it was his boss, *her* boss, too, the man who started Venture Productions, who set Choate up at Manray's. Grace recognized him right away. That's why she smuggled a copy of the film to Emma. It wasn't just that porn had come to Boston, it was who brought it here."

I said, "Yes?"

"It's wild," she said. "You'll never guess."

I touched my closed eyelids for a moment, concentrating like a mentalist. When I opened my eyes I looked at her. I said the name of the man Byron Choate worked for. The man Teddy Span and Sheena Sands worked for. And, as it happened, the man I worked for, too.

I said, "Samuel Dodds."

Beth asked me how on earth I knew that.

Part IV

The
Great
American
Novel

23

My publisher?

In the coming days I tried to delude myself, tried to rationalize, to come up with a list of all the good, sound, plausible reasons why Adage would want to publish my novel—it *was* worthy of publication, wasn't it? But in my heart I knew the truth. Only one press had agreed to publish *Helpless Laughter,* and that was no coincidence. And I was still getting rejections! Christ! I winced when I considered the smug assurance with which I'd been visiting my mailbox.

Samuel Dodds had signed the letter of acceptance himself; he'd even appeared to negotiate the contract. Such interest from the top was unprecedented, but the old guard at Adage Press had judged his actions hopefully; in signing my quirky little book—wasn't that Percy Hotchkiss's label?—Dodds was sending a message of reassurance. He was demonstrating an immunity to the demands of the marketplace and a commitment to serious if not high literary purpose. The truth, I feared, wasn't so noble; their new boss, the empire builder himself, was merely diddling me.

The rejection slip. The damned rejection slip. That had to be the mechanism, I knew; that had to be the catalyst. I recalled the afternoon I left the hospital; Teddy Span had taken something with my address on it, which happened to be a rejection slip. And from him, the slip of paper made its way to Choate, and from Choate to Samuel Dodds.

Just what did Dodds want? A chance to have a look at me, to judge for himself what kind of man Emma Pierce had called for help? If there was some possibility I could do him harm, however remote, well, why not put me under contract? What better way to keep me on a leash? A simple phone call from my editor and I'd come running. And when I arrived, I'd grovel and say thank you.

Once he saw the rejection slip, the rest would have been easy. Every author, and especially a Cambridge author, submits his manuscript to Adage Press. All Dodds had to do was send an underling to fetch mine. That would've been the only hitch, I thought sourly, rescuing my manuscript from the bottom of the slush pile, the mountain of similarly unread and unsolicited novels by similarly deluded authors. All that remained was the gracious letter: Dear Mr. Theron: We here at Adage Press are pleased to inform you . . .

Bile rose in my throat. I had a sickening feeling that I was the butt of a bizarre joke. I was being toyed with, manipulated in some obscure game, played by rules I couldn't comprehend, much less master.

As a precautionary measure, there was a certain logic to it. But I dimly perceived, too, a warped malignity lurking in whatever mind had concocted such a scheme. My mind flew back to the day I'd signed the contract. There seemed to be almost a gleefulness, a perverse pleasure at work, as if the spectacle of my jumping through hoops was being relished. Why else change the title to *Naked Laughter* except for a gratuitous dig? Why else fire Percy Hotchkiss and turn the project over to what's his name—the fat fuck—and put me under his blubbery editorial thumb? And if the offer to publish was merely a ruse, why insist on adding all the sex scenes, except to rub my nose in it? Whose idea was that?

What really got to me, what bothered me most was, well . . . how much it bothered me. I felt foolish. I felt embarrassed. It was painful to concede how much I cared, how much the book mattered. I'd actually permitted myself to believe I'd pulled it off, written a worthy novel—nameless, speechless hero and all. I'd grown accustomed to my new status in the world. Sign on the dotted line, son, and you'll rise out of the morass of academic hacks to join the sweet company of novelists. I saw my youth extended: a writer under forty isn't just young, he's precocious! I saw the weaknesses of my character redeemed: my liabilities as a professor—my drinking, my laziness, my vulgar bent of mind—were virtues for a novelist, even prerequisites!

My heart had been filled with secret pride, and the penalty for pride was swift and sure. What a moron I'd been to believe it! What a horse's ass!

Only one consolation presented itself: I was a moron, perhaps, but not a dead moron. Our adventure to Byron Choate's had brought no dire punishments down upon our heads; in fact, the episode had passed without discernible consequence. Dodds hadn't sent Teddy around asking for Sheena's return, and I began to wonder whether Dodds cared or whether he even knew. He seemed curiously unaware of our visit to Choate's—had Choate assured him, after all, that everything was okay? I had no way of knowing, but as each day passed uneventfully, I began to relax. And late one Wednesday afternoon I felt sufficiently relaxed to visit Adage Press.

The portraits of the literary gods still hung on the mahogany-paneled walls; and there was the bust of Emerson, and the red chesterfield sofas, and the Tabriz rugs. But the reception room had lost its aura of authenticity. Not that it seemed sinister; it just suddenly seemed to lack character. I felt as though I'd walked onto a staged set, recreated with painstaking attention to detail, but ultimately a clever reproduction—a period room at the world's fair, complete with a corporate sponsor. There was a certain griminess, too, as if Samuel Dodds, in handling his new subsidiary, had left it all smudged with his fingerprints.

I'd telephoned two days ago, hoping to speak with the receptionist, the grumpy one who'd been given notice. When I asked for her, there must have been some misapprehension about who I was. "Oh, you mean Mrs. Fowler?" a girlish voice answered. "If you're calling about the farewell party, it's all set for Wednesday afternoon. Remember, it's a surprise, so either get here before four, or sometime after four-thirty. We're hoping for a good turnout. Are you a relative of hers?"

"Only in misery," I replied, and hung up.

I arrived at a quarter to five and almost missed it. In a quiet corner of the room, Mrs. Fowler stood amid a coterie of seven or eight coworkers who quietly reminisced over plastic cups of ginger ale. She held two bouquets of flowers, and near her feet was a cardboard box filled with assorted memorabilia and what appeared to be the contents of a desk. I hung at the periphery of the dismal gathering until the fete began to die of its own somber weight. One by one, her friends stepped forward for an awkward embrace and then left. Soon she was alone, stooping to pick up the box with her belongings.

"Excuse me, my name's Thomas Theron. I doubt you remember me, but I have a book under contract here."

My face didn't register. Her eyes seemed to recede into a distant look of defeat. She appeared much older than I remembered. But she managed a dignified smile and held out her hand.

"Thank you so much for coming, Mr. . . ."

"Theron. Actually, the reason I'm here, I was hoping you could help me with something."

"Help you? No, I'm afraid my days of helping people around here have come to an end."

I said, "It's about Samuel Dodds."

Her eyes stirred and lost some of their faraway look.

I said, "My guess is that you and I have something in common. I think we both have good reason to dislike him."

"A lot of people dislike Samuel Dodds," she said. "Join the club."

"Yes, but there's a much smaller club, a club for people who may be in a position to do something about it. I just may have the goods on him. I think he's a lot worse than most people realize. I think he's up to all sorts of things.''

"Thomas Theron?'' she said. "Oh, yes. Yes. You're the new author Dodds came around to see. No one here could quite figure it. We're still wondering. Nothing personal, but with all the established authors we publish, well—''

"Why me?''

She nodded. "You said something about helping you? I'm not sure what I can do. . . .''

Almost a week had passed since the specter of Samuel Dodds had cast a shadow on my life, and I had yet to develop a plan of action, coherent or otherwise. I could go to the police, of course, even though they considered me less a source of information than an object of ridicule. What options did that leave? An anonymous letter to *Publishers Weekly*? I was more willing than ever to commit a rash act, but the precise nature of the rash act refused to make itself known to me. And even if inspiration should strike, even if I should come up with some plan of attack, I had no idea where to find Dodds. He was based in New York, that much was common knowledge; and he visited Boston from time to time to buy revered local institutions such as publishing houses and, more recently, TV stations. Other than that, I drew a blank. The newspapers gave the impression that he was a hotel dweller, hopping around the country—around the world—making deals with the same restless compulsion that drives lesser beings to eat potato chips.

"Basically,'' I told Mrs. Fowler, "I was hoping you might have access to his schedule. Where he shows up, and when he shows up there.''

"It's easier to get an audience with the pope. You've already had one meeting. That might be it.''

"Maybe,'' I said.

His whereabouts, she told me, wasn't the sort of information to which she was privy. But she asked me to wait, and she would see what she could find out. Catherine might know. Catherine was Mr. Berenson's secretary, and of course I knew how the papers always referred to Mr. Berenson. "One of Dodds's lieutenants,'' she said. "Lieutenant! As if we were some sort of military organization. Those little strutting men with their little puffed-up egos. Well, I'll have a look at Mr. Berenson's calendar. He wouldn't arrange his schedule without first consulting Mr. Dodds.'' And then, emboldened by a conspiratorial thrill, she whispered, ''Mr. Berenson wouldn't go to the bathroom without first consulting Mr. Dodds.''

She disappeared into the hallowed innards of Adage, and as I waited, I contemplated my sudden impulse for revenge. My motives were sound, but the timing of it, I realized, contained more than an element of selfishness. So Dodds had been tweaking me, having a little fun with my book? That insult paled in comparison to the injury he had caused to others, to the havoc he had wreaked in their lives. If what I was thinking was true, he was responsible for several arsons, one of which caused Emma's death and very nearly my own. And he'd used Adage Press as cover while Byron Choate cranked out skin flicks. But what's that you say? He's poking fun at my novel? Stepping on my blue suede shoes?

It was nearing six o'clock, and everyone was heading home. Interesting men and women passed by me, pulling on coats and scarves, all with intelligent eyes and likable faces. They reminded me of my colleagues at Wesley, and I supposed the worlds of academia and publishing had much in common. Ours weren't merely jobs, we were told, but callings. Come, and we'll give to you a sacred trust, the care of our cultural heritage. Come, and you'll live in a community of men and women who value the life of the mind. Come, and we'll start you off at around thirteen-five. How's your typing?

Whoa, there he was. Among the herringbone tweeds and gabardines, I spied a madras jacket and a pair of green checked pants. Ah, Benny Murphy, my editor, the fat fuck. His head was down, and he was lugging a half dozen manuscripts under his stubby, fat-fuck arms. His eyes never left the floor; if I hadn't stepped in front of him, he wouldn't have seen me. He greeted me moodily.

"Oh yeah, yeah, hey."

"So," I said, "what do you think of the sex scenes I sent you?"

"Gimme a chance, willya? Things are getting a little backed up."

Despite his garish clothes, something about him now seemed muted. Subdued. I looked again at the manuscripts he lugged, the huge reams of paper, the mountains of typescript. Was that what oppressed him? Had it finally dawned on him that reading was an inescapable part of an editor's job? Each day required an exhaustive search for new and ingenious excuses to avoid it. In the meantime, the pages just kept stacking up.

I didn't let him leave. I rested my arm on his shoulders and guided him over to a quiet corner and sat him down. I took a seat across from him, leaned forward, and rested my forearms on my thighs. I moved my hands expressively as I talked.

"The title," I said slowly. "I've been thinking about the title."

"Yeah?"

"I've got a couple of ideas I want to run past you. Get your opinion." This seemed to startle him, as if no one at Adage had yet expressed even remote interest in his opinion. "Not that I'm criticizing what we have. Going from *Helpless Laughter* to *Naked Laughter* is fine—as far as it goes. We have to be bold. Decisive. You remember what Pound wrote to Eliot in the margins of 'The Wasteland,' don't you?" I said, "Ezra Pound, T. S. Eliot. You remember Pound's famous words of advice, don't you?"

He just stared at me.

"Learn to spell, asshole!"

I gave it a good three count before I said, "Kidding, sorry, my little joke. No, no, you see, Eliot had used the word *perhaps* in 'The Wasteland,' and Pound scribbled over it and wrote, 'Damn perhaps.' Pick only what is useful, he said, and jettison the rest. You see, don't you? You see his point?"

The only point Benny Murphy saw was that his geek author was finally losing it. His eyes darted miserably, searching for escape. I felt a little silly tormenting him, but I had to confess, the look in his eyes gave me satisfaction.

"It occurs to me," I said, "that we have to do the same with the title of my book. No more half measures. We started with *Helpless Laughter* and we got to *Naked Laughter* and now it's time to go all the way. Pick only what is useful, and chuck the rest. *Helpless Laughter, Naked Laughter*. And then it hit me. I think I came up with a winner."

"Yeah?"

I said, *"Helpless and Naked."*

He just sat there.

"See, the laughing part's always been the problem. We get rid of that, the possibilities really begin to open up. Think about it. *Helpless and Naked.*" I winked lewdly. "Think about that title and then think about a cover. Do you know what percentage of sales the title generates?"

He dutifully recited the now-familiar statistic. I said, "Damn right. Now you're talking." And then I understood the particular variety of fear in his eyes. It was the fear of an evangelist, I realized, who has converted a sinner, only to discover that the new convert's religious fervor far exceeds his own.

Mrs. Fowler reappeared, so I let Benny Murphy escape with a farewell slap on the back. "This is just the beginning," I called after him. "I'm full of ideas."

I could tell immediately that Mrs. Fowler knew something. There was a sly smile on her face, and she touched her forefinger to her lip. She asked me to walk her to her car. I picked up the box with her belongings, and I realized that I was holding yet another Adage Press shipping carton. They were popping up everywhere. As we walked, I mentioned the warehouse in a roundabout way.

"It's funny," she said. "That's one of the first things Mr. Dodds did. Our warehouse had been there for decades, but before you know it, he sent in a construction crew, renovated, put up some storefronts. It's already zoned commercial, he said, so why not let it carry its own weight? Why not get a rent roll going? I guess you have to give him credit. No one had ever given the warehouse a second thought, but it looks like he turned it into a money-maker.''

I thought, You betcha.

Outside, after I pushed the box into the backseat of an ancient Volvo, Mrs. Fowler turned to me, pleased as punch. "Okay," she said, "I think you're in luck. Mr. Boardman is flying to New York this weekend; Catherine made the reservations. He's staying at the Pierre. The first thing Monday morning he has an appointment at the International at the World Trade Center, Suite 3206. Catherine says that always means a meeting with Samuel Dodds. Then they're going to Washington, D.C., staying at the Watergate. They're finishing that TV deal.''

I jotted it all down. "Blue, blue," I hummed, "blue suede shoes." I never cared much for Elvis. Maybe I just never understood him.

Again that night I lay in bed without sleeping. Sometime after two o'clock I got up, poured myself a tumbler of bourbon, and eased down into an overstuffed chair in the living room. The remote control was on the armrest, and I picked it up and aimed it at the TV. The cassette with *The Right Stiff* was loaded into the VCR, just where I'd left it. The TV screen flickered brightly in the darkness, and I manipulated the remote control as if it were a small weapon, recoiling. I fast forwarded through the movie itself, fast forwarded through the electronic snow at the movie's end, and then slowed to normal speed when I reached the video clip that Sheena Sands had smuggled onto the end of the cassette.

By now I'd watched it at least a dozen times. No more than ten minutes of film, beginning to end. The scene is Byron Choate's loft, and the perspective suggests a camera positioned above the entry door, offering a view of the gallery and a portion of the next room.

The gallery itself is well lighted and empty. But in the dark room beyond, at the farthest edge of camera range, there are intimations of wild revels. It is the cast party Gorgeous George described to us. The smoky shadows yield glimpses of men and women cavorting at the boundary of darkness, as in a dream. Some are clothed, some not, some are dancing, some possibly doing more than dancing with movements sensuous and unrestrained. Their faces, too, drifting in and out of the light, are dreamlike; expressions exaggerated and euphoric, mute testimony to altered states of mind.

In the foreground, three guests arrive. Their backs toward the camera, they step into the gallery and then come fully into view. Samuel Dodds first, and after him two business-men, apparently clients. Dodds is conservatively dressed and his manner controlled, but his companions have clearly been in a celebratory mood; ties loosened, gray hair dishev-eled, swaying unsteadily, they grin like boys.

A moment later Byron Choate, wearing a white linen shirt and slacks, appears from the dark room to greet them. He shakes Dodds's hand in the manner of an underling, with too much enthusiasm, pumping it. When he is intro-duced to Dodds's guests, he gushes. He laughs excessively at their soundless remarks. He is the picture of the toady, the groveling host. For their part, Dodds's guests, still grin-ning like boys, leer at the festivities beyond, at the oppor-tunities that await them.

Having watched the tape so many times, I mostly study Dodds. He is much shorter than the other men, shorter by a good four or five inches than even Byron Choate; huge headed and prim, with his neatly cut suit, Dodds looks almost like a ventriloquist's puppet. More than once I notice that the camera catches him unaware. He sneaks a glance at his watch; he stifles a yawn; when no one is looking, the smile that illuminates his face suddenly vanishes. (Had the smile vanished, too, that day at Adage, whenever I looked away?) But he conceals his boredom well. For all his companions know, he is as smashed as they are and looking to get laid.

Choate beckons toward the darkness, and two young women soon appear, smiling, wearing little more than G-strings and cut-off T-shirts, to escort the businessmen into the party. When the happy couples disappear, Dodds hangs back and speaks to Choate. He is all business now, still at work, having performed an unpleasant but necessary chore of his profession. And for those ten videotaped minutes, that profession appeared to be nothing more or less than pimp.

And that was it.

I sipped the bourbon and rewound the tape, feeling again the same curious disappointment I'd felt each time I watched it. I'd been hoping for a bedroom scene. Samuel Dodds, tiny and naked and vulnerable, and caught in the act. Perhaps Samuel Dodds engaged in some exotic deviancy. Powerful men in the boardroom enjoy subjugation in the bedroom, wasn't that how the popular myth ran?

Wrong. I'd fallen into an old habit, thinking sex, not money. I wouldn't have to be reminded again. Only one kind of intercourse inspired passion in men like Dodds, I decided, and that was the intercourse of the business world.

24

The next day I got a call from Rolland Palmer, my friend at Wesley Business School. "I got your message, Thomas. What's up?"

Even though it was noon, he'd wakened me. I spoke very slowly, my voice a hoarse whisper. "Maybe you know," I said, "is it legal to call an ambulance for a hangover?"

"That bad, huh?"

"There's a tiny man standing on my pillow. He has a ballpeen hammer. Every time my heart beats, he hits me right between the eyes."

Rolland offered to call back later, but I said no, if the phone rang again, it might cause permanent brain damage. "I need to ask you a few questions. I want to know about Samuel Dodds."

"What about him?"

"A hypothetical," I said. "Suppose someone could link him to some very sleazy activities. How much of a problem would that cause him?"

"How sleazy are we talking?"

"On a scale of one to ten, I'd say eight."

"What's ten?"

"White slavery," I said. "Child molestation."

"Would you happen to have anything in the way of proof?"

"Enough to give him some explaining to do," I said. "At this point, I don't think the cops will be chasing him with a pair of handcuffs. I've uncovered some peculiar circumstances, peculiar relationships. Whether any of it will stick . . ."

"In other words," Rollie said, "you don't have diddly-squat."

Mostly what I had was the videotape, but whether it constituted diddly-squat, and precisely what kind of diddly-squat, I still wasn't sure. The tape worried Dodds, I knew that much, and it might still be worrying him if he knew I'd carried it away from the bombing intact. He'd gone to extraordinary lengths to suppress it, I just didn't know why. Procuring women for business clients? That was potentially embarrassing, probably illegal, but unless you shared a world view with Gomer Pyle, it wouldn't shatter your illusions about capitalism.

"At this point," I said, "all I have is a circumstantial case for moral turpitude. I'm afraid that's about it."

Rollie thought for a moment before he said, "Well, that's probably all it would take."

"All what would take?"

"You asked me if exposing Dodds as a sleazoid would cause him a problem. Well, it just might. As a matter of fact," he added, laughing, "right now it might put his feet to the fire. That kind of publicity might cook his goose."

"Publicity? Are you sure we're talking about the same man? Dodds doesn't care what people think. When he bought Adage Press, every columnist in town was flipping through a thesaurus, looking for new ways to call him Dumbo. Remember? He boasted that he hadn't read a book in years."

"Being a dumbo is one thing. This is America. You can be a dumbo and president at the same time. Being a sleazo, at least under certain conditions, is another matter."

"What conditions?"

"Thomas, you don't read the financial pages, do you?"

"Of course not."

"That's what I thought. You ought to try it sometime. You'd be surprised what's in there."

"Surprised, or just bored?"

He sighed elaborately. "I'm beginning to understand what keeps you English professors in poverty, not to mention the dark."

"You mean it's not just a general lack of ambition?"

Before we hung up, Rollie agreed to meet me that evening and explain some of the hallowed mysteries of the business world. I left for Beth's, still contemplating what he'd said about the financial pages. Was a daily glance at the business section all that stood between me and prosperity and enlightenment? After the sports world, the world of entertainment, the book world, and usually a minute or two for the world itself, who had time for the business world? To my credit, I did follow one set of financial charts, a group of complicated and highly leveraged short-term investments listed every day on the last page of the sports section, under RACING RESULTS. Even though the stock index remained impenetrable to me, the numerical records of equine performances were like deep pools, shimmering with meaning. But I don't suppose that's what Rollie had in mind.

"I don't know what I was expecting," Elizabeth was saying. "I remember what we heard about the bookworm college girl, but I was still expecting a bubbleheaded nineteen-year-old, all boobs and no brains, someone who didn't have a clue what she was doing. Well, Grace isn't that."

"Then what is she?"

"Wait and find out for yourself. She'll be back in a couple of hours."

"I'd rather hear it from you. It's simpler that way."

I'd stopped by to drop off the videotape. I'd already told Beth what was on it—"an adults-only version of 'Wall Street Week in Review,' " I said—but she wanted to see for herself. I also brought along my VCR to hook up to her

VCR to make some copies. How many copies, and for what purpose, well . . . having a few copies couldn't hurt. As a last resort I could always charter a helicopter and litter the countryside with them.

Beth was sitting upright on the stool at her kitchen counter, her hands on her knees. She took a breath and exhaled thoughtfully. There was a pot of coffee in front of us, and I was listening to the story of how Grace Alice Perry had become Sheena Sands.

"She reminds me of other kids I've known who grew up in the East Sixties in Manhattan. She's smart, in some ways amazingly sophisticated about the world, but there are large pockets of equally amazing naïveté. Both her parents are lawyers, and her family was always politically intense, very socially aware. As far as sex was concerned, she told me that after she reached fifteen, it didn't matter so much what she did as long as she knew why she was doing it and what it meant. Add to that the further complication that she's a very good-looking young woman. She started to feel a lot of pressure, to feel that there was no room for tentativeness, no waffling allowed, that whatever she did made some kind of statement. Even if she did nothing, that meant something, too. She said it was like that with a lot of her friends. There was no middle ground. They either slept with every guy who came along, or they didn't sleep with anybody, or sometimes the girls just slept with each other. The only options were extreme. You either rejected sex absolutely or you embraced it absolutely. Actually, the irony of her situation is scary; she told me she was one of the ones who didn't sleep with anybody until about two years ago, her freshman year at Barnard. And then there was no stopping her."

It was a tale of sexual awakening, I thought, with a uniquely modern twist; a coming-of-age story in a world where quaint talk of reaching first base or second base seemed hopelessly out of place. From virgin to porn starlet without any stages of transition.

"That first year at Barnard she took a course from Emma

and got to know her, and everything seemed to be going fine. She was living at home, and midway through her sophomore year she began to have a few problems at school, with her parents—I'm not sure what kind, but I don't think anything out of the ordinary. During the holidays she was in Boston visiting friends at BU, and she just stayed on. She didn't sign up for the spring semester, her money was beginning to run out, one thing led to another, and the next thing she knew she was stripping at Manray's. That's where she met Byron Choate. He gave her a place to stay. Remember the studio upstairs where we found her? She'd been living there for the last six months. At first she thought Byron was exciting, I suppose, dangerous, fascinating. He'd put in those years at film school in California, and I'm sure he made it sound like he was Francis Ford Coppola. She thought they were kindred spirits. He talked about sex in a way that was new to her. Of course, too, he was telling her how wonderful she was twenty-four hours a day. He convinced her that the movies he was making would be different''—she rolled her eyes—''not porn but erotica, something sensual and politically correct. . . .''

I said, "This is where the naïve part of her personality comes in."

Beth nodded. "Choate had been using the palm reader's technique, watching her carefully, listening to every word, then telling her just what she wanted to hear. Well, it worked, and Grace made a film. Then she made another. By the time she'd made the third, it was pretty obvious to her that whatever Byron was doing, it wasn't a cinematic exploration of the realm of the senses. He was turning out run-of-the-mill skin flicks, and she was a run-of-the-mill smut star." Beth paused and sipped her coffee and looked at me. "I suppose it must sound pretty outlandish."

Actually, it didn't sound outlandish in the least. I'd spent enough time in a university setting to know that in any given year a certain segment of the student population was on the verge of committing some act of sexual anarchy that equaled if not surpassed Grace Alice Perry's brief excursion into the world of adult films. A decade earlier I'd been surprised when I learned that a groundskeeper at Wesley was running a prostitution ring out of a freshman dormitory, but since then I'd gradually become inured to each fresh disclosure of scandal among students or faculty. About the only thing that surprised me now was the administrative skill the college displayed in keeping recurring episodes of sexual adventurism out of the newspapers, and therefore out of the minds of alumni and parents.

"And then a couple of things happened at once," Beth was saying. "Grace already knew about Proposition Six, of course, but then she found out that Emma Pierce was in Boston, working with the antiporn groups. And about that time, too, Byron Choate gave his infamous cast party. It must have been some argument. She was breaking things off, telling him how betrayed she felt, and all that was on his mind was the VIP who was going to be at the party. He said he needed an important favor, and what was the big deal? It wasn't just any man he wanted her to help entertain, it was a very powerful man. It was, in fact, *the* man, Sam Dodds, the man behind all of it. If he was bringing along a couple of business clients, and he wanted her to go to bed with them, well, she ought to be flattered. Grace said that looking back on it, she guessed that Byron figured the name Dodds wouldn't mean much to her. But it did, and it started her thinking.

"She made sure the video camera in Choate's gallery was running that evening, and the next morning she copied the footage with Dodds on it, and sent it to Emma. When she told Choate what she'd done and why, that was that. That put his ass on the line. He wasn't about to let her leave when he heard that. So he kept her upstairs in a Seconal fog, and he must've sent Teddy after Emma and the cassette. And you showed up. And Grace never got a chance to tell Emma exactly what was on the tape."

"Did Grace say what she thought would happen? What did she think the videotape would accomplish?"

"She honestly believed it would cause a furor. If people

knew that the same man who owned Adage Press also owned Venture Productions, wouldn't they be mad? And if they were mad, wouldn't they vote for Proposition Six? *Leaves of Grass* and *The Right Stiff*, just two items in Dodds's catalog. She's naïve, sure, but she believed what we all believed at first. None of us really understood that people just don't care.''

Until Beth told her, Grace hadn't known what happened to Emma. For the past several days she'd been Beth's houseguest, slowly regaining her equilibrium, her emotional state progressing from confusion to depression and finally to anger. She agonized whether to file charges against Byron Choate. What kind of charges? Kidnapping? Technically, we'd found her alone in the studio where she'd been living for the past six months. Charge Teddy with rape? The prospect of a trial was unnerving. What courtroom indignities awaited her, a performer in adult movies, in a legal system that routinely heaped abuse upon even the most cloistered of rape victims?

Amid the uncertainty, one possibility presented itself to her, one forum in which she felt compelled to express her rage. In the last day or two, Beth told me, the girl had been meeting with the Coalition of Women Against Pornography. The coalition had planned a rally for Monday, a final push for votes on the eve of the referendum vote, and Grace had asked to speak on behalf of Proposition Six. Here was an opportunity that focused her mind with clarity and conviction; in it she saw the chance for a memorial to Emma Pierce and for herself a measure of redemption. Beth encouraged her, and the members of the coalition were enthused that Grace should volunteer to tell her story. The testimony of an apostate would inspire new interest in the cause; her mere presence as a speaker would ensure publicity.

We finished our coffee and sat for several minutes without speaking. The videocassette lay on the counter before us, and Beth picked it up and said, "This isn't going to help Proposition Six win ten votes, is it?"

"Probably not." I told her the rally might help, but I didn't really believe it. I said, "Who knows? Grace Alice Perry might turn out to be a very persuasive orator."

"I just get so frustrated, so goddamned angry!" She was off the stool now, pacing. "Everything is so much worse than I thought, it just depresses me. I've been putting in maybe ten hours a week, helping the coalition organize this rally, and God, it's such an eye-opener! You'd think at the headquarters for Proposition Six that you'd be among friends, but some of the groups we attract, some of the people who come around asking to volunteer, it's scary! There's one group, the New England chapter of some animal-rights league, about fifteen men and women, very sincere and concerned, who want to be represented at the rally to speak on behalf of the protection of animals. I guess they have bestiality in mind, but can you believe that? I just want to shake the hell out of them, scream at them, tell them to get their goddamn priorities straight. It trivializes the issue to talk about animal rights. It's demeaning to women. But there they are, all full of concern and sensitivity.

"The religious groups aren't much better. They're as antiwomen as the pornographers, only it's a mirror image, the bondage of chastity. Suppress porn to keep women pure, powerless, and on a pedestal." She stopped pacing and looked at me. "And the worst," she said, "the absolute worst are the men who come in off the streets. You take one look at them, and you know they have some spooky sexual reason for volunteering, some creepy guilt trip, I don't know, but it scares me. Guys who look like Charles Manson coming around grinning, asking me to pin a PORN EQUALS HATE button on their lapel. Thank God Gerald's around."

"Gerald?"

"He's been helping out. All the women at the coalition think he's great. He doesn't talk much, and he's one of the few men I know who don't resent taking orders from a woman. You should see him. One day he'd delivered some materials to one of our information booths, and he stuck around to help solicit contributions. He's got a real gift for fund-raising. People just don't know how to tell him no.''

Beth slumped down on the sofa and sighed. She said,
"What about Dodds? If nothing else, maybe we can stick it
to him.''

"Maybe," I said. "I'm having dinner with a B-school
friend who thinks the videotape will cause him a problem.
He thinks he knows why Dodds has been so hell-bent on
suppressing it. He says it might cook his goose.''

"That's something, at least.''

"I wouldn't bet on it. I think he's untouchable. In
Dodds's world, having your goose cooked probably means
some stock you own plummets a quarter point.''

That's what was beginning to worry me. I had an uneasy
feeling that however things ended up, the result wouldn't be
emotionally or legally satisfying, and it certainly wouldn't
resemble poetic justice. What was happening so far? Beth
was at Proposition Six headquarters pinning buttons on sexual psychopaths. Grace was reluctant to press criminal
charges because a trial might exact a greater penalty from
her than from Byron or Teddy. I was back counting rejection slips. As for Dodds, if he suffered any consequences at
all, they'd probably be the kind you record in an accountant's ledger.

As I was leaving, we paused on the stoop outside, and
Beth asked me if I'd be at the rally. I told her not if it was
on Monday. I'd be out of town on Monday, in New York,
maybe Washington. She was eyeing me now, for a good
reason. I never went anywhere.

"What's in Washington?''

"Samuel Dodds.''

"You wouldn't, would you?''

"Wouldn't what?''

"When you talked about doing something rash, you
wouldn't do something really rash? If Dodds still thinks the
videotape never made it out of the First Amendment, maybe
we should leave well enough alone.''

I smiled. "I thought you wanted to stick it to him.''

"I'm serious, Thomas.''

"I haven't done anything yet. I'll probably come up with something like Grace is doing by speaking at the rally. A gesture. Something elegant and hopelessly ineffective."

"Good," she said. "Stick to what you know best. Ineffectiveness has always been your strong suit."

Every minute or so a couple passed by on the sidewalk in front of the stoop. Everyone seemed to be pushing strollers, all loaded down with baby paraphernalia. We watched them, and I reached for Beth's hand, and we intertwined our fingers, but somehow it felt strange. Forced. We didn't let go—that would've been worse—so we just stood there, self-consciously holding hands. The problem, of course, was all the talk of porn and hate. You couldn't help but feel hardened by it, implicated in it. It didn't offer the most appealing emotional context in which to rekindle old feelings.

I said, "You ever come across those human interest stories in the paper about two people who got divorced, and maybe four or five years later, they remarry?"

"I suppose it happens."

"When you hear something like that, what do you think?"

She looked off into the distance. "I think they're idiots."

Which is what I thought, too.

"Thomas, we need to talk about things, about what we're doing. About us."

"I know."

"All this hopping into bed without thinking. Maybe it's all in the revolutionary spirit, but I'm not sure how good it is for either of us."

Another stroller, this one a two-seater. Two fat babies asleep, heads lolling.

Beth said, "We need to be more careful."

I said, "I realize we haven't given things a lot of thought, but—"

She said, "No, I mean we need to be more *careful*. What I'm saying is, I haven't been on the pill for over a year now. I've been giving my body a break."

When I regained the power of speech, I said, "Beth, you're not . . ."

"I'm not anything. I'm just saying we should be more careful."

I spent the rest of the afternoon in the periodical room at the Wesley College library, surrounded by heaps of back issues of *Business Week, Forbes,* and the *Wall Street Journal.*

The magazines were filled with articles on Dodds, and each gave more or less the same abbreviated history of his meteoric rise. The business world, it seemed, had developed its own special version of the myth of Humble Beginnings. Dodds's father had worked all his life in small-building real estate in New York, and at his death had managed a net worth of only slightly more than two million dollars. From that low perch, his son had vaulted into the more lucrative world of office buildings and commercial real estate, and in no time he had multiplied his father's meager inheritance fiftyfold. And then, as they say, his eyes got big. He looked for a larger, more glamorous arena in which to move. He began buying things and putting his name on them. Newspapers began to refer to him as a mogul, an empire builder. His desires soon fixed upon that transcendent goal to which all ambitious real-estate developers ultimately aspire: the ego-massaging world of communications. He bought radio stations, two national magazines, a chain of theaters, a video franchise. And then he entered the domain of prestige publishing when he bought Adage Press. And now he was assaying the wonderful world of television.

Dodds's plan to acquire Channel Eight hadn't generated the same fear and loathing that attended his purchase of Adage. New England prided itself on a reverence for the printed word and a scorn for the pablum of the small screen. Acquiring the publisher of Emerson and Thoreau was one thing; acquiring a UHF independent that showed "Leave It to Beaver" reruns was another.

Channel Eight was the linchpin in a complicated maneuver that would enable Dodds to purchase a group of six TV stations from a conglomerate called UrbanView. The stations were in various markets across the country, all well managed and profitable, but the plum was Boston's Channel Eight. The price tag for all six stations was enormous—over half a billion dollars, even out of Dodds's price range—but he had structured the deal so that he could have his cake and eat it too. The financing hinged on his intention to resell Channel Eight immediately; he had a ready buyer offering top dollar, and that influx of cash fueled the larger deal, putting it within reach. When the dust cleared and the paper settled, Dodds would walk away with the other five stations at a price far below market.

In the meantime there was a maze of federal regulations to be finessed, a new FCC chairman to be courted, investment bankers to be persuaded. Dodds had been hopping up and down the East Coast, orchestrating the financing in New York, overseeing a smooth transfer of the broadcast license in Washington.

Actually, I kept coming across interesting stuff. For one thing, I learned why TV stations—a few cameras, an antenna, and a small, overpaid staff—cost a couple hundred million bucks. The expense, it seemed, was the broadcast license itself, which was a money cow; a station's physical assets and payroll accounted for only ten percent or so of the total price. And the financial maneuvering wasn't nearly so complicated as I'd first believed. I was secretly pleased to discover that Dodds fell prey to the same economic strategy that saddled my Uncle Billy whenever he shopped for a new car: They both bought more than they could afford and spent the rest of the time thinking up ways to pay for it.

The more I read, the more I began to come across little details that gave me pause, that started me thinking. Hmm. I kept reading and kept coming across more little details— another Hmm, and Hmm again—beginning to feel as if I were holding a Geiger counter that had suddenly begun to register, emitting rapid-fire beeps. Before long I was photocopying some of the articles and by the time I left the reading room to meet Rollie Palmer, I was getting ideas. Maybe I didn't know exactly what was up, but I knew enough to ask some interesting questions.

Since I was buying, we met at HooDoo's. The waiter brought my short ribs and cornbread, a bottle of hot sauce, and two half-pint cartons of chocolate milk. Rollie looked at my plate just as Beth had looked at it weeks ago. He asked me if it was some kind of bizarre torture.

"Hangover cure," I said. "Guaranteed."

"Yeah," he said, "but what do you do if you get terminal runs?"

"All strong medicine," I said, "has side effects."

Rollie sipped his beer and glanced through the material I'd photocopied. He looked up, affecting an Asian accent, asking me, "So, little Grasshopper, what have you learned?"

I said, "TV stations."

"Good."

I said, "Broadcasting licenses."

"Good, good."

I said, "Public trust. Federal Communications Commission regulations."

He looked at me and smiled. "Ah, Grasshopper, I see your subscription to *Weekly Reader* hasn't lapsed."

The only thing I could find that might put a scare in Dodds was a serious review of the transfer of the broadcast license.

I said, "Tell me if I've got it wrong, but FCC policy on broadcast licenses is inconsistent. When the FCC originally grants a license, they make the applicant jump through the public-interest hoop. Pledge to offer good programming, pledge to give community access, pledge to air a wide variety of views, on and on. The FCC holds a licensing hearing, and all the public-interest groups line up, dozens of them, each voicing an opinion about the applicant's financial or ethical fitness to hold a broadcasting license. The process drags on for weeks, months. It even gives red tape a bad name.''

But there seemed to be a loophole. Once a license was granted, the FCC had developed no bureaucratic mechanism to keep track of it. So if someone sold a TV station—to Dodds, for example—the broadcasting license would be transferred with no public scrutiny at all. The transfer was a formality. There was no hearing, no nothing. It didn't really make sense.

Rollie said, ''It's the government, Thomas. It doesn't have to make sense.''

''But there's a catch.''

He nodded. ''There's no automatic review of the license, but if an individual or group petitions the FCC, demonstrating why Dodds is either financially or ethically unfit to hold the public trust represented by the license—''

''In other words, if someone could make a case for moral turpitude—''

''Exactly. Then all bets are off.''

I said, ''So if a group—say, the Coalition of Women Against Pornography, or a lot of mainstream religious groups that are antiporn—started pointing fingers at Dodds and yelling, 'Pornographer! Pornographer!' what would happen?''

''The bureaucratic monster raises its ugly head, opens its huge regulatory maw, and starts working its jaws around Dodds's ass. Something like what a python does to a rabbit.'' He smiled. ''Not to mention the new FCC chairman, I forget his name—''

Orrin Muller. I'd read about him.

''Yeah, Muller, who is supposed to be a world-class hard ass, a real Bible thumper from the Midwest, an ex-judge, a Republican who's heavily into a family-values schtick, who feels that regulating the airwaves is as American as apple pie. If that's who Dodds is trying to avoid, I don't blame him.''

I said, ''Dodds seems to have him snowed so far.''

One of the articles I'd photocopied was an account of an

early meeting between Dodds and Muller. Dodds seemed to be appealing to the chairman's republican instincts. After the meeting the chairman told reporters that Dodds "impresses me thus far as a solid, sober businessman." Asked if he was troubled that the TV deal was just another case of the rich getting richer, Muller responded hotly. "In this country, prosperity isn't a crime, not yet anyway. I like to see a man who has worked hard, and whose efforts have been rewarded with financial prosperity. That is the backbone of the American system, and I don't think Mr. Dodds should apologize for it."

Rollie said, "If Dodds keeps it up, he's home free. Once the license is transferred, you could publish photos of Dodds in bed with a sheep and it wouldn't matter."

I contemplated it all, trying not to feel disappointed again, trying not to feel the disappointment I'd felt when I first saw the videotape of Dodds, not naked and vulnerable and humping away, but merely soliciting. Was this the best I could hope for now, throwing a wrench in his TV deal? It would cause him some pain, but how much pain?

I said, "So that's it? That's cooking his goose?"

"No, no, you still don't understand. It's much better than that. The whole deal is set up with the presumption that the license transfer is merely a formality. The financing side of these deals, even for Dodds, can be a roller coaster of terror. He's already *bought* the stations, Thomas. He's paying for them right now. He made the deal using short-term money, and it's very expensive. Right now he's shouldering a staggering debt burden, and the only way he can relieve it is to sell Channel Eight. But he can't sell it if he can't get the license transferred. His ass is on the line."

"So if someone yells 'Smut Lord' and Chairman Muller listens?"

"Dodds will be the proud owner of six TV stations he can't afford. Unless he's quick on his feet, he's looking at Chapter Eleven. He's back selling one-bedroom condos in North Bumfuck."

"Oh," I said, "that's different."

• • •

Thursday was the first day of the fall term. When I arrived at my classroom in Sever Hall, I found a packed house waiting for me. About two hundred students had showed up for Am. Civ. 265, ''The American Novel in the Nineteenth Century''; students spilled out into the aisles, and there was standing room only at the back of the room. Ordinarily the course drew about thirty, thirty-five students, and I'd brought maybe fifty reading lists. For a moment I wondered if someone had switched classrooms without telling me, but then it dawned on me. The students were checking out the mysterious Peeper Prof.

I squeezed through them, took my place at the podium, and opened my lecture notes, business as usual, as if I were accustomed to attracting hordes of auditors.

There is a basic rule of lecturing during the first week of classes, when students are still shopping around, undecided about which courses to take. You must resist your natural urge to be liked. You must be neither charming nor witty nor even particularly informative. You must, in fact, make every effort to be the most tedious lecturer that you can possibly be. It's a matter of survival. If you fail to observe this rule, you will be punished with overflowing classes, sentenced to spend every weekend grading armloads of papers and exams, while constantly reminding yourself that you don't get paid by the head.

Once your class gets down to a manageable size, of course, there's plenty of time to show a dramatic improvement in your oratorical skills and end up having everyone like you, pleasantly surprised.

Today, with two hundred students crowded in front of me, I knew the rule was even more important than usual. And I must admit, I did a pretty good job. When I picked up my lecture notes at the end of the hour, only about a hundred or so students remained, and another fifty were having trouble staying awake. Well, their curiosity was satisfied. As they left the lecture hall, I could just hear them: The only mystery about the Peeper Prof, they'd be whispering, was how he got to be boring as shit.

On the whole, not a bad start to the semester.

At a little past noon, I took the T downtown, surfaced on Boylston Street, and headed north until I came to number 172, American Courier. I went inside. The man behind the counter was wearing shirtsleeves and a bow tie, suggesting efficiency, and when I told him what I had in mind, he said, "We can do it any way you want. Same day, overnight express, door to door."

I said, "How about hand to hand? Can you have someone take it up and put it in his hand?"

"Sure, we do it all the time. It's just more expensive. Who's it for?"

"Orrin Muller. Chairman of the Federal Communications Commission."

He copied the address of the headquarters of the FCC on the delivery form. At the bottom of the form, he began filling out the blank spaces under Special Instructions.

"If he's not there, we should leave it?"

"I called. His secretary said he'll be there."

"Okay to leave it with his secretary?"

"As long as she says she'll take it in to him right away."

"You want this insured?"

I shook my head. "I have copies."

I sealed the package with the cassette inside, along with a letter I'd typed. I'd tried to keep the letter brief and low-key, but even so I couldn't disguise what it was, the epistolary equivalent of pointing my finger at Dodds and yelling "Smut Lord."

It was Thursday afternoon now, and Chairman Muller would get the package sometime tomorrow. He'd watch the movie past the end and have the entire weekend to work himself into a righteous fury. And first thing Monday morning, I'd be there in his office, ready to answer questions. Maybe I should bring along a Bible, and if he started thumping his, I could thump mine along with him. Get a little rhythm section going.

Thomas Theron, character assassin.

I kept the original cassette of *The Right Stiff*, the one Emma had shown to me that day, the one I'd clutched to me before passing out. The one with the history. The one with the bloodstains on it.

Looking at the cassette now, it occurred to me that if I'd been smarter, if I'd been more observant, I might have guessed its secret much sooner. A small piece of cellophane tape had been affixed to the edge of the cassette, covering a square hole in the plastic. The aperture, I knew now, was a safety feature; it prevented accidental erasure of a movie, or recording over a movie by mistake. To add anything to the cassette, someone had to stick the cellophane tape there first. And that's what Grace Alice Perry had done. Before she copied the footage of Dodds onto the end of the reel, she'd covered the small aperture with Scotch tape. And then she'd mailed the cassette to Emma.

The cellophane tape had been there all along, only I hadn't noticed it. A good detective would've spotted it immediately; hell, it was a clue. A good detective would have taken his time, held the cassette up before his eyes, slowly turning it around, and said, "Hello, what's this?" Seeing the small square of tape, he would have suspected something, would've carefully explored the bit of evidence the cassette offered to him.

But there are two kinds of detectives, I supposed, with two ways of looking at the world. One kind looks at the world and sees what is actually there. The other kind sees only what he expects to see or what he hopes to see. That was the kind of detective I was. When I looked at the world, mostly what I saw was myself.

25

So here, finally, my rash act. Professor Theron goes to Washington.

Late Sunday evening, after I'd packed a single, conservative suit, I took a cab to South Station and bought a ticket for Amtrak night service to Washington, departing Boston at 10:10, with stops in Providence and New Haven, a brief layover at Penn Station, New York, then on to Newark, Philadelphia, Baltimore, eventually arriving in the capital at 7:55 Monday morning—a mind-numbing, ten-hour haul. The Amtrak Night Owl, the carrier of choice for anyone too cheap or too afraid to fly, and I qualified on both counts.

Just before I left, Rollie Palmer had called again. Something I'd said about Samuel Dodds had puzzled him, had triggered a vague memory.

"When you said arson," Rollie said, "I thought that was a little off the wall, but something clicked in the back of my mind. I'd heard it or read it somewhere, something about Dodds's father, describing his career as 'checkered.' Nothing more, just checkered. So I went down to the microfilm and looked up a few contemporary newspaper accounts. You know how the old man made his money, right?"

Real estate, I recalled, but strictly small potatoes. Low seven figures. And now his life represented little more than a brief footnote to his son's story.

"It was in New York right after the war," Rollie said,

"and Dodds, senior, was speculating, buying and reselling small buildings, and I gather doing all right for himself. The checkered part turns out to be pretty interesting. No one ever proved anything, but at least a couple of times he was investigated. Apparently his buildings experienced more than their fair share of suspicious fires, fiscally advantageous fires. Had all the insurance companies in a snit. So at the time, in the real-estate community in New York, there was a general feeling that when Dodds the elder brought out a match, it wasn't necessarily to light his cigar."

Hearing that, I felt a lot more confident that I hadn't been imagining things. The slenderest of circumstantial evidence, of course, but if my task now was merely to plant the seeds of moral doubt, the rumors about Dodds's father invited the classic strategies of defamation: guilt by association, the sins of the father visited upon the son. Why should I play fair?

I'd talked to Beth, too, dropping by to see her earlier in the day. I found her with the telephone cradled on her shoulder, busy with last-minute arrangements, preparing for the rally tomorrow afternoon. She was excited, her spirits high. Everything seemed to be going much better than anyone had expected. Grace Alice Perry had been the final addition to a distinguished roster of speakers, but she'd quickly become the featured attraction; suddenly, momentum was building. There was growing interest in what an ex–porn starlet might say. Some of it lurid interest, certainly, but there was a potential, too, for sympathy. Her story seemed to be provoking the curiosity of the huge numbers of people who had yet to give Proposition Six a single thought. And if they were curious, they might listen; and if they listened, they might be persuaded. Anything seemed possible. One news poll even hinted at a close vote.

At first the coalition had worried that the site of the rally—the small park on Duffy Street, adjacent to Choate's porn factory—was too remote to attract much of a crowd; now the concern was that the park might be too small to accommodate the anticipated throng. Each new estimate of the turnout exceeded the last; some guessed thousands, some guessed tens of thousands. There was talk of moving the rally to Boston Common, but the city permits were already in place, a stage had been constructed, and a sound system rigged.

And now Beth was saying that even the weather was cooperating; a forecast of clear skies for the rally, and on the following day, the day of the vote, a cold drizzle. If bad weather lowered voter turnout, she said, that could only help Proposition Six, whose supporters would show up at the polls even in a blizzard.

As I listened, I stood off to the side, studying my ex-wife from an angle, trying to keep my mind from drifting. Just what did she mean the other day about being careful? Just how careless had we been? Was it just a general warning—we've been lucky so far, let's not press our luck? Or were we talking a missed period? Buh-buh-buh-babies?

I couldn't think of an appropriate way to broach the subject; it wasn't an easy question to ask, even under less emotionally ambiguous circumstances. Just what would I say? So, Beth, how are things, you know, menstruation-wise? And even if I got past that hurdle, I knew she'd get defensive. I could just hear her saying, Don't worry, Thomas, it's not your problem. And I'd say I didn't say it was a problem. I wasn't worried, I'd say, I was just curious. And she'd say, Curious? You mean the same way you're curious about today's sports scores? That kind of curious? And then I'd get pissy and before long we'd be saying some pretty shitty things to each other.

So I kept my mouth shut.

I heard her say, "You're not really taking the train to Washington? Isn't that an all-nighter?"

"I happen to like trains. Nice, slow pace, a return to a simpler—"

"Spare me," she said. "If you ever come to your senses, I know some people who could help you with this phobia about flying. I have friends who get good results with behavior mod. It's a very good technique."

"Behavior modification? Are you sure that will work on someone who never does anything?"

That got a smile, which encouraged me to say, "Beth?"

"Yes?"

"Remember what you said the other day about being care—"

The phone rang. She answered and I massaged the back of my neck while she told someone that yes, every single seat on the stage had been assigned, and no, not to promise anyone anything, because she'd be onstage checking, and about ten minutes later the conversation hadn't advanced very far beyond that. She looked over at me with an apologetic shrug, so we said good-bye with her palm covering the phone receiver.

She said, "Call me when you get back."

I nodded.

"Maybe on Tuesday we'll go over together and vote."

"Sounds good," I said, heading out the door, knowing it would've sounded a lot better if I'd sent in my voter registration card.

Outside I passed a young woman on Beth's stoop, and by the time I was out in the street with my hand raised to hail a cab something clicked in my mind and I realized that the young woman was Grace Alice Perry. I turned and looked back and saw that she'd paused at Beth's door and was looking back, too. She wore no makeup, and I recognized her black running outfit as Beth's. She appeared to be very much what she was, a pretty, well-scrubbed young college student. Her face seemed untouched by experience, sordid or otherwise. Your past, I knew, didn't begin to make public service announcements on your face until much later.

She stood there studying me for a couple of seconds before calling out, "You're Thomas Theron, aren't you?"

I retraced my steps and met her at the bottom of the stoop. "Yeah, hi," I said. "How're you feeling?"

"Pissed off," she replied matter-of-factly.

It occurred to me that this was our first meeting unmediated by drugs or videotape, the first time I'd seen her with clothes on. Oddly enough, the ordinariness of this sidewalk encounter seemed far more complicated and challenging. For a moment I wished I hadn't turned back.

She said, "I guess I should thank you."

"To tell you the truth, I was mostly helping Elizabeth. I sort of helped you by accident."

"Beth said the two of you used to be married."

"Yep."

"I like her."

"Me too."

"She said the two of you were seeing each other again."

"I'm not exactly sure what's going on."

"Join the crowd. Sounds like my life."

We didn't seem to have much else to say to each other. We stood there a few moments longer, until Grace finally headed up the stoop again. At the top she turned back.

"Beth told me that you wrote a novel."

I nodded.

"I've been trying to think of what I should say tomorrow, and then she told me about your book, and I don't know, I started thinking that writing a novel is probably a lot like acting in a porn movie."

"How's that?"

"It sounds dumb, I know, but . . ." She stopped, gathered herself, and started again. "You're kind of driven to do it even if it's not the smartest thing or the most responsible thing to do, and the need that drives you is very private, and all along you convince yourself that you're being an artist, that you're the one controlling everything, that everything is your idea. And when you're finished and these private needs—whatever they are—have been satisfied, you stop looking inside yourself and start looking around, and that's when you're in for a real shock. What you find out is you're not an artist at all, you're just a worker bee, and all this stuff you thought was your idea wasn't your idea at all. All you've been doing is generating merchandise, only you didn't know it. And what's really weird about it, what I still can't figure out is, this art that you think was all your idea, well, it turns out to be exactly the product the boss ordered, as if he'd been standing over you and telling you what to do every step of the way. Does that sound crazy?''

I smiled at Grace Alice Perry and she smiled back.

"Yeah," I said, "until it happens to you."

Three o'clock in the morning, and I had the club car to myself. Even in daylight, the northeast corridor isn't a scenic route. At night it offers only brief glimpses of gloomy urban decay, the dimly lit, saggy ass of every metropolis along the eastern seaboard. As we approached New York, I remembered the theory of a celebrated sociologist, from Columbia, maybe, or NYU. There are no unexplored lands, he claimed, only unexplored regions of time. He impressed this notion upon his students by leading them on walking tours of New York City at just about this time of night, in the hours before dawn. The familiar turf of noonday existence, they soon learned, is transformed into the dark province of the night, unknown territory ripe for scholarly discovery. There they encountered new and interesting populations, new and interesting economies, new and interesting codes of behavior. They were frequently mugged.

Which led to the demise of the walking tours, I recalled, and a return of the discussion to a safer, more theoretical basis.

Just south of Philadelphia I fell asleep. Less than two hours later I was wakened by an infant's yawlp and the odor of synthetic bacon as my fellow travelers began to arrive in the club car for breakfast; the motion of the train caused them to stagger forward along the center aisle, grinning sheepishly, grasping at headrests for balance.

I should've stayed awake. Dazed and squinting, I lifted my head from the small café table, a patient coming out of a coma, a zombie coming out of a grave. I was getting a couple of hard stares. I checked my watch—a quarter past seven—and took a few minutes to gather myself. Eventually I managed to bring back to my table two large coffees, plus a fresh pack of cigarettes. Twenty minutes later we pulled into Washington, and I'd achieved some semblance of consciousness, my head abuzz with nicotine and caffeine, not so much awake as wired, shell-shocked. Poor man's jet lag.

Once in the terminal I carried my suit bag into the men's room and hung it on the door of a bathroom stall. I'd worn jeans and a sweatshirt for the train ride, but now I changed into my black suit with the narrow lapels. My funeral suit. I splashed my face with cold water, rehearsing aloud what I planned to say to Orrin Muller. I paused to examine my image in the mirror. Gaunt, haggard, dark circles under my eyes, but that was okay. That could work in my favor. If I showed up in Muller's office looking like an Old Testament prophet, so much the better.

At precisely nine-thirty, I approached a bank of high-tech pay phones and dialed the number for the FCC. Only then did I fully appreciate the tenuousness of my mission. Was I serious? Did I really think I could just ring up the FCC chairman, waltz into his office, and ruin Samuel Dodds's life?

"Chairman Muller's office," a woman's voice answered. "Good morning?"

I was so full of apologies and explanations that I must've sounded deranged. But I kept talking, kept getting it out bit by bit until she finally interrupted me.

"Thomas Theron," she said. "Yes, yes, I have it right here. The chairman was in early this morning, and he left a note on my desk. He said if you called to tell you that he'd be pleased to meet with you."

"He did?"

"He's in a meeting right now, but I can fit you in next if that's convenient. Could you be here in half an hour?"

"I think so. I'm at the train station. Is that far?"

"That should give you plenty of time. Tell the cabbie it's just off Dupont Circle."

I took a moment and returned to the men's room mirror for a last look at my ragged features. I reknotted my tie, patted my hair wet, then combed it with my fingers. I took a few deep, calming breaths, telling myself: Spiritually tortured is fine, Thomas, just don't overdo it. Just don't walk in his office looking like an addict suffering withdrawal.

The Federal Communications Commission occupied a squat, gray granite office building of seven stories on Avenue M; its utilitarian design offered a spare, bureaucratic contrast to the city's more imposingly monumental structures. Standing on the outside steps, I guessed how a cutaway might appear, the guts of the edifice laid bare like an ant farm; I imagined hundreds of cubbyholes, and in each of them a single worker composing memorandums, and other workers carrying the memorandums from cubbyhole to cubbyhole, and when the memorandums had made the rounds to all the cubbyholes, a worker in green coveralls loaded them into something like a laundry bin, took them down to the basement, and put them in a huge incinerator. Wasn't that how government worked?

Inside, I studied the directory, found Muller's office number, and took the elevator to the top floor, feeling good now, alert, even euphoric. The odds might not be completely in my favor, but nothing seemed like such a long shot anymore. Orrin Muller had asked to see me, that was the key. If he thought I was a crackpot, if he didn't want to be bothered, he could have easily put me off. No, I was sure he'd looked at the tape and wanted to know more.

He didn't keep me waiting. I stepped inside a sleek outer office—no cubbyholes on the top floor—and his administrative assistant, the woman with whom I'd spoken on the phone, announced my arrival. Before I knew it Orrin Muller himself had come out to greet me.

He was a middle-aged man, nearing sixty, with long arms and big hands. An angular face, full of sharp rural features that seemed at odds with the soft lines of a very expensive haircut. Not so much tanned as windburned. He wasn't wearing a jacket, only a light blue short-sleeved dress shirt and matching tie that reminded me of the prepackaged tie-shirt combos that K mart sold in small sizes to children and in large sizes to church elders. Though the office was cool, even chilly, half-moons of sweat dampened his armpits.

Pumping my hand enthusiastically, his left arm curling around my shoulders, he began asking me about my trip, telling me what a wonderful city Boston was, how he looked forward to it whenever he had a chance to get up there. Was this how it felt if you were from Idaho and came to Washington to meet your congressman?

I was doing my best to play my role of concerned citizen, indignant, yes, but uncertain what action might be warranted. I displayed whatever gift I possessed for sincerity, not to mention shameless flattery. "It isn't for me to judge," I concluded, "whether Sam Dodds is morally unfit to hold a broadcast license. So I bring this matter to you, Chairman Muller, to seek your guidance, to receive the benefit of your counsel."

"Well, you did the right thing, Professor Theron. Rest assured, you did the right thing. Most people won't. Most people'll just sit back, let the other fella speak up. It's not my problem. Let the other fella get his hands dirty. Let him worry about it. Now, if everybody thought like that, where would we be then? Where would this country be?"

I was about to offer some appropriately dismal speculation where the country might be if everyone refused to come forward with sex tapes damning their fellow citizens, but Muller wasn't listening.

He said, "We'd be going to hell in a handbasket, that's where. We'd be up that well-known creek, heh, without a paddle."

The chairman had the country-boy routine down pat. A former federal judge, Rollie had said, and a state rep before that. I was beginning to wonder if he was the kind of man who'd spent his entire life in officialdom, in some administrative or elective office, but he liked you to think that just yesterday he'd been out in the fields on his tractor when he got the call from Washington to come East and run the FCC. I looked again at the wet patches at his armpits; maybe he gave himself a quick douse with the plant sprayer between appointments.

He ushered me into a spacious office; one side of the room held an enormous oak desk with executive chair, and on the other was a sitting area with a black leather sofa and two wing chairs. At the far end of the room, beyond a portrait of the president, was a media wall, a floor-to-ceiling bank of high-tech electronic equipment; after all, this was the office of the head of the FCC.

I counted six television screens, all of them blank except one. The cassette I'd sent him was playing, only the tape hadn't reached the end, the incriminating scene with Dodds and Choate and the business clients and the midnight revels. What was playing was *The Right Stiff,* and we happened to walk in at the commencement of a scene of energetic fellatio. We stood there a moment, staring, and I tried to put myself in some posture of conspicuous disapproval.

"Look at that," the Federal Communications Commission chairman said. "My God, will you just look at that," the tone of his voice intending a note of censure, of course, not praise.

Orrin Muller stood before the screen, fast forwarding through the movie, and I took the opportunity to supplement some of the suspicions I'd outlined in my letter. The videotape, I said, very clearly shows Dodds pimping for business clients, but that's just a detail of a larger picture, a far more disturbing picture. I think Dodds organized and financed a company that produces adult films. I think he hired an arsonist who torched some buildings in Boston's Combat Zone and tried to pass it off as the work of a mad antiporn bomber. And I think he ordered the kidnapping of a young woman who was trying to bring these activities to light. To this point I don't have legal proof, I said, but there's more than enough here to support a license review, enough to initiate an FCC hearing. . . .

I don't know if he heard me or not. He remained in front of the TV screen, moving the images quickly forward, then

stopping for a moment, then moving forward again. Over
the weekend, I wondered, had he developed a fondness for
certain scenes?

He said, "Professor, you ever see a deer in rut?"

"Beg pardon?"

"A deer in rut," he repeated. "When that scent gets out,
nothing else matters. That's what brings the buck out in the
open so you can draw a bead on him. Not a hunter, are you?
But maybe when you were a kid you had a dog and it got
around a bitch in heat. Male dog just loses its personality,
like you don't know it and it don't know you. Sometimes a
man can get that way. He just can't help it. He can lead a
good life, an honest life, but it won't amount to a hill of
beans when he's on the scent, when his sex drive kicks in
and takes over. I guess it's sort of what it must be like to
lose your mind. You don't know yourself. You can't think.
You hate yourself for it, but that don't matter."

I listened politely as he reflected on man and the natural
world, and then I attempted to steer the discussion back on
course.

"Don't get the wrong impression, Mr. Chairman. I'm
not saying that Dodds himself is sexually obsessed. I don't
know whether he is or not. All I'm saying is, at the very
least he's engaged in some extremely unsavory business
activities."

By now the videotape had advanced to the end of the reel,
and the final scene appeared, Byron Choate and Samuel
Dodds and the girls coming out from the dark revels to join
Dodds's clients. Muller stopped the tape.

He was talking again, not so much to me, really, as to
himself, asking how a man could get like that, just like a
deer in rut. You wouldn't think of holding it against a buck,
so why would you hold it against a man? Saying, the buck
gets on the scent and comes bounding out into the open, not
even mindful of his own instinct for self-preservation, and
the next thing you know he's splayed across the hood of a
pickup truck, and then stuck up on the wall in somebody's
den, watching college football. And why? For what? What

was the terrible thing the buck'd done to deserve that punishment? What had the buck done that was so wrong that his enemies should rise up over him? What?

"Chairman Muller?"

No answer.

I said his name again, and he looked at me with a kind of agonized hostility. He said, "Why don't we cut through the bull hocky, Professor. Just what do you have in mind?"

What was in my mind was simple—putting Dodds's ass in a meat grinder—but I was beginning to have serious doubts about what was in Muller's mind and whether any of it made sense.

"I'm suggesting," I replied patiently, "that a serious review of the transfer of the broadcast license might not be a bad idea."

He jerked his head toward the TV screen. "How many copies of this thing are around?"

"Only a couple. None of them are actually around."

Muller walked over and sat behind his desk. He didn't lean back into the chair, but perched at the edge, and he began rocking slightly, initiating the rhythmic motion by dipping his head forward, not unlike a child on a swing or a demented person on a subway. Muller was losing it. The veins at his temples bulged; his forehead beaded with sweat. I was thinking I should fetch his secretary, thinking he was experiencing some recurring medical episode, and his secretary would come in and know just what to do, know just where he kept the vial of tiny pills that restored him to back-slapping mediocrity. Something was horribly wrong, I just couldn't figure . . .

I looked at the image frozen on the TV screen and then I looked at him. I looked back at the TV.

For maybe twenty seconds I kept looking back and forth, back and forth from the TV screen to him, and only then was I sure. A queasy sensation swept through my gut, a sinking feeling, as if I were on a carnival ride and my stomach had suddenly dropped to my feet. And oddly enough, I felt a kind of exhilaration, too, the thrill that gets mixed in with the fear whenever you are confronted with something extraordinary and unforeseen.

I was in the process of committing a blunder of legendary proportions. My recent past was little more than a chronology of mistakes—I conceded that—but my presence in Muller's office represented an entirely new level of accomplishment. I had entered an epic realm.

Orrin Muller was on the videotape. Orrin Muller was one of the men for whom Dodds had been pimping. I sat staring at the frame where Muller had frozen the tape, and there was no longer any doubt whose image was recorded there. Orrin Muller was standing just behind Dodds, showing up at Choate's party, a rumpled old buck drunk and grinning and eager to get laid. For Dodds, of course, it made perfect sense; a brilliant stroke, really. Maybe the license transfer was considered a formality, but if you had a fortune riding on it, and if you had the opportunity to remove even the tiniest element of risk, to leave absolutely nothing to chance . . .

My first impulse was to laugh, which I suppressed. My second impulse . . . I didn't have a second impulse. I hadn't the vaguest idea what to do. I just sat there, watching the Federal Communications Commission chairman rocking in his chair like a demented child, until I heard a voice from somewhere behind me.

"Ah, Professor."

I turned and what I noticed first was the business suit, coming through a private entrance to Muller's office. A shimmering light gray, exquisitely cut, perfectly encasing the diminutive physique upon which rested the huge, immaculately groomed, telegenic head of Samuel Dodds. At his sides were two less impressive suits, worn by large young men, clean-cut and unsmiling.

Dodds entered the office comfortably, as relaxed as if it were his own. He crossed the room to Muller's desk, turned, and propped himself against the front edge of it, facing me, oblivious to the old man behind him. Muller stopped rocking now and slumped back in his chair, holding his head in his hands. The last time I'd witnessed an expression of such melodramatic despair was the final act of a student production of *King Lear*.

"Professor, Professor, Professor," Dodds sighed, casting his eyes upward, bemused. "Excuse me, but I find your naïveté almost charming. So many people would have given anything to get wind of this cassette, so many enemies, business enemies, political enemies, all so eager to have a weapon against me, to do me harm. And where have you placed it, into whose hands? I'm sorry, but sending it to Orrin is so astoundingly inept that really, truly, I'm touched." Still looking at me, he leaned back slightly, saying, "Aren't you touched, Orrin?"

The chairman sat mute. Dodds gave a curt nod of his head, and one of his young men walked over to the bank of TV screens, ejected the cassette, and placed it in Dodds's open palm. He inspected it for a moment, then looked up.

"It's interesting, don't you think? In many ways, pornography is an ideal product. No matter what standard of evaluation you might apply, it meets or surpasses every criterion. It's repetitive in content and easily produced. Most of it's legal, but there's no quality control, there are no complaints, and there's almost no limit on the markup. Plus there's no need to advertise. But the thirst for it is unquenchable. In the hinterlands, there is a great, unceasing hunger for pornography, as constant as the hunger for shelter and clothing and food. Yes, I suppose that's what it is, finally, the dark, addictive rations of the night."

Dodds grew expansive, pushing away from the desk, pacing about the office as he spoke.

"My involvement, you know, was little more than a whim. I'd just acquired a franchise of video stores, which got me thinking. I was trying to imagine those stores as they'd be in three or four years, trying to imagine who would be in them, and what they would be thinking. In my mind I saw a picture of frustration, unhappy customers browsing those depressingly familiar aisles, and I could hear them saying, 'No, I don't want to watch *The Seven*

Samurai, any more than I wanted to watch it the last time I came here, or the time before that, or the fifty times before that.' What the future holds, I decided, is obvious. Eventually in every video store across the country, there will be only two movies. Hundreds and hundreds of cassettes, perhaps, but for all practical purposes, only two movies from which to choose. One of these will be called *Hollywood's Latest with Big Stars, Part II.* The other will be called *Sheena Takes One up the Wazoo.* Really, it's as simple as that.

"And so I asked myself, if there'll be only two movies, why shouldn't one of them be mine? Pornography is a money cow, Professor. It generates pure profit."

Finally, a tiny flaw in his perfect facade. As he pronounced the words *pure profit,* a little bubble of spittle appeared at the corner of his mouth. But he kept explaining himself, and the spittle vanished, and I listened, wondering why I should be the beneficiary of his odd confession, until I realized it wasn't a confession at all, but something far more satisfying to him, an expression of his complete control, the arrogance of his absolute authority; the emotion that drove him to explain, to tell me what had happened and why, and what would happen next, was childlike in its simplicity: Dodds was proud of himself.

"And about that time along came Byron Choate. He'd been pestering some of my people in California, trying to secure financing for some outlandish feature-film project, which, of course, was out of the question. But I made a counterproposal. Develop a few adult titles, and we'll see about the other. He jumped at the chance, of course. I bought a small company, Tele-Techniques, for the hardware, set Choate up at Manray's for a talent pool, and gave him all the space he needed at the warehouse. And that was all there was to it, really. A modest investment that I thought one day might bear fruit. My video stores, stocked with my videos."

Dodds circled the oak desk and stood next to Muller, smiling down at him with playful menace. He raised his voice, as if he were speaking to someone hard of hearing or feebleminded. He shamelessly affected a corn-pone accent.

"You haven't been boring the professor, have you, Orrin? Going on and on about livestock in heat? You know what you are, Orrin? A character. You're what they call a colorful character."

Muller suffered silently, offering no resistance; he appeared oblivious to what was happening around him.

"There, there, Orrin, don't be depressed. Don't let your troubles get you down," Dodds said, placing his hand on the chairman's shoulder with the feigned concern he might show a household servant. "We have to be going now. We'll leave you to your work, let you collect your thoughts. You remember the work you have to do, don't you? The government business that must be attended to, the airwaves that need to be regulated, the broadcast licenses that need to be transferred. . . ."

A moment later we left through the private entrance, moved down a short hallway, then squeezed into a private elevator, Dodds and I forward and the two clean-cut young men behind. Dodds, a full head shorter than the rest of us, was completely at ease in close quarters, saying, "Orrin has some interesting ways of interpreting his libido. He's very much like Byron Choate in that sense, although Choate tends to find meaning in his childhood rather than the barnyard. But they're both libidinous men, and they'll always find themselves at a disadvantage. I'll tell you frankly, Professor, the appetites that drive me are enormous, but they're not sexual. I don't like the risk. The more risk you remove, the more control you gain, and you can never have too much control."

"People obsessed with control," I said, "get ulcers. Have heart attacks."

It wasn't much, but at least I said something.

"No, no, people who *fail* to control get ulcers. People who control live well and prosper."

Outside, we walked toward a black stretch limo hogging an embarrassing portion of the curb. Dodds slipped on a

pair of aviator sunglasses, and a couple of passersby paused
to study him, wondering which ambassador, which politi-
cian he might be.

"So you want to be a writer," Dodds said, his voice
dripping with the same ridicule he'd unleashed on Muller.
"Since I bought Adage, I've met a few novelists, and I
can't say I'm impressed. I'm having a hard time understanding all the fuss. Sitting in a small room with pad and
pencil, making up worlds that don't exist simply because
the one out there displeases you. It's such a pathetic thing,
really, a puny thing, drifting from delusion to delusion. You
know what I think? You want to know who're the real
artists in this world, the real geniuses? Businessmen. Cap-
italists don't just imagine a different world, they recreate the
one that already exists. That's what the Great American
Novel is, and it's been here all along. The entire goddamn
country is a novel, and—"

"And you wrote it."

"You're damn right I wrote it. Me and men like me. Men
with vision."

I said, "And that vision includes fuck films?"

He removed his sunglasses, and his eyes were full of
contempt. "You make me sick," he hissed. "You make me
want to puke. Correct me if I'm wrong, but you were only
too happy to top off your dismal little book with a few fuck
scenes. Didn't think twice about it. Tell me, Professor,
what muse inspired you to do that? You're in good company. Byron Choate was no different. All eager to direct
some pseudo-Frog film, until someone comes along and
says to forget that and try porn, and he's so beside himself
to get to it he's about to pee in his pants.

"You know what I think? You know the only person who
comes away from this with any room to talk? That little girl,
Sheena whatever. When she found out what was happening,
at least she had the gumption to get out, to try to do something about it. I can admire that. To tell you the truth, I'm
a little disappointed she won't get her chance for revenge."

"Maybe she will," I said. "We'll just have to wait to read the papers tomorrow."

"She may make the news, but it won't be about anything she says."

"Why's that?"

"Do you think I'd let her? Less than a week before Orrin does his thing, and you really think I'd let her get up and call me the great Satan pornographer with the cameras running? All I've been through with this, do you think I'd permit that?"

"What do you—"

Dodds ducked inside the limo, and I started in after him, but one of the young suits blocked my path and closed the door behind him. Dodds looked up at me through the passenger window.

"Run along now, Professor. I'm through with you. If you don't like what's happening, you can always go back to your typewriter and make something up."

An electric motor whirred and the tinted window began rising shut, and I stuck my hand in just before it closed. It hurt, it hurt a lot, but I was pleased to find that it didn't take my hand off, either. A moment later the window opened again, and I pulled my hand back and rubbed my wrist.

"What do you mean you won't permit it?"

The two young men were up front now, the doors were closed, and the engine was running.

"Why don't you ask Teddy? I probably don't have to remind you, he has a rather bizarre sense of humor. For the past week or so Theodore has been volunteering his services at the coalition. I bet you didn't know that, did you? Yeah, well, Teddy's been volunteering his technical skills. He's something of an artist himself when it comes to wiring things. He's set up a very good sound system for the rally, a first-rate system to carry the antiporn message to the world. Sheena's not the only one who's planning a dramatic revelation; I think Teddy has a flair for the dramatic himself." Dodds glanced at his watch. "Maybe you still have

time to catch it. Teddy assures me that Sheena's speech''—
he smiled coldly— ''Sheena's speech will be quite explosive.''

The motor whirred again and the tinted window rose
shut, and Dodds's face disappeared behind it. Just before
the limo pulled away, I found myself staring at my own
reflection, watching my expression as it registered the significance of what he'd just told me. Then watching my
expression change some more as I realized who else would
be on the stage with Grace.

Seeing how scared I was scared me even more.

26

Airborne for less than five minutes, the nose of the jet thrust upward, still climbing to cruising altitude, and I was already preparing to violate a cardinal rule of passenger etiquette: under no circumstances utter the word *bomb,* not even jokingly, and certainly not with sweat dripping off the tip of your nose, a crazed look in your eyes. No one will care that the bomb you're referring to is four hundred miles away in Boston, and that you didn't plant it, and your only interest in it is to figure how to keep it from going off—none of that matters. Reporting a bomb is like having a terminal disease. There is a stigma attached to it. Somehow in people's minds it reflects badly on you.

The moment Dodds's limousine pulled away, I'd jumped into the first taxi that came along—not hailing it so much as running out in front of it—yelling at the cabbie to take me to the airport, and the cabbie taking his time, asking which one, Dulles or National? And I said the nearest one, the nearest one with shuttle flights to Boston. Did he have any idea what the shuttle schedule was?

"Pan Am leaves on the half hour."

It was five minutes past noon. "Can I make the twelve-thirty flight?"

"No problem."

"Good," I shouted, "let's go! Let's go!" and after we'd

gone no more than twenty yards, I shouted, "Wait, stop! Wait! Pull over!"

I shoved a ten-dollar bill across the front seat and said, "Can you gimme some quarters? No, don't count 'em out, just a handful. Come on, hurry!"

I jumped out of the cab and ran to the pay phone on the corner, fumbling with the change, dropping every third coin as I jammed them into the slot. I got about three dollars' worth to fall, and I dialed Beth's number, hoping to God she hadn't left. Her answering machine came on, and I waited through her message. When I heard the beep, I said, "Beth, pick up, pick up, you there?" But she wasn't, and I hung up, the quarters cascading out as from a slot machine, and I caught maybe half and recycled them, then dialed Boston's area code, and then 911.

I didn't know if the call would go through—911, long distance?—but a woman answered and I asked if she could connect me to Lieutenant Cryder, the detective at the South Everett station who'd found my kidnapping story so amusing. Cryder and I might not have much of a rapport, I was thinking, but at least I wouldn't have to waste time explaining. If someone asked me to start from the beginning, I wouldn't finish till sometime next week.

She said, "You have to dial that direct."

"Can't you help me out? This is an emergency."

"If it's an emergency, you tell me about it."

"Okay, listen, I'll dial him direct, just give me the number."

"You have to call the precinct for his number. I don't give out numbers. This is an emergency line."

"That's what I'm telling you! This is an emergency."

What kept us from going around in another circle was a recording threatening to cut me off if I didn't put in more money. I didn't have more money, and I didn't have much of a choice.

"Listen to me," I said evenly. "You know the Proposition Six rally this afternoon? You'd better get some people over there, because a bomb's gonna go off."

"Is this a joke? Because if it's a joke, you should be fully
aware that—"

"I'm not joking. I know. I'm sure, so—"

And then I heard a dial tone. I rushed back to the cab, out
of change and running out of time.

Concentrate, I told myself. Block out everything else.
The rally was scheduled for two. I wasn't sure what preliminaries were planned, or how many speakers were on
before Grace, but there was a good chance she wouldn't
begin before three o'clock, probably closer to four. That
gave me at least three hours to get there. If I made the
twelve-thirty shuttle, that would put me on the ground in
Boston by two or so, say another half hour to get to the park
. . . Jesus, that was cutting it close.

I couldn't count on the police; they'd been getting Proposition Six bomb threats for weeks, and my call might not
elicit anything more than a jaded groan and a weary roll of
the eyes. They might do something—Kevin, who can we
spare for this one?—but I doubted my brief warning had
sent officers sprinting out to their squad cars, roaring off
with sirens blaring to alert twenty thousand people to a
bomb threat.

We made it to Washington National in less than ten minutes, and the taxi skidded to a stop in front of Pan Am.
There was a curbside check-in and only a couple of businessmen standing there with briefcases and *Wall Street
Journal*s, and before I knew it I'd reached the counter,
bought my ticket, and was on my way. I even had enough
time to stop at a newsstand for more change and one last
shot at the telephone. I called information in Worcester and
got the number for Gerald Valentin.

After five rings a woman answered, her voice tremulous
with the timbre of old age. Gerald, I remembered, lived
with his sister.

She said, "Gerry's not home right now."

I told her who I was, told her it was important, and asked
where Gerry was.

"Oh, he's in Boston again, helping those nice young

girls. I think it's so wonderful he has the chance to get out and help people. It means so much to him. Excuse me, but aren't you the charming professor he's been telling me about?''

I expended the last seconds of my last call politely praising Gerald to his sister, and then I excused myself and boarded the plane.

An overwhelming surge of adrenaline was coursing in my blood, the same hormonal rush that enables a mother to free a child trapped beneath a car's wheel, but I had to suppress it, I had to sit there trying to appear normal. Normal? We were just about to take off, and all I wanted to do was stand up and scream, Bomb! Bomb! Bomb!

Fear of flying? I couldn't wait to be in the air! Had I stumbled on the cure for the countless, debilitating phobias of modern life: bomb therapy? Vanquishing one fear simply by presenting the specter of a far greater danger? Scared of heights? Not when you see what's waiting below. Scared to leave your house? Not when I tell you who's coming to visit. Scared of spiders? Not if that huge fucking snake gets any closer. . . .

Easy, Thomas, I told myself, easy. Rein it in. You can't help Beth or Grace or anyone else if you don't keep it under control. Come on, now, that's a boy. Keep the lid on.

Fifteen minutes into the flight, a stewardess leaned over me, her hand on my headrest.

"Sir, there's no smoking on domestic flights, so I must insist—"

I put the cigarette out.

She hesitated, studying me. "Is everything okay?"

"Maybe you could tell me—is it true that the captain can call ahead from the cockpit, be patched through by telephone to someone on the ground if there's an emergency?"

Under certain circumstances, it might have seemed a fairly routine question, but I could tell I was making her nervous. I knew what she must be seeing in my face, because I'd seen it too, in the window of Dodds's limousine.

"Is there some kind of problem, sir?"

"Actually, there is a problem, quite a serious problem, but I don't want to alarm anyone, so perhaps if I could speak with the captain for a moment."

I hadn't said "bomb" yet, but I was saying enough to get her attention, and I could see her mind working, already reviewing what she'd been taught in flight-attendant school, the passenger profile that helped you identify potential problems. Going down the list, ticking them off one by one. Yes, he's sweating bullets; yes, he's nervous as hell; yes, eyes wide, not really blinking . . .

"If you could just tell me what's the matter, sir, perhaps I could—"

"Seriously, please, if I could just have a word with a member of the flight crew."

She was about to reply but decided against it and headed forward. Perched rigidly on the edge of my aisle seat, I was aware that I'd begun to rock—short, rhythmic, obsessive rocks—and I felt a sudden empathy for Orrin Muller. Dodds had pushed us all to our outer limits, had us all rocking on the edge of our seats like maniacs.

The seat next to me was vacant, the window seat occupied by a young man with his jacket off, showing his paisley suspenders. He was staring down at a magazine, and he was gripping the edges of it so tightly that his fingertips were white. He hadn't turned a page for a couple of minutes now. I guessed he'd overheard my exchange with the stewardess, and he was probably wondering how he could get past me when the time came to make a break for the emergency exits.

Now a crew member was coming down the aisle toward me. He wore a short-sleeved white shirt with chevrons, was tall and slim, gangly as a cowboy, his expression affable, as if he'd just strolled back with nothing particular on his mind, maybe find somebody to talk sports—How about them Aggies, that little freshman receiver they got?

"How we doin' there, buddy?"

He was the flight navigator, he said, his tone of voice calm and soothing, a verbal sedative administered once the

problem passenger had been identified. I followed him to
the rear of the aircraft, and I said everything I needed to say,
and I made it sound as reasonable as it could be made to
sound. And then I told him, "Look, I don't blame you if
you're skeptical, but why not play it safe? And if the police
are skeptical, it won't hurt them to play it safe, either.
There'll be police officers at the rally anyway, for crowd
control or whatever, so there's no reason not to check it out.
Just in case . . ."

It was impossible to tell what the cowboy-navigator was
thinking; he listened calmly, without the slightest hint of
alarm, as if I'd been telling him Yeah, that little Aggie
freshman receiver was great, but what they really needed
was somebody who could get the ball to him.

"Don't worry, Mr. Theron, we'll take care of it. Just be
calm. I'm sure everything will turn out just fine."

"One other thing," I said, "tell Cryder to keep an eye
out for a guy with scabs on his face. He's the one."

The navigator nodded solemnly, as if this were the sort of
identifying feature he dealt with all the time. Height,
weight, hair color, facial scabs . . .

For the rest of the flight, every time I glanced up to the
forward cabin, one of the flight attendants happened to be
glancing back toward me. Eventually a microphone crackled, and we were told that we'd begun our final descent into
Boston. The approach was over water, the runway itself on
a narrow peninsula jutting out into the harbor, so that you
didn't see land beneath you until four or five seconds before
you touched down. So what? Why should that bother me?

The plane taxied off the runway, and as it slowed to a
stop near the terminal, I timed it so I was halfway through
first class before anyone else stood up to reach for the overhead racks. I pushed past the few passengers still ahead of
me, a worried-looking stewardess calling after me, "Good-
bye, now!"—probably the only time she'd said it with genuine enthusiasm—and then I was in the connecting tunnel,
free and clear, sprinting unencumbered, hitting the terminal
first. All eyes were on me as I sprinted through the roped-off

passage leading into the waiting area, everyone no doubt relieved that I wasn't the out-of-town guest they'd come to meet, still running when . . .

The cowboy-navigator had called ahead after all.

Up ahead three uniformed police officers were waiting, and standing in front of them was a man in a rumpled suit. I didn't recognize him, but he was acting as if he recognized me, stepping forward, smiling, his hands out in front of him, patting the air.

I stopped in my tracks, still fifteen yards away. Why the hell was he patting the air? He wasn't patting the air to say, Okay, Mr. Theron, we got your call and we're ready to move and we need your help. No, he was patting the air as if he were calming a man on a ledge, telling him, Relax, buddy, don't jump, trying to keep him occupied while someone else snuck up from behind with a straitjacket.

I turned around and sure enough, a police officer was creeping up behind me, giving me a new respect for air-patting analysis.

I leaped over the rope boundary and fled, thinking if I ran fast, I wouldn't hear them when they told me to stop, and so I wouldn't have to stop. But I heard them anyway, so I figured I'd just have to lie about that later. I knocked into people as I ran; a woman screamed, a child cried, grown men gave me plenty of room. I was wild, as out of control as I'd ever been in my life.

A huge clock hung high above the main terminal floor. It was two thirty-five. A horrible thought: Maybe I'd get there in time to identify the bodies.

A quarter mile from the park, the traffic on Duffy Street was already bumper-to-bumper, so I jumped out of the cab that I'd literally dived into at the airport. I started running, flinching at each street noise, as if it portended the end of the world. But nothing bad had happened yet. The sidewalks teemed with women, and everyone was still happy, laughing, caught up in the camaraderie of the moment. I ran past the familiar brick building at number 29 and wondered if Choate was back there at this very moment, filming among the cartons of books, indulging in the sort of irony that would've amused him. Vendors lined the sidewalk out front, conducting a brisk trade in antiporn buttons and T-shirts.

As I neared the park itself, I was stunned by the number of people. Thousands of women had gathered. I'd had some vague notion that I'd just run up to the stage, discreetly warn Beth, who would organize an efficient evacuation of the speakers. Run up to the stage? I couldn't see the stage. I couldn't even see the park! I saw the tops of trees, I saw the tops of the reproduction 1890s streetlamps that encircled the park, and beneath that I saw only a vast ocean of women. I plunged in—what choice did I have?—a swimmer preparing to battle the surf.

Teddy had done a good job on the sound system; a woman was addressing the rally, her voice impassioned and clear, easily subduing the noises of the crowd.

". . . we must change the law first; perhaps later we can change minds. But don't be fooled. The law isn't a set of absolute principles, eternal and just. If that were true, we would have always had the right to vote, we would have always had the right to educate ourselves, to own property . . ."

Five minutes of hard work, pushing, squeezing, insinuating my body sideways through the close throng, and I wasn't even sure if I was getting any closer. I picked out a landmark, an elm tree that I thought might be near the stage, and headed for that. As I weaved farther into the crowd, nearer the boundary where people were straining for a glimpse of the speakers, my advance began to pose a territorial threat. I began to mark my progress not so much by distance as by the number of times someone called me an asshole or a selfish jerk.

". . . no, the law is a weapon, a bludgeon that enforces the authority of men. If you doubt that for even a second, think back to the latest rape trial, call to your mind a picture of the rapist and of the victim, and remember whose face was smug and grinning, and whose face burned with hot tears. . . ."

I spotted Gerald. Through the heads bobbing in front of me I saw him maybe thirty yards away, standing just beyond a middle ground where groups of women were sitting on blankets. I started waving my arms above my head and shouting his name as loudly as I could, and the longer I shouted, the more I enraged the women around me, their worst fears confirmed, a man in their midst trying to shout down the speaker, trying to drown out the truth.

A heavyset woman wearing khaki pants and a dress shirt suddenly appeared and began to pepper my ribs with sharp pokes.

"Shut the fuck up, asshole."

But I kept shouting and waving my arms and a moment later Gerald looked back, scanning the crowd until his eyes paused and seemed to focus on me. He saw me; I was sure of it.

By now the heavyset woman looked as if she wanted to murder me, but she settled for cursing me and shoving me backward, hard shoves that knocked me off balance, until I turned and escaped by slipping a few feet back into the crowd, thinking I would resurface a few yards away. But I got trapped again, and so I started pushing my way back, but I wasn't making any progress, and I began jumping into the air, trying to catch Gerald's eye over the sea of heads. I couldn't see anything. I wasn't even moving forward now, but getting turned around, getting pushed back. I tried to keep up my spirits, tried to ward off morbid thoughts, but it was becoming increasingly clear that if I had any hope of getting near the stage, I was going to have to wait until the bomb went off and everyone scattered.

Finally I just stopped. Confronted by the enormity of the crowd and my helplessness in it, my resolve began to wane. A depression was coming over me, a disquieting desire to give up and let events take their course; no longer a parent with a miraculous surge of strength to free a trapped child,

I now felt like a man lost in a blizzard, preparing to lie down and curl up in the snow.

I found a dead spot in the crowd and lingered there, asking myself, Why had I run from the police? If I'd stayed, at least I would have had the chance to do something I was good at: talking. I knew why I'd run. I was still suffering from a delusion, some secret fantasy that whenever the time came that I *had* to act heroically, at least competently, I'd be up to it. I actually believed that my life of watching from the sidelines was simply a matter of choice, a conscious decision. Well, now I was learning the truth, and guess who was going to have to pay for it? Heroic? I couldn't even fight my way up to the goddamn stage.

What interrupted this reverie of self-loathing was the sound of thunderous applause as the woman onstage concluded her address. Would Grace Alice Perry be next?

I took a couple of deep breaths and tried to think, tried to put myself in Teddy's position. Where was he? He'd planted the bomb somewhere on the stage, and I assumed he was just waiting for the moment when Grace walked up to the podium. He'd trigger it by remote control, that seemed obvious; remote control was his pride and joy. But what restrictions would it impose on him? How far away could he be? Wouldn't he need a direct line of sight? I tried to think of the electronic beam as an invisible thread, and my job was to trace it to its source. No way, I thought, no way he'd be where I was, swamped by the crowd, where his line of sight might be cut off at any moment. No, he'd be farther out, near the perimeter. And he wouldn't be at ground level, either. He'd be up, on top of a car, maybe, or even in a tree. . . .

He'd be up.

And suddenly I knew exactly where Teddy was. I knew the perfect vantage, the one spot that offered a clear line of sight, the one spot he'd have all to himself. What I remembered was the roof scene in *The Right Stiff*, the scene Beth and I had studied so carefully, the one with the park in the background, the library sign visible down below through the limbs of the trees. That's where he'd be, across the street at the warehouse, on the roof.

Backing out of the crowd was a lot easier than pushing into it—everyone was happy to stand aside and let me pass—and with each step I increased my speed, starting to make good time. Less than a minute later I'd already reached the side street between the park and the warehouse, and when I made it to the spot where the Boston Public Library van parked three times a week, I stopped. I leaned back and looked up to the roof, hoping to see some subtle sign of Teddy's presence, a little glint of reflected sunlight, the sort of glimmer that in Westerns signals the presence of outlaws in the hills above the pass.

I brought my hands to my forehead to shade my eyes and squinted into the blue sky. No glint of light, no darting movement that left me wondering if I'd only imagined it, I saw nothing at all like that. What I saw was a man standing there at roof's edge, gazing out over the masses of women in the park, conspicuous, not trying to hide. It was Teddy, and he was just watching, waiting; he didn't seem the least bit concerned.

I started running again, circling to the rear of the building, and as I entered the parking lot, I heard another round of thunderous applause, and I was aware that Grace was being introduced, and then I heard still more applause.

Up the concrete steps at the end of the truck bay—Teddy's red Buick parked right there—looking ahead at the steel security door, thinking, Shit! but it was open and then I was inside the shell of the building, among the walls of shipping cartons. Byron Choate wasn't on the soundstage filming; in fact, there was no soundstage and nothing to suggest one had ever been there. I looked around until I spotted a metal stairway against the brick wall behind me; it led up to a narrow catwalk that extended the length of the wall, halfway up. And there, at the far end of the catwalk, a ladder that rose and seemed to disappear into the ceiling.

Up the metal stairs, across the catwalk, and halfway up the ladder. Looking up, I could see sky through the open hatch. I'd begun to breathe hard, making noise, so when I reached the top I took a second to catch my breath. I oriented myself, tried to visualize where the park was, and facing in that direction, I very slowly raised my head and peered through the opening.

A tar roof, a maze of aluminum duct work, ventilation pipes, exhaust fans. Teddy Span was maybe twenty yards away, wearing a black T-shirt and jeans, still gazing out over the rally, his back toward me. He appeared to be holding a black object in his hand. There was a lot of open space to cross before I got to him, and there was the further problem of what to do when I got there. If he stayed where he was, of course, if he didn't hear me coming, I'd just give him a push, send his scabby ass flying. I was feeling strong again, my adrenaline pumping once more, the man rising out of the snow, telling himself, Keep walking. You can make it. You can do it.

My head out in the open air now, I could hear Grace on the loudspeakers from across the park.

". . . and the lesson is bitter. Because the lesson is bitter, we resist it. We are despised. We resist every time this is made clear to us, but it is true. The bitter lesson of pornography is that we are hated. . . ."

I eased out of the hatch, not thinking, not planning, only noticing with relief that the tar roof muffled the sound of my sneakers. Soon there were only ten yards between us, and Teddy still hadn't moved, and he was definitely holding something black, adjusting it in his hand, tensing up, as if he were preparing to use it. Another step or two and I could just rush him, and I steeled myself for this event by uttering violent curses in my mind, pumping myself up, saying, Yeah, fucking run over and fucking launch his scabby ass, see if that motherfucker knows how to fly. . . .

And that's when he turned around. Which rattled me, but what rattled me even more was his expression: he wasn't shocked, he was grinning. A guttural howl rising in my throat, I rushed him anyway, in that instant knowing but not caring that my momentum might carry us both over the side. And as I reached him, I saw that the black thing in his hand was a leather sap, and he swung it heavily against the side of my head, thudding the bone behind my ear, stopping me cold. A shower of nerve stars exploded before my eyes. I was down.

I struggled to one knee, and he brought the sap down again, and this time he laid me out good. On my back, I now aspired to a more modest goal: simply trying to maintain consciousness.

Teddy stood over me, a dark profile against the blue sky.

"Where the hell you been, Professor? For a minute there I didn't think you were gonna find me. I been standing up here right where you could see me. Jesus, I thought maybe I was gonna have to shoot up a fucking flare."

I tried to lift my head, but the pain stopped me.

"Mr. Dodds gave me a call around noon. He said you might be showing up. He said if I could work it out, try not to start without you. Mr. Dodds said tell you hello."

My brain was slowly beginning to function, but when I tried to speak all that came out was a moan.

"Dooon't . . . don't . . ."

He looked at me and smiled. "Don't what? You mean don't blow that little slut's ass to kingdom come? Mr. Dodds and I talked about that. This may be your lucky day, Professor. We decided that maybe you're right, maybe I shouldn't do it." He leaned down and grabbed me under my armpits and dragged me toward the edge of the roof, propping me up against the low brick wall, saying, "It was kind of like a flash of inspiration. We decided that the smart thing would be for you to do it. We decided we should let *you* blow her ass to kingdom come. How does that sound?"

He sat down next to me, the leather sap in his lap, and he brought from his pocket a remote-control switch no larger that a cigarette case.

On the loudspeakers across the way, Grace Alice Perry's voice carried as clearly as if she were standing next to us.

Teddy said, "You hear that? Can I rig a public-address

system or what?'' He laughed. ''What do you think, Professor, is it live, or is it Memorex?''

''. . . Pornography is the proof of their hate. We are despised. This is what we must understand before we can ever understand anything else: from the nice guys to the bad guys, from the mama's boys to the lover boys, they hate us.''

Teddy leaned back against the low wall, saying, ''I don't hate you, honey. That's not hate, that's love. You're just fucking confused, that's all. If you come up here I'll show you.'' Happy, starting to sing, '' 'Show you my love, baby, uh-huh, show you my big love . . .' ''

I said, ''Listen to her! Listen! She's not saying anything about Dodds. There's no reason to—''

Teddy shushed me. ''Give her a chance, let her talk. You want to interrupt her, just wait a second''— he held up the remote-control switch—''I'll let you interrupt her real good.''

He was looking at me and shaking his head sadly, as if I were a complete disappointment to him.

''You're still not up to speed on this one, are you? You know what you make me think of? One of those club fighters, one of those pugs who walks right into every punch that gets thrown. Gets hit by everything. What do you think the cops'll think? If I lock you up here on this roof, there's no way down except to jump. Everybody down below screaming and crying, and the police find you up here with the little doodads I'm gonna leave you with, what're they gonna think? Give it a chance. Let it sink in. Just what're they gonna think?''

Some compartment within my brain saw the answer with perfect clarity. They would think I was guilty. I didn't know how long they would think it, but for a while they would think I was guilty. Less than three hours ago, I'd placed a bomb threat to 911. The maniac on the plane, running like hell when I landed, running so I could do it before they stopped me.

And that was just for starters. The more I thought about

it, the more my mind filled with an endless number of details that would conspire against me. I'd been there when the bomb went off at the First Amendment. I'd been asking about Sheena, trying to track her down. Didn't that sound like an obsession? Tabloid perfection: the professor and the porn star. I'd even tried to get a part in one of her movies.

And then they'd search my apartment. "Come 'ere, take a look what's on this guy's desk. A goddamn list of dirty words, and in his typewriter all these descriptions of people fucking. I tell you, it's eerie. And hey, over here, there's a videotape! He's on the videotape with the girl! She's out of it, and he's acting nervous as hell. . . ."

And when I started to think of all the reasons it wouldn't work, all the reasons they wouldn't believe it, I realized that nothing really came to mind.

Teddy stood up. "Okay, Professor, that little slut is beginning to get on my nerves. What do you say, is it time to give her the old hook?"

I feigned grogginess, sandbagging for a moment, and then I lunged for the remote switch, but he was too quick, pounding me again with the sap. I sank down and clung weakly to his knees. Teddy held the remote control away from me, above his head as if it were a bit of food and I was the dog that he was teasing.

And then I heard the horrible sound.

The explosion was abrupt, concussive, not at all the thunderous rumbling I'd imagined. Had I forced him to trigger it by accident, in the act of warding me off? I concentrated on the horrible sound of it so I wouldn't have to think about anything else. I kneeled there clasping Teddy's knees, and a moment later he sat down on top of me.

". . . For men, the Combat Zone is just a place to visit. For women, the Combat Zone is the place where we live. It is the place we take with us, everywhere. We live there whenever a man says, Oh baby, you sure you won't gimme a taste of that? Whenever a man says, Oh baby, where'd you get those nice tits. Whenever a man says . . ."

Grace Alice Perry was still speaking, and Teddy was still

on top of me, no longer sitting, but reclining now, heavily on top of me, prone, and I managed to look at his face. His scabbed cheeks were red, more livid than ever, and his neck was red, too, and his forehead. Especially his forehead, red and wet. I turned away from the ghastly sight of it and that's when I saw Gerald.

Gerald was coming toward us from the roof hatch, a pistol in his hand. With one hand he pulled Teddy off of me, the other hand still holding the gun on Teddy, just in case Teddy moved. Judging by the size and placement of the bullet wound in his forehead, and by the amount of blood that had spewed out of it, Teddy wasn't going to move without supernatural intervention.

I just lay there, not moving, now understanding that the sound I'd heard wasn't a bomb, but a gunshot.

I watched Gerald at work, his movements efficient but nonchalant, as if this were a necessary but not uncommon activity. When he'd satisfied himself that Teddy no longer posed a threat, he squatted beside me.

He said, "Thanks."

I just stared at him.

"That's why I was following you up here, to tell you thanks. I almost lost you."

"Thanks?"

"My sister said you called. She said you were real nice to her."

When I recovered my powers of speech I said, "Don't mention it."

Epilogue

A fall day in Wesley Square, and I'm sitting alone at an outdoor café, bundled up in my old sweater with the shawl collar, drinking coffee, enjoying a cigarette, watching the leaves blow across the brick plaza, just seeing who might pass by. The Indian summer of the past few days has gone, and now there's a chill in the air, the white sky a premonition of winter. It's the sort of weather and the time of year that always inspires in me an odd feeling, an intense sensation of both optimism and dread. I know why, of course; I know the source. It's simply the adult residue of a childhood emotion, a six-year-old simultaneously frightened and hopeful on the first day of school. And thirty autumns later, here I was, still going to class. It occurred to me that I'd conducted my entire life by the academic calendar.

Almost a month had passed since the Proposition Six vote, and I couldn't remember the exact tally. Eighteen thousand or so, yea. Twenty-seven thousand or so, nay. Somewhere in there.

As soon as the final vote was tabulated, the result seemed utterly predictable. Inevitable. Why had there been such a sense of anticipation the day before? After all, it was a free-speech issue, wasn't it? That was the consensus. When the moment came to cast a vote, that was the issue you had to keep in mind. What good was the First Amendment if it

271

protected only the things we liked, things that didn't bother us?

An exit poll revealed a final irony. Interviews with voters who favored Proposition Six showed that a certain number of them had been confused. So relentlessly had the tabloids labeled the ordinance the "Porn Prop" and "Proposition Sex" that many supporters instinctively believed they should vote no. No to the Porn Prop. Not enough confusion to affect the result, the analysis showed, but just one last wrinkle, just one more thing. The media responded to the exit poll with a brief flurry of introspection. One tabloid editorial lamented the finding, solemnly warning that the media "too often become players in the events that they are charged with reporting."

Oh? You don't say.

The story that made the news reports identified the murderer of Emma Pierce and the mad Proposition Six bomber as Theodore Spanelli, sometime film techie, disgruntled employee, and disgruntled lover, a New Yorker with a history of erratic behavior. There was some evidence that the bombings were part of a real-estate scam, but the reports suggested the greater likelihood that Mr. Spanelli had initiated the violence on his own, with the ultimate intention of casting suspicion on his employer, Byron Choate. Byron Choate wasn't talking, except through his lawyers, who dismissed the entire story as laughably baroque. Where's the proof? they wanted to know. There's not one iota of proof.

Disgruntled. So that's what Teddy was. When I thought back to everyone who'd played a part, from Emma and Grace to Beth and me and even to Byron Choate, Teddy alone among us seemed not the least bit disgruntled, but more or less happy as a clam throughout. The same for Dodds; by no stretch of the imagination was he disgruntled, and the only conclusion I could draw was that the two people most responsible were demonstrably the least disgruntled. What the police and the FBI should do, I thought, is track down the handful of people in the country who weren't disgruntled and keep an eye on *them*. Wiretap their phones. And maybe in the transcripts of those conversations we would discover why the malefactors of the world were so goddamn happy while the rest of us were so miserable and disgruntled and pissed off.

The stories went on to say that Mr. Spanelli had met his end while committing his final act of extreme disgruntledness—why hadn't reporters come up with a scientific term for it, *disgruntia dementia*?—when he was shot in the head by Gerald Valentin, a volunteer security expert working for the Coalition of Women Against Pornography. Found in Mr. Spanelli's possession were electronic triggering devices and bomb paraphernalia, and beneath the podium an unexploded bomb powerful enough to have left a sizable crater where the stage had been.

Gerald Valentin had been recommended by a number of citizens groups for their citizen-hero awards. Only two stories even mentioned that I'd been on the roof, and neither account left a particularly clear impression of what I was doing there. Even so, rereading the stories always gave me a perverse pleasure, and I would think, Sure, sure, that's how I remember it.

Of course I'd been a responsible citizen and told the homicide detectives, and afterward an assistant DA, every detail of every event insofar as I understood what had happened to me. I told them all about Samuel Dodds, but I had no idea what they thought about it; the assistant DA said he would get back to me, but the weeks were passing, and I was still waiting to hear from him.

The rest of the story was in the business section, but you had to read between the lines to make any sense of it. Orrin Muller had suddenly resigned as chairman of the FCC, citing failing health. The transfer of the broadcast license had been delayed, but I wasn't sure to what extent Dodds was hurt by it. The TV deal was still pending, and there were rumors of financial setbacks, hints of impropriety, but not much more than that. His power of recovery, I suspected, his flexibility in the face of economic reversal was extraordinary. His control seemed fully intact.

One article quoted Dodds himself, capturing him in his homespun mode. The article was entitled, "Debt-Driven Deal Falters," and Dodds, after an expression of mild dismay at the progress of the TV deal, conceded that "we've been taken down a notch," but "sometimes a little taste of humble pie can work wonders." And then he began going on about organizational well-being, offering assurances of financial health, general optimism for the future, confidence in the economy, a renewed call for American excellence, so that by the end of the quote you didn't have the slightest idea what he was talking about. Which I suppose was what he wanted.

All in all, I decided, it was about what you would expect. Once the newspapers had worked their reductive magic, it was hard to believe that there was genuine human activity behind the events or that I had somehow been connected to them.

I was sick of thinking about it. I had other things to think about, some pretty good things, and as I sat here on this autumn day with this invigorating chill in the air, I fully intended to relish them.

The number of students in my Am. Civ. 265 class had dwindled to thirty-eight, each of them relieved that I'd turned out not to be boring as shit, but actually, a sort of interesting guy, you know, sort of fun. Mostly what that meant was I wasn't above telling the occasional literary anecdote of a bawdy nature, just to keep their attention.

One day last week I'd come home to find a message on my machine from Percy Hotchkiss. As it happened, he hadn't been out in his backyard mulching gladiolas, but had landed on his feet, taking a senior editor's position at a very hip little press in Cambridge. I returned his call, and after we brought each other up to date, he asked me what was happening with my novel.

"I may do what poets did in the Renaissance," I said.

"Circulate the manuscript among a few close friends. Then, at my death, leave instructions to burn it."

Percy Hotchkiss said he might have a better idea. He couldn't make any promises, at least not yet, but he thought his hip little press might be interested in publishing a hip little novel whose main character didn't talk.

I said, "Got any ideas for a title?"

He said, "I've always had a sentimental regard for *Helpless Laughter*."

I said, "Do you have any plans for naked women on the cover?"

"Nope."

"Then I'll have to think about it."

And finally, there was Beth. She wasn't pregnant; menstruationwise, nothing out of the ordinary had happened. But in recent days we'd been a lot more careful in bed. We'd been working at it, practicing being careful, just seeing how really careful we could be, sometimes two or three times a night. Well, at least one time two or three times a night. We'd reached such a level of expertise that we could share almost two bottles of wine and still be extremely careful. If we were any more careful, I was going to have a heart attack.

I don't know why things were better between us, but they were. My birthday was just last week, and she'd given me a present, a package with a dozen pairs of white boxer shorts. The pair on top was embossed with the logo "Teeny Tiny Thomas." The card read, "Wear these for a couple of months and get your sperm count up. Then we'll talk."

And so this was how I spent my morning, with coffee and cigarettes at the pleasant outdoor café, in a wonderfully good mood in the wonderfully chill air, when I began to hear voices raised, an argument from a nearby table. I eavesdropped, aware of the illicit pleasure that comes from overhearing a private conversation, but mostly what caught my ear was the content. The argument was about Proposition Six.

I glanced over to a young couple who, like me, had been

drinking coffee and watching people. I'd noticed them earlier; their discussion had begun quietly and reasonably, but now there was an edge to it, a nerve had been touched, as if suddenly the stakes had been raised. Now they were playing for real.

"Say they got rid of every magazine and every adult video and every image that demeans women, just what do you think that would accomplish? Pornography is in the brain. It's in the brain, so unless you're prepared to start giving men lobotomies—"

"I don't have a problem with lobotomies."

"Be serious."

"What makes you think I'm not serious? This is war, and women are losing. We're getting killed. Literally, we're getting killed."

"I know you don't mean that—"

"Stop patronizing me—"

"Look, all I'm saying is pornography is a symptom, not the disease."

"Then let's treat the symptom. Doctors do it all the time. Let's ban pornography. We can worry about the disease later. I kind of like your idea about lobotomies—"

"While you're at it, why don't you shred the Constitution?"

"Great, here we go with the Constitution, the favorite refuge of every secret porn lover. Show me a strict constitutionalist, and I'll show you an inveterate masturbator."

"That's bullshit. What about the Bill of Rights? Have you ever heard of the First Amendment?"

Have you ever heard of the First Amendment?

As the question reverberated in my ears, the hairs on the back of my neck stood out, and my spine tingled. It seemed like years ago that I had lain hung over in bed, and Emma Pierce had telephoned to ask me that very question.

I paid my bill and left the café, left the disgruntled couple there, not wanting to hear any more. Before I returned home, I strolled around Wesley Square and preoccupied myself with an activity that was completely new to me. I was noticing children. Since I got Beth's note, it was hard not to think about them, hard not to notice them, and what surprised me most was how many of them there were. They were everywhere.

At the large newsstand in the center of Wesley Square, I watched one little girl in particular. Her father looked like a professor, and he was buying a stack of newspapers and periodicals, and she stood quietly beside him, holding his hand. I wasn't sure how old she was—two? three?—and to tell the truth, I wasn't even sure it was a little girl; I'd only been noticing children for a few days now, so I wasn't experienced enough to know what to look for, and they all seemed so ambiguously dressed. But I think it was a little girl, and she stood there in a classic pose of childhood innocence, both bashful and curious. Toes inward, one small hand rising up to her father's hand, the other hand in a fist on top of her head.

As her father paid for the newspapers and journals, I noticed that she was staring at something at eye level, a magazine on one of the lower racks. On the cover was a photograph of Sheena Sands, one of the stills from *The Right Stiff*, another of the stories featuring her that had been appearing everywhere. I'd read this one, too: IVY-LEAGUE PORN QUEEN RECANTS. The cover photo was an image of submission, Sheena Sands nude, looking up to a clothed man.

I wondered what the little girl was thinking. What passed between her mind and the photograph? What information was communicated? I imagined the image projected onto her retina, upside down; transformed to electrical impulses, onto a network of synapses, and somehow into a thought, later a memory, and stored in some enormous reservoir of unremembered thought. What was that thought? When it coalesced in her brain, the naked woman on her knees, the clothed man above, what was that thought?

Even now, I had no idea.

About the Author

Robert Reeves is the author of *Doubting Thomas*, which *The Kirkus Reviews* called "a zesty, classy original." A former teacher of English at Harvard University and a longtime Boston resident, Reeves now lives with his wife and son in New York City, where he is at work on a third Thomas Theron novel, *Thomas Solves the Mystery of Life*.